Desire's Chase

ANA E ROSS

DESIRE'S CHASE

(Chase & Desire)

Beyond Granite Falls #2

Copyright © 2016 by Ana E Ross Books

All rights reserved. All rights reserved. Except for brief quotes used in reviews, no portion of this story may be used or reproduced in any form by any electronic, mechanical, or any other device now known or invented hereafter without the written permission of the author. These forms include, but are not limited to xerography, photocopying, scanning, recording, distributing via Internet means, informational storage or retrieval system.

This story is a work of fiction. All names, characters, and incidents are the products of the author's imagination and are used fictitiously. Similarities to actual events, locales, business establishments, or persons living or dead, are purely coincidental.

To learn more about Ana, visit her at: www.AnaERoss.com

Edited by Crazy Diamond Editing Services
Cover Design by Niina Cord
Formatted by Ana E Ross Books

ISBN: 9780986339943
ISBN-13: 9780986339943

DEDICATION

For Nicoya, Duanna, and Tamika, three beautiful young ladies, who
are destined to make the world a better place...
I love you!

CHAPTER ONE

He was back and hell was begging to be paid.

Chase Hunter stared through the cockpit windshield as the small private jet made its final approach into Granite Falls Regional Airport.

Nestled at the foothills of New Hampshire's White Mountains, and bordered by the Aiken River on the west, Lake Crystal in the northeast, and Lake Aubrey in the southeast, Granite Falls had always been a picturesque town. In twelve years, it had flourished into a little metropolis that matched the glamour and excitement of any of the big cities Chase had visited around the world.

The majestic mountain ranges in the north and west provided breathtaking backdrops for the sprawling billion-dollar estates at the peak of Mount Reservoir, and for the multitude of modest family homes scattered across its foothills. Directly below him, the glowing sunset bounced off the tops of historical landmarks and the mass of modern high-rises in the downtown area—many of which had been erected since Chase's absence from Granite Falls and its sister town of Evergreen to the east.

It was hard to imagine a town, especially one located in a

remote mountain range, expanding at this rate, but when the population included four billionaires with growing families—all of whom were dedicated to making Granite Falls, and now Evergreen the best little towns in the region—then anything was possible.

A mixture of rage and pride spread through Chase like a California wildfire as his eyes scaled the tops of Fontaine Enterprises, Fontaine Towers #1 and #2, and Fontaine Conference Center—the tallest buildings in Granite Falls. That son of a bitch had stolen so much from him. Not only his ideas and his reputation, but also his chance to make a life with the only woman he'd ever loved. The woman he'd had to put out of his mind for twelve heartbreaking years.

It was bad enough that he'd been chased out of town, but even worse was the evidence that had sentenced him to being forever scum in her eyes. If a picture was worth a thousand words, the incriminating video featuring Chase as the star of the show was worth ten thousand. There was no argument that Chase had been a willing participant in the private homemade movie.

No siree, he thought, as the plane touched down and sped along the runway. He could, however, argue that he'd had no idea the video existed, much less that it would be shown to a room full of the elite residents of Evergreen and Granite Falls.

Irresponsible. Narcissistic. Degenerate. These were just a few of the names the love of his life had hurled at him in front of all those people that night. And those were the nice names, Chase thought, as his gut contracted at the memory of the contempt that had flashed in her eyes.

Stay away from my daughter, you repulsive reprobate. You come near her again, and I swear to God I will shoot you, her father had threatened when Chase had attempted to see her the next day.

It hadn't taken Chase long to figure out who'd set him up, and why. Chase had confronted the SOB and sworn to make him pay, but his enemy had another ace up his sleeve. Somehow, he'd gotten wind of a Hunter family secret—a secret Chase hadn't known existed until that day. And if that secret were made public, it would have destroyed Chase's mother's world.

With his love's contempt for him, and her father's threats against him, Chase had had nothing more to lose when he'd been given two days to leave Evergreen, forever.

Forever, for Chase, turned out to be twelve years—twelve years during which he'd had time to plan his revenge, build up his arsenal to take on, and now take down the bastard who'd robbed him of his life and his happiness with his one true love.

"Welcome home, Mr. Hunter." The pilot turned and gave Chase a big grin once the jet came to a complete stop.

"Thank you, Hector. And thanks for the ride." He unbuckled his seatbelt.

"It's Mr. Fontaine you should be thanking. He paid for the gas and the Scotch, sir."

Chase smiled at Hector's *sir*. That's one name he'd never been called before, at least not in these parts. "The ride was smooth. You're topnotch, and if you weren't so happy at Fontaine Enterprises, I'd hire you in a flash."

"Make sure you share your sentiments about my value with my boss. I can do with a raise."

"I'll mention it the next time I see him," Chase said with a chuckle, as the pilot began his post landing procedure. Hector's family was one of the few Hispanic families that lived in the twin towns when Chase was growing up. Chase had had a short fling with Hector's younger sister, Celia, during their senior year at Granite Falls Prep.

Since Hector never mentioned it, or gave him attitude, Chase assumed he wasn't privy to that information. But even so, Hector worked for Bryce Fontaine, and no smart Fontaine employee would consciously offend someone Bryce considered a friend or a colleague. Luckily for Chase, he was both, all because of a chance meeting several years ago.

Hector was Bryce's most valued and trusted pilot, so when Chase had voiced concerns about his own private jet landing at GFR and thus defeating his element of surprise, Bryce had sent Hector to fly him from Iowa.

He wasn't overly concerned about being recognized as Chase Hunter since most of the people he'd grown up with had left the area. It wasn't as if he had many male friends, anyway. His companions had been predominantly women, and many of them had either married, moved away, or both. The younger generation and new blood that now occupied the twin towns had probably never heard of him, and if they had, they wouldn't be able to pick him out of a lineup.

The cockpit door opened and the inflight attendant stuck his head in. "Mr. Hunter, your driver is here. We've loaded the duffel bags into the car and dispatched your other luggage to your hotel as you instructed."

"Thank you, Nigel."

"See that you stay out of trouble," Hector warned as Chase vacated the seat.

"I'll try, but you know me. Trouble just seems to find me no matter how hard I try to avoid her," he said, as he squeezed his large frame through the cockpit door.

In the plush cabin, he gathered a leather satchel and the rolls of tracing paper—drawings he had been studying before moving to the cockpit—disembarked, and made his way across the tarmac, through the sprawling terminal, and out the other side.

The air was cool, as was expected for a mountain town— much more tolerable than Iowa's evenings, and it smelled a lot better, too, Chase thought, as his nostrils picked up the mixture of floral scents heavy on the westerly evening breeze.

His heart skipped a beat as the memories of Evergreen's Flower Maze—located just across Granite Falls' southeastern border—finally caught up to him. During the approach, Chase had astutely kept his eyes and thoughts away from that garden. There were just too many...

"Chase!"

Chase stopped short as he approached the line of limos on the curb outside the terminal.

"Chase Hunter. It *is* you. Oh my God."

There went his element of surprise. Chase groaned when

the young woman wearing a classic chauffeur uniform—white blouse, black skirt, and cap—alighted from the driver's side of a limo and began running toward him.

Damn it. It was Lisa Yarwood, his true love's cousin. Curvy, attractive with a moon-shaped face and straight black hair, bleached blond at the tips, Lisa hadn't changed much from the woman Chase remembered, except for the fact that she looked older.

"Well, well, well, if it isn't Chase Hunter in the flesh," she said, smiling up at him. "Only one man I know who walks like a jungle cat," she added, as if to answer the first question that popped into his head.

"Lisa." Chase raked his fingers through his wind-tossed shoulder-length hair, wondering how he'd gotten so unlucky fifteen minutes after his return. This town was really too damn small, and seemed to be filled with too many bags of bad luck with his name written on them.

"Oh my God, you remember me. It's been like—how long, ten—"

"Twelve years," he provided, forcing a grin.

"Oh my God." She threw her hands around his neck and gave him a big squeeze. "Welcome home, Chase." She stepped back and frowned up at him. "Desire is going to chip a nail when she sees you. Did she know you were coming home? We had dinner at Francine's last night. You remember Francine's, that ritzy French restaurant in Evergreen where I used to waitress? Desire talked about some big changes she will be making in her life." Lisa sped on without giving him a chance to respond to her questions. "But she didn't specify—" She clasped a hand over her mouth. "Oh my God, is it about you? Was it supposed to be a surprise?"

Chase's heart raced at the mention of Desire's name. It was the second time in twelve years that he'd heard someone utter her name, and it fueled his excitement to see her. But what kind of big changes could she be making to her life—changes that she hadn't shared with her cousin with whom she used to be very close? "Nope, Desire's life changes have nothing to do with me."

"Then it must be about her business. She's been thinking of expanding, but didn't have the money to do it until last year when she planned that big wedding. Yeah, it must be about her business."

I hope that's all it is. The thought of Desire making big personal changes that involved another man tore at Chase's gut, even as the fact that she was still single stunned him. Could she subconsciously be waiting for his return? After all, she'd been calling him *My Chase* since the day they met.

It had been a hot Saturday afternoon, and Chase was carrying a box of comic books to his bedroom in their new house when a butt-naked little girl burst through the hedges that bordered the two properties. Well, butt naked except for a pair of red cowboy boots.

"Hi," she'd said, staring up at him with large brown eyes and a pearly white baby-teeth grin.

"Hi," he'd replied, wondering where her parents were, and more curiously why she was naked. "What's your name?" he'd asked.

"Desire," she'd said, tugging on her two long ponytails. "What's your name?"

"My—" He'd stopped at the sound of a woman's voice calling out to Desire from the other side of the hedges. "Chase," he'd said, returning his attention to the little girl, who had climbed up the steps and was now tugging on his T-shirt.

"My Chase," she'd said.

"No. Chase."

"My Chase," she'd repeated stubbornly.

"Desire, where are you?" the voice had asked.

"Coming, Mommy," she'd yelled before descending the steps and darting back across the lawn and disappearing behind the hedges.

Chase had hurried inside, not wanting anyone, especially the child's mother, to know that he'd seen her naked. But from that day on, he'd become *Desire's Chase.* When she was old enough he'd told her about their first meeting, but she refused to believe it. He wondered if she still consider him her Chase and if she…

"Mmm. That Iowa farm has been *real* good to you, Chase Hunter. You look scrumptious, as always," Lisa said, pulling him back to the present.

"So, this is what you do for a living?" Chase asked. He needed to keep the conversation on the straight and narrow. The Lisa he remembered from their elementary school days used to be pretty smart. So how had she ended up driving people around town?

"Heck, no. I'm the regional manager for Eye Spy."

"The eyewear company? They are the biggest in the northeast. That's impressive."

"Thanks. I've been working for them since I was nineteen. Got the promotion about six years ago. I drive for Twin Town Limo Services at nights and on weekends. It's my second job. My play money job."

And he just had to pick her limo company. Chase wished he'd taken Bryce's offer to have a Fontaine car pick him up and drive him to Evergreen. He'd turned it down, thinking the man had already gone above and beyond favors to help him onto his feet, and now back home, even though Chase had to consider that Fontaine Enterprises had a lot to gain from his return to the area.

"Is Chad or your mom picking you up?" Lisa asked.

"They don't know I'm here. I wanted to surprise them." *Surprise the whole damn town.*

"I'm sure they'll be happy to see you, especially your mom."

"I guess you're my driver," he said, noticing the name sign on the windshield of her limo.

"Nope. Would have been cool, but I'm here to pick up a Mr. Bennett." She glanced around. "They already loaded his bags, but he hasn't shown up yet."

"I'm Mr. Bennett."

Her mouth popped wide. "Why the alias?"

"It's a long story. Shall we?" He took a step toward the limo in an attempt to ward off her questions.

"Ohhh, Mr. Bennett. Very mysterious. Does it have anything to do with why you want me to take you to the

Forsythe mansion on Mount Reservoir, then pick you up at nightfall to take you home?" she asked, before walking ahead to open the door for him.

"It has everything to do with it."

"Are you friends with the Forsythes?"

Of all the questions anyone could have asked Chase upon his return, this wasn't one he was expecting or was prepared to answer. He managed to keep his cool as he searched his mind for a simple explanation. "No, we're not friends. The house has been vacant for some time now. My boss is planning to purchase a home in Granite Falls, and he asked me to check out the property for him while I'm here, take pictures and so on."

"Oh, that makes sense."

It didn't really, but he was happy she thought so. Chase slid into the backseat. "Lisa, can you keep all this between us? I don't want anyone outside of my family to know I'm back, or about what I'm doing. Not until I'm ready to make my presence known. That goes for Desire, too. And no one is to know that I'm using the alias Bennett."

She gave him an animated grin. "No problem, Chase. Your secrets are safe with me." She pulled a card from her blouse pocket and handed it to Chase. "Call me if you ever need a ride."

"Thanks, Lisa. I might take you up on that offer." Chase shoved her card into the back pocket of his jeans.

***

Under cover of twilight, with two duffel bags in one hand and his key ring in the other, Chase stole across the front lawn of 72 Crawford Avenue, past the two parked cars in front of the closed garage, and made his way toward the back of the house and the stairs that led to the private entrance to his bedroom. The kitchen was the only room lighted, which meant it was the only currently occupied room in the house.

Chase smiled. His mother had a thing about not wasting

energy. When he and Chad were little, she used to make them turn off the lights of the unoccupied rooms in the house. If they'd fallen asleep, it didn't matter what time she came home from her shift at the hospital, she would wake them up and make them go around the house and turn off all the lights. Eventually, they had learned to check before they went to bed.

"Thank you, Mom," Chase whispered as his key slid smoothly into the lock of his bedroom door. Some things still fit and worked. From force of habit, before turning the knob, he glanced across the lawn to the wraparound porch of the house next door. It was pitch dark. No one was home.

He tucked away the sweet memories and let himself quietly into his bedroom. He waited a few seconds for his eyes to adjust to the darkness, and his nose to the smell of pine-laced Pledge. Warm feelings of affection enveloped Chase at the thought that even in his absence, his mother never neglected to dust his room and polish his furniture. Those simple acts of filial love had made it easy for Chase to sacrifice his own happiness for her. *He loved his mother.*

Placing his bags on a chair in one corner, Chase tiptoed across the floor and opened the door leading into the hallway. As expected, the doors to the other two bedrooms were closed, but he could distinctly hear the murmur of voices—one male, one female—coming up the hallway from the kitchen.

Taking a deep breath, Chase began his stealthy walk toward the stairs, praying that the floorboards hadn't begun creaking in his absence. He breathed a sigh of relief and began his descent. His mother's and brother's voices grew louder as he got to the bottom step, but it wasn't until he was halfway across the open living and dining area that he was able to make sense of their conversation. The mention of one name in particular halted Chase in his tracks.

Pain ripped through him as if someone had hacked his chest open and torn his heart out of him.

His mother's scream and the screech of a chair against the tiled floor were simultaneous. "Oh my goodness, Chad, I'm so happy for you, son. That is the best news a mother could hear tonight. You know I love her like a daughter. Of all the women you've dated, she is the only one I've ever envisioned as the mother of my grandchildren."

"So you don't mind the color thing, or about what happened eleven years ago?"

"Chadwick Hunter, when have you ever known me to be concerned about the color of anyone's skin? As to what happened all those years ago, every family has its secrets and its shame to bear. We all live in glass houses, so none of us should be throwing stones."

Chase's gut tightened.

"When did you propose?" his mother asked Chad.

"Three days ago. We had dinner at Odyssey, the Greek restaurant on Remington Drive. Afterward, we drove over to Cedar Lake. I proposed there under the stars. I wanted to make it special, you know."

"Three days ago? Why are you just telling me?"

"We decided to give ourselves time to think about it, and if we were still in agreement at the end of three days, we would inform our families, separately."

Chase frowned. Who does that? People in love don't wait. *Oh yes, they do. He'd waited, and now...*

"She's telling her family tonight as we speak. We'll make it public in a day or two, and then she'll begin wearing that big rock I gave her. Wait till you see it, Mom. I went all out. It set me back a bit, but—"

"Oh Chad. That is absolutely wonderful. We have to call Chase right away. He's going to be so thrilled."

CHAPTER TWO

Soft chuckles drifted through the open window on a warm draft of morning air.

Chase's eyelids fluttered as the sounds slowly drew him out of a restless sleep. Groaning, he turned onto his stomach, hugged his pillow, and tried to fall back to sleep. Then the town's clock pealed out the morning hour, bringing him fully awake.

"Seriously?" Rolling on to his side, Chase tossed the rumpled sheet aside and swung his legs over the side of the bed. Evergreen, unlike Granite Falls, hadn't changed much since he'd been gone. He staggered toward the window and the sounds of the chuckles, flinching as his aching muscles reminded him of the previous night's activities.

Damn! Damn! Damn!

What the hell had he been thinking, sleeping with Lisa? He'd been home for one night and he'd already screwed up— *royally*. Hector had warned him to stay out of trouble, and like a bull seeing red, he'd charged right into it without batting an eyelash.

Chase groaned again as he peeked through the shades at the house across the lawn. Just as he'd feared, Lisa was busy blabbing to the young woman who lived in the house. Chase didn't need to imagine what they were talking about. The gloat on Lisa's face and the scowl on her companion's said it all.

Chase leaned his shoulder against the window frame as his eyes lingered on the other woman. She was slender, with long black hair brushing her gentle sloping shoulders, prominent cheekbones beneath a smooth coffee complexion, a sexy wide mouth featuring succulent lips, and enchanting brown eyes that took Chase's breath away each time he gazed into them.

Her name was Desire.

And he desired her.

But now, instead of just one obstacle standing between Chase and his Desire, there were two.

Chase's heart did a flip as Desire raised her head and stared across the lawn as if she sensed he was watching her. They might not have seen each other for twelve years, but that special bond they'd shared growing up next door to each other was still there. He released a soft moan, and his shaft tightened and slapped against his stomach as the morning sunrays splayed across Desire's face, drawing out the golden undertones of her skin and illuminating the cherry richness of her lips. It was a taste of both heaven and hell to see her in the flesh.

For the first few years after he'd been forced out of town, Chase had tried to keep up with news about Desire through his mother. He'd waited with bated breath for her to say that Desire had asked about him, had enquired about his whereabouts, when he was coming back so they could talk. But he'd eventually had to push her to the back of his mind when she'd begun dating. It was just too painful thinking of Desire with other men, and besides, he could not afford to wallow in self-pity, or harbor any other type of distraction from his master plan until he was ready to return to Evergreen and take back all that had been stolen from him.

Desire included.

He'd kept an ear out, though, for any news of her becoming engaged to some other man—an event for which he would have abandoned his plan for certain. Desire was far more important than revenge.

Several months ago when Chase received his edition of *Granite Falls People News*, he'd almost blown a load when he'd opened up his copy to page four and had seen Desire Summers in a black floral print dress posing in Evergreen's famous Flower Garden Maze. Her company, Weddings by Desire, had gained global attention for coordinating the extravagant fairy tale group wedding for four billionaires from Granite Falls.

Chase had thought Desire beautiful at eighteen—the last time he'd seen her—but the woman who'd stared back at him from that magazine page was unbelievably stunning. At that moment, Desire had stepped out of Chase's dreams and right back into his heart. The fact that she'd chosen to pose in the garden, in the exact spot where she had kissed him for the first time twelve years ago, had renewed Chase's hope that she might still be in love with him.

Chase rubbed the pad of his thumb across his lips at the heated memory of Desire's soft, luscious, and barely legal lips pressed up against his in the garden that night. He remembered the lingering taste of peppermint and chocolate ice cream on her tongue.

He'd always loved her, respected, and adored her, and that night in the garden when she'd made the first move, indicating that she was ready to step into his adult world, Chase had unleashed all the emotions he'd been holding back and allowed himself to fall head-over-heels in love with Desire. The need to make love with her had been severe, but he'd had to slow the pace because of her tender age, her inexperience, and the fact that her father didn't like him very much.

Now he'd returned, determined to change her father's opinion about him, and hopefully convince Desire to give him—give them—another chance. But Chase's world had once again fallen apart when he snuck into his mother's house last night, only to overhear the worst news of his life.

Desire was engaged to—of all people—Chase's younger brother, Chad.

Anxiety tore at Chase's insides as he recalled the moments following his mother's remark about calling to tell him about his brother's engagement.

"No need, Mom," Chase had said, stepping into the kitchen. A recent graduate of the School of Deceit, Chase conjured a hearty smile. His gut was ripping apart as he took in the mixture of joy and surprise on his mother's oblong-shaped face and the twinkles in her lively gray eyes. Average height and curvy, she was strong and beautiful, and he loved her.

So instead of spoiling her happiness, Chase had made a mental date to drown his pain in a bottle of Scotch later that night. Cheap tequila had been his friend when he'd first left Evergreen, but as time passed, he'd graduated to Scotch. The good, expensive kind. They hadn't spent a lot of time together in the past few years, but they would be picking up where they'd left off before the night was out. He was certain of that.

"Chase! Chase!" His mother flew across the floor and threw herself into his arms, hugging him so ferociously, breathing had become difficult for Chase.

He hugged her back, kissing her plump cheeks over and over again.

She reluctantly released him and gazed up at him, grinning from ear to ear. "You're back in Evergreen. We weren't expecting you. We didn't know you were coming home. Oh, my heart is so full tonight to have both my sons here with me, at last." She hugged him again, then asked, "Are you hungry? We just had baked chicken, rice, some grilled broccoli with pumpkin seeds, and a salad. There's plenty left."

Chase glanced at the stove where some covered pots were hanging out. "No, Mom." He was starving, but anything he sent down his esophagus would be back up in seconds. "I stopped in town and had something to eat." He hated lying to her, but it was better than vomiting all over her freshly scrubbed kitchen floor, or worse, her kitchen table.

"Hey, Chase." Chad rose from the table.

"Hey, little brother." Chad's brief hug wasn't as enthusiastic as their mother's, but Chad had never been an overly affectionate child. Chase remembered their mother begging her youngest son for hugs when they were growing up. Chad was fifteen when Chase left home, and from what he'd observed from the times they'd visited him in Iowa, Chad's aloof personality hadn't improved.

That's why Chase couldn't believe what he'd just heard.

"Come on, sit." His mother pulled him down into the chair next to her. She held on to his hand as if she were afraid he'd run off again. *"I'm obviously happy you're here, son,"* she said, her eyes beaming from the ceiling light, *"but I'm dying to know what made you decide to come back home."*

"It was time, Mom." That wasn't a lie.

"Well, you picked the right time," Chad said, returning to his chair on the other side of the kitchen table. *"I'm sure you heard the news."*

Chase swallowed the knot in his throat. *"Yep. So when's the wedding?"*

"We haven't set a date yet. We only got engaged three days ago."

Three days ago. He was three days too late. Talk about bad timing. He should have returned for love instead of revenge. If love had been his motivation, he would have been home long ago, before Chad had the chance or even the idea of proposing to Desire. Hearing that she'd pledged herself to another man at the very time his hopes for them had begun to resurface was hard to take.

But to his brother?

Had it been any other man, Chase would have viewed her engagement as a challenge, one he would have moved heaven and earth to break up, but when it came to family…that was one road Chase dared not take. It would be history repeating itself—the contemptible history Chase had fled from in order to keep it hidden. Not that he thought his and Chad's rivalry over the same girl would have ended the way Chase's father's and his uncle's had ended. Nonetheless, if that secret ever got out, everyone would have been looking at Chase, shaking their heads, and thinking: *Like father like son.*

Nope, Chase would have to sit out this one and let it fall apart on its own. He hoped Desire came to her senses before it was too late. Maybe if she saw him face-to-face, the feelings she'd once had for him would come rushing back, just as poignantly as his had the moment he'd seen her picture in the magazine.

Chase would bet his jet that it was Desire's burgeoning professional success and not her physical beauty, or even the unique qualities of her heart and soul that interested Chad. No, his brother, who was quickly rising to the top of the twin towns' elite chart as one of the most influential lawyers in the area, and who had several times mentioned his interest in running for office, was as pragmatic as they came.

Last night, as he'd talked about Desire, Chase had been waiting for Chad to get that giddy look in his eyes, that catch in his voice, that stupid grin on his face that men got when they were truly in love. He was still waiting.

Since the billionaires' wedding, Desire had been in high demand. Hollywood celebrities, and business executives and politicians across the nation had solicited her services. Chase knew his opportunistic brother well enough to know that he planned to ride Desire all the way to Washington, D.C. Through her business, Desire was acquiring a long list of connections that would be more beneficial to Chad than it was to her.

Chad's reasons for marrying Desire were as clear as crystal, but why Desire had chosen to marry Chad was the billion-dollar question. The one question Chase knew he had to ask *her*, and depending on her answer, he would either…

"Chase, are you up?"

Speak of the devil.

Chase swung away from the window and grabbed a pair of jeans from the footboard of his bed, just as his bedroom door flew open.

"Oops." Chad grinned as Chase hauled his jeans over his hips.

"Will you ever learn to knock before barging in?" Chase carefully eased the zipper over his morning erection. "You always barged in, even as a kid."

"I'm glad you're home. It's been a while. A boy needs his big brother."

"Like he needs a hammer smashed against his head." Chase gave Chad's six-foot, lean frame a once-over. Fully dressed in a suit and tie, with a pretty face and green smiling eyes, Chad looked sharp and articulate. Always did. "What do you want?"

Chase was irritated beyond words, and he made no effort to hide it. If he weren't still trying to keep a low profile, he would have been waking up in his recently rented penthouse suite at Hotel Andreas in Granite Falls. Nobody was supposed to know that he'd joined the ranks of young, wealthy bachelors on the global market. And until he was ready to go public, he had to keep pretending that he was the same *poor old Chase* who'd been chased out of town—even to his family.

"I was wondering if you wanted to ride into Granite Falls with me this morning. We have a lot of catching up to do."

"Chad, we saw each other at Easter when you and Mom visited me in Iowa. We've seen each other frequently over the years. So cut the crap."

"You hurt Mom when you left so abruptly, you know? She was depressed for weeks, months, but you didn't have to stay away this long. You didn't have to leave because of that video. It would have blown over quickly like everything else around here. In fact it did in a few months when Victoria shot—"

"Is that what you came in here to discuss? My past transgressions?" One long stride and Chase towered a good three inches over Chad. He flexed his muscles and narrowed his eyes as he stared down his brother. "Because you have a couple of your own we can take a swing at. One in particular."

Chad took a hasty step away from Chase and dropped his gaze.

"Have you told her?"

"It was a long time ago, Chase. I was a kid. It only happened one time. There's no reason to tell her anything. You, of all people, should understand."

Yeah, he understood. He understood a lot more than his devious little brother thought he did. "I ask again, what do you want, Chad?"

Chad pushed his hands into his trouser pockets and sent Chase a sheepish look. "Well, since you've been away, a lot has changed around here."

Like you moving in on my girl.

"New businesses and people have moved into the twin

towns. The old roads have been rerouted and new ones built. Lots of new suburban residential communities are being built. The mill buildings down by the Mannis River are being renovated to accommodate the influx of investors and new businesses. They're putting in an esplanade like the one on the Aiken River in Granite Falls. Two marinas and million-dollar lakeside mansions are going up along the Evergreen side of Crystal Lake and on Cedar Lake, too. Your old employer, Carron Architecture, won the bids for most of the projects, but I heard another company, D&C or C&D Designs, out-bid them for the major projects."

"And?" Chase asked, when Chad stopped to take a breath.

"The point is, I have some free time this morning and I'd like to show you around. You don't have a car and your old Yamaha has been sitting so long, it probably needs a tune-up." He looked Chase up and down. "How long are you home for, anyway? You never said. Do they need you back on the farm in Iowa anytime soon?"

The question was legit since Chase's family thought he'd spent the past decade working as a farmhand down in Iowa. They had no idea that he owned Carver Farm, and had been using it as a cover to mask his true identity in the corporate world for the past eight years.

"How long are you staying?" Chad repeated.

"I have no idea. Maybe until another video of me surfaces," he said, surprised that his heartbeat didn't accelerate at the mention of his worst blunder. The sweetness of revenge had definitely taken over the pain of embarrassment and the loss of his love.

"See that you don't. Mom won't survive another disgrace like that one."

You don't know the half of it.

"I'm serious, Chase. You disappeared without a trace. A whole year went by before Mom and I knew where you were. We thought you'd gone off and—"

"What? Killed myself?"

"We were worried."

"Well, I'm not dead." *But you might soon wish I were.*

"Desire and I are having lunch with a reporter from *Twin Town Times*. Our engagement will be public by tomorrow morning. I thought you'd like to join us and give—"

"No, thank you." Chase picked up his duffel bags from the floor, dumped the contents out onto his bed, and began stuffing the drawers of his bureau and dresser, one huge handful at a time, even as he wondered why he was unpacking since he was only staying a couple days in the house. Oh, yeah. *Appearances.*

"You don't need to be so antagonistic toward Desire, Chase. I'm sure she's forgiven you. She's not an immature teenager anymore. She's a woman with a level head. You can't avoid her forever. She'll be family, your sister-in-law. Once we have kids—"

"Do you love her?" Chase jammed a handful of underwear into the top drawer of his dresser and slammed it shut. He turned to face his brother. What he wanted to ask was if they'd been sleeping together and for how long. But he didn't think he could deal with a positive response.

"Love?" Chad chuckled on his way to the window Chase had been staring out of earlier. "Desire and I are practical people. We're not governed by silly notions like love and romance. Many of the couples she helps tie the knot end up in divorce court at some point. She'll help put them together and when they're ready, I'll assist in breaking them apart."

Ever the cynical bastard. "So it's a business arrangement."

"It's a good match."

"A good match? Where are we, in seventeenth-century England?"

"That's the problem with you, Chase. You let your emotions rule you. You've always been hotheaded. You must learn to use your head. Well, the one on your shoulders," he added with a snicker.

"So you're telling me you feel nothing for Desire." It was more of a statement than a question.

Chad shrugged. "I won't say *nothing*. She's the first friend I had, ever, even though she's three years older than me, and after you left, our friendship blossomed. We respect each other. She knows I'll never hurt her or embarrass her."

Like I did.

"We're fond of each other, and..."

Fond?

Chase took his travel case to the dresser and began unloading his toiletries as Chad went on and on about why he and Desire were perfect for each other. By admitting that love wasn't a factor in his impending marriage, Chad had given Chase tacit consent to derail his plan.

From what Chase remembered about Desire, love was important to her. That hot July night when she'd kissed him in the garden on her eighteenth birthday, she'd told him that it was the place where she wanted to get married. She'd even gone so far as to lay out the plan for him. She wanted a harp and violin orchestra, the release of butterflies during the exchange of vows and white doves after the ceremony while she and her new husband walked down the garden path hand-in-hand. As she'd described the perfect romantic wedding, Chase's twenty-one-year-old heart had begun speeding like an Indy 500 race car dashing for the finish line.

"I want to be your Desire, Chase Hunter," she'd said in a tremulous voice, her beautiful brown eyes gazing with love, affection, and hope into his. "I know I'm young and you've had a lot of women and experience, and my parents might disown me because of your wild reputation, but I don't care. You're the man I want standing by my side on my most special day. I'm giving you my heart, hoping you'll give me yours. Will you be My Chase for real?"

Chase was young. The night was hot. Her breath smelled like peppermint and chocolate ice cream, and tasted just as sweet. He'd promised to be her Chase, and kissed her again and again and again that night as the moonlight bathed their faces.

Chase closed one hand around the wooden pendant hanging from the black hemp cord around his neck. The wood was fashioned into the shape of a heart with a butterfly painted on the top side of it. Desire had been fascinated with butterflies as a little girl. She'd given him the necklace on her fifteenth birthday, just before he left for college, and had asked him to keep it for her until she was all grown up. She'd grown up that night in the garden. Chase swallowed as his thumb slid along the engraved words on the bottom of the heart: *Desire's Chase.*

"…perfect for each other. Desire won't have much time to hang out with her after we're married. She will be busy hosting business meetings and such. You know, you should marry her, take her back to Iowa with you, settle down and raise a bunch of little Chases."

Chase whipped around. "What the hell are you talking about, Chad?"

"Lisa. I heard the two of you last night." Chad turned with a grin. "That old trailer in the backyard was rocking off its axles and—"

Chase growled. "Don't you have anything better to do than sneak around in the middle of the night watching other people f—"

"Stop. Stop." Chad raised his hands. "Remember where you are, brother. You're home, not in some cornfield in Iowa. So hold the expletives, please. As to my sneaking around on you, Mom still forbids me to smoke in the house, so I went out back, and that's when I heard Lisa's, 'Oh God! Oh Chase. Oh God. Oh…' I wouldn't be surprised if that isn't what Desire and Lisa are talking about. You know women share their sexual experiences, right? They might even be planning a double wedding. From what I heard last night, you two seem to really enjoy each other. She's a good match for you. I can picture you working side by side on the farm in Iowa. You should—"

Chase charged toward his brother. "Get the hell out of my room, Chad!"

Chad made a dash for the door and turned to face Chase from the other side. "You should reconsider having lunch with Desire and—"

Chase slammed the door in his face. He shrugged out of his jeans, and as he headed for the bathroom, he chastised himself for allowing Chad to get under his skin—the way he used to when they were kids. Chad would always find a way to get Chase all riled up, then sit back and laugh while Chase ranted and raged out of control.

They were so different, like chalk and cheese, he thought, as he turned on the shower and stepped into the tub. Chad wore silk suits; even though he was wealthy now, Chase still preferred old jeans and T-shirts that had been worn so many times that even after he came around to washing them, they still maintained his form. Chad gave himself a close shave every morning and visited the salon every other week to trim his sandy hair, while Chase clipped his beard with a pair of scissors, and wore his dark locks at shoulder length. Chad enjoyed fancy restaurants, fine wine, and that classical crap for music. Chase felt right at home in a burger joint with a draft of cold beer and the jukebox blasting some country and western singer's sad lyrics about somebody who done did somebody wrong. Chad liked the opera and ballet, while Chase preferred hard-action thrillers, rough football, and wrestling.

The only thing they had in common was their high IQs. Straight-A students, they had graduated top of their individual classes from Granite Falls Prep High School. Chad had been eager to attend college, and had earned his law degree from the University of Pennsylvania.

Chase, on the other hand, had enrolled at Dartmouth College just to get his mother off his back. Bored stiff sitting still for all those long lecturing hours, he'd dropped out after the first year. It just wasn't his thing. He already knew what he wanted to do with his life and he didn't need a college degree to verify it. Despite the wild sex with a great number of college women, and one or two adventurous female professors, Chase had been glad to get the hell out of there.

It had broken his mother's heart, but she'd learned to accept his decision. His mother believed in her children choosing their own paths and had always backed up their choices whether she liked it or not. She often said that folks learned only from their own mistakes. Chase had made a lot of mistakes—as recently as last night. It seemed he still had a lot to learn.

Chase lathered up his washcloth and kicked himself mentally for the umpteenth time since he'd limped out of the trailer and snuck into his room after his romp last night. Back when he used to roam the neighborhoods, Lisa must have been the only girl who'd never thrown herself at him, probably because Desire had told her how she felt about him. But after hearing that Desire was engaged, Lisa probably figured that the one reason she'd denied herself a piece of Chase Hunter didn't exist anymore. So when Chase had called her up and told her about Desire and Chad's engagement, Lisa had been all too happy to help him ease the pain in his heart.

But a roll in the hay—in this case, a hump in the camper— was as far as his relationship with Lisa went. Chase scrubbed at his skin as if trying to eradicate the evidence of his indiscretion. He hoped Chad didn't say anything to their mother about him and Lisa, and of Chad's stupid idea of a double wedding, especially because their mother had questioned Chase last night about his plans to settle down and raise a family. Her questions had sent Chase running from the house in search of therapy. He couldn't lie to his mother about the matters of his heart. It was his love and protection toward her that had sent him in search of the truth and his roots that she'd buried a long time ago.

For the past twelve years, Chase had wished that the only family history he knew began thirty years ago when he was three, and his mother, Azura Bennett, moved from Iowa to New Hampshire to work as a nurse at Granite Falls General Hospital. She'd fallen in love with and married Dr. Chadwick Hunter, a dermatologist who worked at the hospital. Chadwick adopted Chase as his own son and then a few years into his marriage with Azura, he suffered a stroke and died.

Unbeknownst to Azura, Chadwick had been addicted to gambling and was almost bankrupt when he died. Azura had immediately sold their house in upper suburban Granite Falls and purchased a home in the less affluent town of Evergreen.

Luckily for Chase, she'd bought the smallest and most affordable house on Crawford Avenue, right next door to Gerald and Ruth Summers and their two daughters, sixteen-year-old Victoria and three-year-old Desire.

Shortly after their move to Evergreen, Azura left Chase with one of her friends, went to the hospital for a couple days, and returned with a squirming little baby boy. She placed him on Chase's lap and said, "Chase, this is your little brother, Chad. You're the man of this house, so you're responsible to look after him. See that he stays out of trouble."

And that's exactly what Chase had done. He'd looked after Chad. He had fought his battles with the older boys at the playground. He'd taught him how to pitch, and how to kick a ball. He'd taught him how to ride a bike, how to swim, how to hook a line. He had taught him how to read, and the trick to mastering algebra and geometry. And he'd taught him about girls.

Azura hadn't been too happy about the way he'd handled the latter subject. Especially after Mrs. Connor from next door had rung the doorbell one afternoon with a crying eight-year-old Susie hiding behind her skirt. Mrs. Connor had accused Chad of playing doctor with her little girl. It didn't matter to her that Susie was a year and a half older than Chad and that she might have been the one who had initiated the game. Mrs. Connor had caught them playing, and as far as she was concerned, Chad was at fault.

Somehow, Chad had pinned the blame on Chase, and Chase had been punished. How the hell he'd done that was still a mystery to Chase. Yet, in spite of all their childhood quarrels, and even those that had followed them into adulthood, Chase loved his younger brother, and he knew Chad adored him.

What his mother and Chad didn't know was that years later, a teenage, guilt-ridden Susie had approached Chase. She said she was sorry that he'd been punished for something Chad had done and wanted to make amends. Chase had helped her ease her guilt countless times up against the side of Mrs. Connor's house, securely secluded by her drying wash flapping in the wind.

He'd enjoyed Susie. She was probably the sweetest girl he'd been with up to that point. They'd started up again after he dropped out of college, but then Desire had brought an abrupt halt to his relationship with her. Surprisingly, he never missed Susie. How could he miss her when he'd found the love of his life?

Chase sighed. It had been hard for him to choose between his love for Desire, and ruining his mother's life, but he nonetheless believed that he'd made the right choice. If he had to do it again, he would have made the same decision, but he would have made sure Desire understood why he had to leave. And he would have asked her to go with him or simply wait for him.

Chase sighed again as he turned off the shower and stepped out of the tub. When they were growing up, Chase had always stepped aside and let Chad have his way, let him win whatever games they used to play, because winning always made Chad feel better.

Those days were over. They were playing grown-up games now, and Chase would be damned if he would sit back and let Chad rob him and Desire of a second chance at love, the kind of love that lasts forever.

He was Desire's Chase and no one else's.

CHAPTER THREE

"You don't still have a thing for Chase Hunter, do you, Desire? I mean you can't, otherwise you wouldn't be marrying Chad. Oh my God, I didn't even know you two were dating. What a surprise!"

Desire furrowed her brows. "Why are you asking me about Chase? He's been out of my life for twelve years. And how do you know I'm marrying Chad? We haven't made it public yet. I just told Mom and Dad last night. Did Mom tell you?" Desire stared at her cousin—her mother's niece—as they sat on Desire's porch swing, enjoying the early morning breeze—just as they used to do when they were children and Lisa would sleep over. Lisa was a few months older than Desire, and they had always been close—more like sisters than cousins, really.

"No, I didn't hear it from Aunt Ruth," Lisa said. "Chase told me. Oh my God, that's the life change you mentioned the other night."

Shock rippled though Desire. "Chase?" she asked, when she finally found her voice. "You talked to Chase?" She cleared her throat. "Did he call you from Iowa?"

"No, silly." Lisa slapped her arm playfully. "Chase is here. He came home. He's in Evergreen. Probably sleeping in his bedroom, right across the lawn as we speak," she added with another giggle, nudging her chin toward the Hunters' house.

"Chase is home. He's here. Across the lawn." Desire swallowed the bile that rose to her throat.

"Yeah, and oh my God, girl, you won't believe what we did last night…"

That was how the most difficult conversation of Desire's day had begun this morning.

Chase slept with Lisa. Chase slept with Lisa. Chase slept…

The words bounced around in Desire's head as she backed her Audi out of her driveway and began her twenty-minute drive from suburban Evergreen to her place of business in downtown Granite Falls.

It was a full hour and a half before her usual time of departure, but she couldn't stay in her house one minute more, not with Chase occupying the house next door.

For the hundredth time this morning, Desire wished Lisa hadn't told her about her tryst with Chase, or had at least spared her all the gory details. It was as if Lisa was gloating that she'd finally been with Chase, the boy every teenage girl had swooned over when they were growing up together on Crawford Avenue. Maybe Lisa was gloating. Maybe it was payback for Desire not telling her about her engagement to Chad.

Desire had been anxious to share her news with the only true friend she had in this unforgiving town, but she and Chad had agreed not to make it public for three days and not until after all their parents had given their blessings. She didn't want to make anything public until all her ducks were lined up in a row.

And they were finally in a row—well, all except for one— she thought, as she made a right turn onto West Street and then a quick left onto College Road. She was thirty, the age that most women settled down and began raising families. In fact, she was probably the only unmarried woman of her age on her street. She'd helped many of her neighbors get married, first as bridesmaid or maid of honor, and then as a wedding planner. Most of them were still happily married and raising families. A few, including Lisa's—Desire's first wedding, eight years ago—had ended in divorce.

But such was life. There might not be a lot of sparks between her and Chad, but at least she didn't have to worry about him dumping her. He already knew that she was related to Victoria Summers, the crazy woman who'd fatally shot the wife of her employer, eleven years ago. It might as well have happened yesterday since no family in Evergreen or its neighboring towns wanted Victoria Summers's younger half sister as an in-law.

And now that she'd finally decided to settle down with the only man in town who'd never scorned her because of her family's transgressions, Chase had returned to screw up her life. Again. Of all the times in the last twelve years when he could have returned to Evergreen, why had he chosen to do so now, just three days after Chad had proposed to her? Why hadn't he come back a month ago when she was still available, or three days ago before she'd agreed to marry Chad, or even next year after...

Desire's hands tightened around the steering wheel as she took the entrance ramp to Route 80 West and merged into the flow of traffic speeding toward Granite Falls. It was bad enough to learn about Chase's unexpected homecoming this morning, but hearing that he'd slept with her cousin had brought on nausea like Desire had experienced only one other time in her life—the night Chase, her dearest and closest friend, and the first love of her life had humiliated her in a room full of people.

Three years apart, Chase and Desire had been playmates since the day Chase and his mother, Azura Hunter, moved next door. Her cheeks warmed as the story Chase had told her about their first encounter surfaced in her mind. According to him, it was the day she had begun calling him *My Chase*.

Whether the story was true or not, Desire had had Chase's undivided attention for a few months until Chad came along. And even though Azura, a single mother, had placed a lot of the responsibilities of taking care of Chad on him, Chase still found time for Desire.

She'd adored him, although he was constantly getting into

trouble, and had been suspended several times in elementary school for pulling off stupid pranks: pretending to sleep and snore in class, and sneaking into the school office to make bogus announcements about extended recess and lunch periods, and pulling the fire alarm during school-wide standardized testing, were among his list of innocuous misadventures. He'd even set a mousetrap under a teacher's desk once. Thank goodness she hadn't been wearing open-toe shoes that day. Poor Azura had spent more time in the principals' offices than she did at the hospital where she worked as a nurse.

Desire caught herself smiling with pleasant memories. Chase had been a mischievous little boy, but he was so cute that his teachers had had difficulty doling out harsh punishments on him.

"That boy is going to end up in jail or in the grave at a very early age," Desire had often heard her father say in regard to Chase. "There isn't one good bone in his body. He's a bad seed."

"Oh give the boy a chance, Gerry," Desire's mother, who was the principal of Evergreen Elementary School at the time Chase was enrolled there, would respond. "He just needs attention. He recently lost the only father he ever had."

"You shouldn't make excuses for him. Boys like him grow into men who never learn to respect the law."

"Chase is a good boy. He's gentle with Desire. He's like the big brother she never had. He looks out for her, in case you haven't been paying attention."

"As long as that's all he does," her father had huffed. "If he ever lays a finger on my daughter, I'll—"

"Oh, stop it, Gerry. You're being foolish now. Chase would never hurt Desire. He just needs some male guidance in his life. He's a smart kid. He has natural intelligence beyond his years."

So true, Desire thought. Since he was the top student in every grade, the faculty and staff of Evergreen Middle School had perceived Chase's disruptive behavior as boredom, and so they had given him extra and advanced work to keep him occupied. No one was surprised when he'd gained a full merit scholarship to Granite Falls Preparatory High School, a private institution known in the entire country for its high standards and excellence. As expected, Chase excelled to the top of his classes.

When Desire hit puberty and her female hormones kicked into gear, her sisterly adoration for Chase turned into girlish infatuation. Tall and muscular, teenage Chase was impulsive, spontaneous, and wild. Sneaking into movie theaters without paying, taking his mother's car for midnight rendezvous before he got his license, diving off forbidden areas into the region's two rivers, and skinny-dipping by moonlight in Crystal and Cedar Lakes were just a few of the kinds of trouble Chase Hunter constantly got into. Luckily for him, his stepuncle-in-law was the twin towns' Chief of Police, so he always got off with a slap on the hand, and none of his pranks had gotten back to Granite Falls Prep, or else Chase would have surely been expelled.

Desire had loved the aura of danger and excitement he exuded even though she didn't understand the feelings running rampant through her teenage body at the time. She used to look forward to getting home from school and hanging out with him as he helped her with her homework and science projects. She'd pretended not to understand geometry and algebra, just so Chase could tutor her for hours. She was certain he knew she wasn't that dumb, but he never let on. He was always patient and gentle with her.

Chase's charisma grew with him, and, unfortunately for Desire, she wasn't the only girl in Evergreen or Granite Falls Prep who'd begun to notice his sexual magnetism. The older girls had begun looking at him with dreamy eyes, and he would always look back and smile at them in a way he never looked or smiled at Desire.

Eventually, he'd stopped hanging out with her and Chad, and would disappear for hours at a time, returning with rumpled clothes, a twig or two embedded in his dark hair, a gleam in his gray eyes, and a satisfied smile on his ruggedly handsome face. Having already taken sexual education in school, Desire had known exactly what Chase was doing with those girls, some of them older than him—women. Green with envy, she'd vowed to make him notice her when she was old enough to partake in his adult games.

Desire caught herself smiling as she took the Highland Avenue exit off of Route 80 and drifted into the flow of traffic into downtown Granite Falls. On her eighteenth birthday, she had asked Chase to accompany her to the Flower Garden Maze, her favorite place in the entire world. He'd recently dropped out of college and had been splitting his time between working as a landscape artist at Carron & Son Architecture Designs in Granite Falls, and washing and polishing the motorcycle he'd bought at age sixteen with money he'd saved up doing odd jobs around the neighborhood since he was ten years old.

Desire had been surprised that Chase had broken off a date with Susie Connor, his current girl at the time, and her former neighbor and childhood playmate. The fact that he'd stood up Susie to spend time with her was Desire's first clue that Chase cared about her in a grown-up way. That knowledge had given her courage to kiss him and share her dreams with him that night.

Desire's heart began a rapid beat as she recalled walking between a row of sunflowers and daffodils with Chase while licking the ice cream cone he'd bought her at the maze café. They'd talked about her going off to college to study marketing in the fall of that year, and returning home to work at Fontaine Enterprises where she'd interned for two summers, and where her sister, Victoria, worked as a personal assistant to Bryce Fontaine, CEO and founder of the billion-dollar company.

That night, Chase had shared his passion for architecture and had told Desire about his plan to present his ideas and sketches at the upcoming Youth Talent Night at Granite Falls Country Club—an annual event where the winner of each category was awarded fifty thousand dollars to start their own companies or further their interests. Desire, who happened to be on the planning committee, had agreed to be Chase's presenter since all candidates needed one. In her excitement, she'd hugged him, and before either of them knew what was happening, their lips had been locked in a deep, passionate kiss that had left her breathless.

It was Desire's first kiss, ever, and she'd been so mesmerized, she'd had visions of walking through the maze in a white wedding gown with a mile-long train toward Chase, who would be dressed in a white tuxedo. She'd shared her dream with him just as freely as she'd shared her first kiss.

"Would you be My Chase for real?" she'd asked in a breathless whisper against his lips.

"Yes, Desire. I'll be your Chase. I'll be yours. I promise."

"What are you going to tell Susie?"

"Susie, who?" he'd asked, before capturing her lips again and kissing her so passionately, Desire's skin had felt like it was on fire.

She'd wanted to make love with him right there in the garden, but he'd said it wasn't the right time and place with people mulling around. He wanted her first time to be special and memorable with candles and flowers—no wine because she wasn't old enough to drink yet, he'd jokingly added. He'd booked a room at a nice hotel in a town north of Evergreen where they would spend the night after the talent show was over. But alas, their plans never materialized.

The thumb drive that was supposed to hold Chase's architectural designs turned out to be a short video of Chase and two women—a mother and a daughter—having sex in the women's home. The time stamp was two days before the event—a week after she'd kissed Chase in the garden and after he'd promised that she was the only girl in his heart.

Desire swallowed as she remembered standing at the podium, her mouth frozen open as she stared at the video. The initial gasps from the audience had been thunderous and the silence that followed had been deafening. Desire had prayed for the floor to open up and suck her into a deep black hole from where she could never escape. Tears had stung her eyes as she'd looked at Chase, dressed in the suit she'd picked out for him, sitting in the front row with all the other candidates.

He'd had the audacity to walk up to her, attempting to apologize while his porno clip was running. Humiliation, disgust, and contempt were just a few of the emotions that had been rioting in Desire. Her hands had itched to slap him, her feet to kick him, but because lashing out at him that way would alert the world that she cared, she'd contained herself to telling him what a vile, contemptuous, less-than-human scumbag he was.

People had talked about that clip for months. Some had even asked Desire for the entire movie and wondered if she knew where it could be purchased. Overnight, Chase Hunter had become a sought-after porn star and Desire had been labeled his pimp. The image of Chase having sex with two women had been stamped in Desire's brain for a long time. But she had been forced to put it aside a few months later when her sister shot and killed Bryce Fontaine's wife before turning the gun on herself. Chase Hunter's junk had become old news as the media vultures began hounding her family about Victoria's crime of passion.

Two hideous stains had been placed on the Summers family name in the space of a few months. All of Desire's socialite friends began avoiding her as if she had the mark of the devil stamped on her forehead. Cursed was what they'd called her family. The only person who'd shown compassion for what had happened was Lewis Carron, Chase's old boss's son. He'd expressed his regrets that one of his father's employees was that contemptible. He'd said that Carron Architecture's reputation had suffered just as much as she had. Desire had been grateful to have one person who understood what she was going through.

Except for Azura, all of her parents' friends had dropped them, too. They were no longer invited to social events nor welcomed at the Country Club. Her father had had to resign his role as Mayor of Granite Falls, and then he'd suffered a heart attack that almost killed him.

Life had become so miserable that Desire had often fantasized about escaping to another corner of the world where nobody knew her—just like Chase had done. But escape was not an option for her. She'd even had to give up the luxury of leaving home to attend college. She couldn't abandon her sick, grieving father and her heart-stricken mother. Instead of attending NYU as initially planned, she'd enrolled in Evergreen Community College, and then spent the last eleven years of her life trying to redeem her family's name.

Since Victoria's crime, and suicide, Desire had been a "good girl," doing everything her parents wanted and expected of her. She'd loved her half sister dearly, and she missed her terribly, but many times Desire wished she wasn't related to Victoria and that she hadn't been expected to clean up the mess her father's oldest daughter had left behind.

She'd become a poster child, above reproach, avoiding anything with even a hint of scandal in it. In essence, she'd had to put aside the desires of her own heart to become the desire of her parents' hearts—especially her father's, who'd been diagnosed with prostate cancer, seven years ago. He'd beat the disease with chemotherapy, lots of prayers from their church, and TLC from her and her mother. He'd been in remission for the past seven years, but his oncologist had warned that he could succumb to the cancer within six months to a year if it ever returned.

Desire suppressed a groan. She was so grateful that she'd finally had the chance to redeem her family's name before her father died. Her chance had come last summer when, due to a twist of fate, she'd been hired to plan the elaborate group wedding for Bryce Fontaine and his three, billionaire friends. Because of that wedding, Bryce had come around to forgiving Victoria for killing his first wife, thanks to his second wife, Kaya, who'd convinced him to let go of his animosity toward the Summers family, so they could all move on with their lives.

Planning that wedding had opened up doors of opportunities for Desire—both personally and professionally. Her business had grown so big, she'd had to hire extra help. She couldn't go it alone anymore, especially now that she was thinking of expanding beyond Evergreen and Granite Falls, not only as a wedding planner, but also as a coordinator of other events.

Lori, her personal assistant and food connoisseur, who kept her on task; Jacques her brilliant and talented floral designer; and Gillian, her advertising and marketing consultant, all worked diligently to keep Weddings by Desire's flag flying at the top of the wedding planning totem pole.

Her personal life had come full circle as well. She was making new friends—most significantly, the wives of the billionaires, she thought with a pleased smile. Folks were beginning to show her respect, and a couple of the guys who'd dumped her had the audacity to try to get back with her since she began associating with celebrities and politicians around the country.

She'd sacrificed her dreams to take care of her parents and make them happy. In hindsight, Desire could admit that not going off to college in New York had worked out in her favor. Staying home and attending a community college with a lighter workload, less stress, and a nonexistent social life had afforded her a lot of time for some deep soul searching, and figuring out what she really wanted from life.

Yes, it would have been awesome to have an MBA in Marketing from NYU, and maybe follow in her sister's footsteps working at a global, billion-dollar company like Fontaine Enterprises. She'd had to abandon that first dream, but now, instead of being an employee, she was an employer. Nothing could compare to having her own company, being her own CEO, and hopefully one day becoming the most prosperous wedding planner in the world, or the country at least.

Desire's second dream, her true life's dream had begun materializing when she'd served as Lisa's maid of honor. Desire had gone above and beyond her duty and had planned a fairy tale wedding for Lisa from start to finish, including writing her vows. Everyone had been impressed, and soon other brides-to-be—even those who'd shunned her after Victoria's crime—began asking her to plan their weddings.

They didn't want to be friends again. They just wanted her professional expertise, and they were willing to shell out insane amounts of money for it.

Desire had quickly realized that she didn't need friends to run a successful business—a hard fact to accept, but a sound one, nonetheless. All she needed to do was earn the trust and respect of her clients and provide the best services on the market. Weddings by Desire had been delivering for the past six years, and even more so in the past year.

Her good-girl façade had paid off, way beyond her wildest imaginations. But could she maintain that level of decorum now that Chase Hunter—the one man in this world who still had the power to make her want things and be willing to do things that in no way, shape, or form aligned with the new principles she'd had to create and live by—had returned to Evergreen?

That was the question bouncing around in Desire's head as she pulled off Main Street and into the parking lot of the building that housed Weddings by Desire.

With an hour to spare before Lori, her personal assistant, and Trinity Newman, her first client of the day, showed up, Desire made herself busy by making some calls to her regular caterers, photographers, and deejays for two weddings that were scheduled for early fall. Lori usually undertook those chores, but Desire needed something to keep her mind off Chase Hunter. Those tasks accomplished, she arranged three table settings, complete with some of the most expensive bone china dinnerware, sterling silver utensils, and crystal glasses on the market—specifically requested by Trinity.

At thirty-one, Trinity was embarking on her third marriage. One would think that by the third attempt at happiness, a bride-to-be would avoid the fuss and just head on down to City Hall, but Trinity was the exception, a true romantic and believer in forever-after fairy tales. She wanted the white dress with the long train, bridesmaids, ushers, and flower girls—the works. Trinity was the daughter of a Hollywood producer who'd attended the billionaire wedding last year. Since the

Newmans owned a summer villa on Crystal Lake, Trinity had opted to meet with Desire in Granite Falls instead of flying her out to Hollywood. Trinity had ordered the expensive dinnerware samples and offered them to Desire at no additional cost.

Desire knew for a fact that those samples cost four times as much as a first class round-trip ticket to California, but truth be told, she would much rather have the items in her collection. She was sure she would have the opportunity to present those brands again before long.

Forty-five minutes later, with a freshly brewed mug of coffee in hand, Desire was in the middle of setting out the customary daily munchies—an assortment of fruits, crackers, cheeses, and sweets—on a coffee table when the guttural *burrrrrooom* of a motorcycle drew her attention toward the parking lot in the front of the building.

A few seconds later, her heart began to gallop as the towering dark figure of a man stepped from behind an SUV, and began a tiger-like stride toward her business.

The cup in Desire's hand tipped as she placed it on the table, spilling the hot black liquid over the snacks she'd so carefully arranged. Sweat ran down her armpits, drenching her silk coral blouse. Her heart pounded in her ears. Her skin itched. Butterflies fluttered around in her stomach, and her throat dried up. But worst of all, to her dismay, she felt a pool of fluids soak her panties as she took in his massive, six-foot-three-inch physique.

His yard-wide shoulders served as a springboard for his thick mass of dark hair with every step he took toward her. His formidable pectorals, his guns, and the muscles of his washboard stomach, vibrating with vitality, were barely contained beneath the cotton material of his white T-shirt. His narrow hips tapered off into strong powerful jeans-clad thighs and legs.

Desire trembled as he came to a stop at the door. His lips that had transported her young inexperienced body to heaven that night in the garden were pressed tightly together and his gray enigmatic eyes stared her down through the glass. She noticed with conflicting emotions that he still didn't shave his facial hair, but wore it trimmed close to the surface of his smooth tanned skin. Even from a distance, Desire could see the strong muscles of his chin and jaws twitch, and even through the glass, she could feel the rage emanating from him. He was pissed. There was no doubt about it.

He tried the door and, realizing it was locked, he made a motion with his hand for her to unlock it.

Desire hesitated, even as she felt compelled to obey him. He was a Chase she did not recognize, yet one with whom she felt an unnatural familiarity and synergy. Chase had always possessed a ruggedness and vital power that attracted her, but in his absence, he'd acquired a polished veneer that made him even more dangerous and irresistible. Bad boy, Chase Hunter, a gardener with no real purpose in life, had left Evergreen in the wake of a repulsive scandal. He'd returned, a man with an air of authority that demanded instant compliance.

What had happened to her Chase? How could a farm in Iowa equip him with such commanding power, Desire wondered as her pulse careened out of control.

He made the *unlock the door* motion with his hand again.

Desire contemplated ignoring him, but common sense told her that it was best if she confronted him now and sent him on his way. Trinity and Lori were arriving soon and the last thing she wanted was to expose more Summers family dirty laundry to the public, especially in front of a high-end client. Plus, there was no way she would be able to concentrate on work with this much tension in her body. She needed release. And if release was confronting Chase Hunter, then so be it.

Wiping her sweaty palms down the sides of her white linen pencil skirt, Desire forced her wobbly legs to take her across the floor.

CHAPTER FOUR

Chase stepped inside and closed the door, his gray eyes narrow and hard as he looked her over from her head to her ivory heels.

In spite of the barely contained rage emanating from him, Desire's breath caught in her throat as the scent of his cologne wafted up her nostrils. *Straight to Heaven*, aka *White Cristal.* She recognized the woody, spicy fragrance with distinct hints of musk, jasmine, patchouli, cedar, amber, nutmeg, and rum that reminded her of a warm sunny day on a tropical island. How could Chase Hunter, a field worker on an Iowa farm, afford *Straight to Heaven*?

Desire had first encountered the fragrance on one of her wealthy clients and had liked it so much, she'd bought a bottle for her father last Christmas. He wasn't impressed and had passed it on to Chad with her permission. Maybe Chase had swiped some from Chad.

The scent had been pleasing on other men, even Chad, but on Chase—God, the ingredients mixed with his own masculine pheromones was sending Desire sliding into a state of concupiscence, evoking feelings she'd long ago stopped dreaming of ever experiencing again.

"Why are you marrying my brother?"

Desire startled and took two steps back as his deep vocals pulled her out of her spell, turning the pleasure churns in her stomach to fury. *Just like that?* No, *Hi Desire, how are you? You look great. It's been a while. I'm sorry I screwed up. Can you ever forgive me?*

She held his glare, even as she willed her lower lip to stop trembling. "Why did you sleep with my cousin?"

"Because you're marrying my brother."

Oh, he'd turned honest. Despite her fears of what his presence meant in her life, Desire felt a hot and awful joy at seeing him, of hearing his voice, of being this close to him, of smelling him, of having the chance to reach out and touch him if she wanted—and God she wanted to. She wanted to grab him, pull him in, lock her arms around his neck and glue her lips to his. But he'd done her wrong and then disappeared without an apology.

Pushing the lustful temptation aside, Desire squared her shoulders. "Well, if you hadn't run away, and then stayed away, I wouldn't be marrying your brother, would I?"

He flinched.

Desire dropped her gaze to his chest, rising and falling with his labored breathing. Why the hell had she said something like that to him? Chase was the one person in the world who had the power to turn her life upside down, make her say stupid things that might come back to haunt her. The words *Carver Farm* printed in bold black letters on the front of his T-shirt seemed to taunt her for feeling vulnerable to a mere farmhand, a boy her father always thought was beneath her, and a man who would definitely not fit in with the kinds of people with whom she now kept company.

"You'd be marrying me instead. Probably be married to me already," he stated matter-of-factly, as if he was reading her mind and dared to challenge her opinion that he wouldn't fit into her world. He took a step toward her.

Desire took another step back—her third away from him—and found her back against the wall, the satiny floor-to-ceiling drapes brushing against the backs of her thighs and her legs, adding to the sensuous sensations Chase's proximity and his scent were causing from the front.

Inadvertently, her gaze wandered down to the huge bulge in his crotch and the outline of his shaft against his left thigh. She shivered from the memory of feeling Chase's erection pressed into her belly for the first time in the garden that night, and then more intimately against the soft heat of her sex in the following week. He'd pulsed with life while she'd stroked him through his jeans, and she'd burned with untapped passionate hunger as he'd molded her breasts, kissed her neck, and fondled her through her clothes. She'd felt his excitement several times, but she'd never had the opportunity to *see* what Chase Hunter really had to offer. His private parts had been blurred out in the video, thank God, but the vision of him with those women was still very much alive in her mind.

Desire sucked in her breath as she felt the inner walls of her sex vibrate and spew more warm fluids into her panties. She couldn't believe she was getting turned on at the twelve-year-old vision of Chase having sex with those women. See, that was why she needed to distance herself from him. He brought out the worst in her. She couldn't afford...

"At least let's be honest and truthful about our feelings. That has never been a problem for us."

His comment pulled her out of her stupor. She met his stare head-on. "You have no right to talk to me about feelings nor about the truth after what you did, Chase. You humiliated me in front of all those people, the most esteemed in the region. They all thought I was part of your sick scheme. You have no idea how I've suffered because of what you did. They called me a pimp. *Your pimp*! I lost all my friends because of you."

"I'm sorry."

"If you were sorry, you would have stayed and cleaned up your own mess, explained to me why you had the need to embarrass me like that. What was your game? What did you expect to gain?"

His chest rose and fell on a deep sigh and the muscles of

his jaws twitched under his facial hair. "I tried to explain. You wouldn't see me. Your father called me a repulsive reprobate, and threatened to shoot me if I showed up at your house again."

Desire's eyes narrowed. "My father threatened to shoot you?"

"Yes."

Her father was a gun collector, and he used to love going to the shooting range with his friends. But he always kept them locked away in a safe when she and Victoria were growing up. Ironically, it was one of his guns Victoria had used to kill Bryce Fontaine's wife—a fact that still haunted her father, and probably what had caused his heart attack. He'd gotten rid of his guns after the tragedy, but he, like everyone else, knew it was too little too late. He couldn't bring Pilar Fontaine or Victoria back to life.

"I don't blame him," Chase said, tugging her back from the unpleasant past. "Without the facts, his reaction was justified. If I were in his shoes, I would have done the same thing. A good father would protect his daughter from the kind of man I used to be. I was a rebel. I would want the best for my daughter, too."

And her father's best for her, and her best for her father, was Chad, Desire thought on a tremor.

Last night, her parents hadn't seemed surprised when she'd told them that Chad had proposed and that she'd accepted. They'd been overly excited, especially her father. And why not? She and Chad had maintained a healthy friendship throughout their lives, even while they dated other people. Perhaps it was their families' closeness that had subconsciously led Chad to propose. Desire knew that her father's one wish before he died was to walk her down the aisle. It was the reason she'd accepted Chad's proposal—subconscious though it was.

Would her parents still be elated about her engagement to Chad if they knew that she and Chase had expressed their love for each other since she was eighteen? Would they encourage her to give her hand to one brother when she'd already given her heart to the other? Would her father still want to give her to the one man he thought wasn't good enough for his baby girl?

"How long have you and Chad been—" He waved his hand in the air as if he were afraid to voice the word.

"Close?"

"If that's what you call it." His eyes narrowed and hardened.

"Why does it matter?"

"It matters. And if you're worried about hurting my feelings, I can take it. I'm a big boy."

That you are. Desire shifted her focus to the parking lot that was slowly filling up with the cars of the employees who worked on her block. She knew exactly what Chase wanted to know, but how could she be honest without admitting that she still had feelings for him, still loved him?

Chad's and her relationship had remained strictly platonic until last Christmas when he'd kissed her on her lips while they'd been standing under the mistletoe in her parents' Granite Falls home during a holiday party—the first one her parents had hosted in years. Maybe he'd kissed her because they were both unattached, and were feeling lonely at such a festive time. Nevertheless, after the shock of his unexpected advance had worn off, she'd recoiled, mainly because she'd been thinking of Chase at the very moment Chad had kissed her.

She'd longed for Chase, pined for him, even though he'd made a fool of her. He'd toyed with her emotions, made sweet promises to her, and then he'd gone and had a *ménage à trois* a few days later, made a video, then showed it to the world—her world.

What disgusted her most was that he'd had sex with those women during the time he and she had been sneaking around to keep their romance a secret. Innocent, eighteen-year-old Desire was still dependent on her parents back then. Chase was almost twenty-two, a grown man and very experienced when it came to women and the ways of the world.

Her overly protective father would have definitely shot Chase if he'd known what the two of them had been doing on a mat on the floor of an abandoned building down by the Mannis River at the edge of town. It was their own special place for making out until the night of the talent show. Chase was supposed to be the man to make her a woman.

She was sure Chase never expected her to ever find out what a lying, two-timing louse he was. He'd made a mistake in giving her the wrong thumb drive, and she'd made a mistake in trusting him. The fact that he'd broken off a date with Susie so easily and then kissed her a few hours later should have alerted her to his despicable character. But she was young and in love, and love, as they say, is blind.

The hopeful part of Desire had waited for Chase to come back and apologize, explain his side of the story, but he never did. And so as time passed, she'd tried to forget him by dating other men, only to be disappointed in each of them because none of them was *her* Chase, or when they dumped her after discovering she was one of *those* Summerses.

He plucked a strand of her hair from her cheek, and placed it behind her shoulder, making her quiver from the light brush of his knuckles against her skin.

She gazed up at him, speechless that his simple touch could still make her melt inside.

"I've changed," he said in a husky voice. "I'm not the same man who left Evergreen. I changed that night in the garden, the night I kissed you and promised to be your Chase. I meant every word I said to you that night. I still mean them. Look." He pulled a hemp string from inside his T-shirt, and held up the white wooden pendant she'd given him on her fifteenth birthday. "I still wear it. I've never taken it off. I'm still your Chase."

Desire shuddered outwardly as she stared at the words on the heart-shaped pendant: *Desire's Chase*. She'd been so infatuated with him. He'd been her only crush since she was eight years old. Her infatuation had grown into love and passion, but after being hurt, she'd had to trade that kind of love and passion for something sure and stable—the kind of relationship Chad brought to the table.

Chase's nearness, his intoxicating odor, and the heat from his body were proving that it was impossible to forget the ecstasy that had begun in the garden and had lasted for one full week. Why had he shown up now, out of the blue, when things were going great for her? If she didn't get back on the defense, she would be bringing down another scandal on her family name. One from which her father might never recover. She would be a fool to trust Chase again.

Taking a deep breath, Desire straightened her shoulders and raised her gaze to his. "I find it hard to believe that you've changed when you slept with my cousin the first night you came back home. And then here you are, less than eight hours later in my face telling me about our feelings for each other. You are still the repulsive reprobate my father called you, Chase Hunter. Why don't you just go on back to your corn farm in Iowa and leave us all alone?"

Desire's attempt to walk away was halted by Chase's hands on her arms. Her back was against the wall and his hard, muscular body was pressed up against her front, his erection burning a hole in her belly. His face was mere inches from hers, his breath warm on her cheek.

"Why don't you just tell me how you honestly feel about me?" he dared her. "Tell me why you're marrying my brother."

Desire swallowed. "Why do people get married?"

"For all kinds of reasons. Greed, pregnancy, money, status, desperation. You name it. What's your reason? And why Chad?"

"Why not Chad? He's a good man. The kind of man my father wants for me."

"So, you're marrying Chad because your father thinks he's the best man for you."

"Yes. He'll make a good husband and father, and he—"

"Desire."

Desire's heart ricocheted to her throat at the sound of her name on his lips—the first time in twelve years. It was a whisper, soft and feathery like a lover's lips lightly brushing her cheek. Only Chase could say her name with such sensuality. Her knees buckled. Her heart began to thump in her ears again.

Taking advantage of her weakness, he trailed his hands down her arms, all the way to her wrists. He laced their fingers together, like he'd done countless times in the week leading up to the talent show. He raised their hands above her head and pressed them against the wall. "Do you love my brother?"

"Yes." She swallowed.

"I don't mean like a friend. When he stands near you, like this—" He crouched down and rubbed his erection against her heat, causing a pitiful moan from her lips. "Do you tremble and sigh into his mouth like you're sighing into mine now? Does he make your heart beat faster, out of control? Does your breath come out harsh and shallow like it does now? Do your throat and your mouth dry up, and does your tongue come out to lick your sweet luscious lips, over and over again?"

Desire yanked her tongue back into her mouth and squeezed her thighs together as the walls of her sex began vibrating and pulsing and aching and her body began to melt under his lewd questions. She moaned aloud this time when his hands traveled slowly down her arms, across her quivering belly. He tugged on her blouse, releasing the hem from the waist of her skirt. His fingers brushed the bare skin of her stomach, sending tingling sensations whooshing through her.

Dear God, she was about to have a mini orgasm right here, right now, fully clothed, up against the wall in her place of business with her door unlocked where anyone could walk in at any moment. She whispered his name, not knowing if it was a plea for mercy or an acceptance of pleasure as his fingers brushed against her thighs. He began lifting the hem of her skirt, slowly and sensuously. "Chase…"

"Desire." His lips brushed one side of her mouth, making her moan and shiver. "You can't marry my brother. It will be a mistake. You know it. I know it. He needs to know it, too. It's best if you end it now rather than wait for this very *thing* to happen between us once you're married. Is this what you want, Desire?" He trailed his lips from one side of her mouth to the next, his low beard tickling her skin, his warm wet tongue making light contact wit her lips, just enough to tease, to show her what she'd be missing if she married Chad.

"You want to commit adultery with your brother-in-law?" With her skirt bunched high on her thighs, his fingers crawled up her heaving belly, his destination clear to her. "You want to start another scandal in this godforsaken town?"

Scandal. The mention of that word was all Desire needed to pull her out of her second lustful stupor of the morning. She placed her hands against Chase's hard chest, and pushed with all her strength. "You disgusting farmhand!"

He went flying back into the table of munchies. Miraculously nothing fell to the floor.

"So that's it, huh? You don't think I'm good enough for you?" he asked, nonplussed.

Desire pushed off the wall, yanked her skirt back into place and tucked her blouse back into her waistband. "You're not good enough for any woman, Chase Hunter. You just tried to seduce your brother's fiancée, and—"

"Not seduce. Save from a life of regret and unhappiness."

"You slept with my cousin last night and here you are, hours later, trying to score with me."

"You keep going back to me and Lisa. Are you jealous that it wasn't you in the trailer with me last night?"

Desire was grateful that she'd stayed at her parents' home last night. It wasn't the first time Chase had taken a woman to that trailer, yet he had never taken Desire there during their week of bliss. He'd told her she was too good for a trailer. That trailer needed to be hauled away and burned.

"At least Lisa doesn't pretend she doesn't want what she wants," he said, taking a step toward her.

"And I'm sure you helped her not pretend."

"I did my best. But you already know about it since I imagine she gave you all the gory details on your porch this morning."

Desire's eyes flashed and her hands balled into tight fists. "That's why I'm marrying Chad instead of you. Chad's a gentleman. Something you can never be. You're a—" She searched for a new adjective to describe him, one that would cut to the core. "You're a—"

"A what?" he asked, taking another step toward her. "What am I, Desire?"

"Get out!" she barked. She was jealous, and mad at herself for allowing him to get under her skin like this. He was taking her back to that night, the worst night of her life.

"Gladly." He turned and stormed toward the door, almost colliding into Lori as she came in.

"Oops. Excuse me," Lori said, staring up at Chase, who'd stopped for a split second before continuing his charge out the door. "A new client?" she asked Desire.

It wasn't unusual for Desire to entertain a male client. Many grooms had made initial contact in the past. She stared at Chase's back, watching the powerful muscles in his shoulders and arms pump with anger as he stormed through the parking lot toward his bike. "No," she said. "Just an unhappy in-law."

Lori's eyeballs widened as she dropped her tote on the floor.

The second she heard Chase's motorcycle roar to life, Desire fell into a chair. She dropped her face into her hands and forced air into her lungs.

"Desire, are you okay?" Lori sat in the chair next to hers.

Desire raised her head and stared out into the parking lot at the sound of Chase's motorcycle sputtering away, leaving a trail of smoke behind him. That bike probably had its own stories to tell, Desire thought, recalling watching one girl after the other climb on and off of Chase's bike. Desire had longed for her chance, but her parents had forbidden her to ever get on that bike.

Desire's blood heated up as she recalled the day when her dream had come true. Her parents were out of town, and her sister, who was supposed to pick her up from a friend's birthday party on the other side of town, had gotten stuck at work and had asked Chase to bring her home. He'd been happy to oblige, and had promised to keep it between the three of them.

Desire smiled as she remembered snuggling up to Chase's back, and wrapping her hands around his waist as he whisked her through town. His body had felt so hard and warm, and even though it was her first time on a motorcycle, she hadn't been afraid. She'd felt safe with Chase, as safe as she always did when they'd done less risky things together.

Desire sighed. Something monumental had happened during that ride, and once she'd climbed off, both she and Chase had seen the evidence of her first period on his seat and on her pink shorts.

Chase had given her a peculiar look and said, *"Desire, you're a woman now."*

It was around that time that he'd stopped hanging out with her. He'd avoided being alone with her as much as possible. And when they were alone—which was mostly to help her with her homework—it was all business. No more boxing or karate lessons, no more doing anything that would require touching her. She was a late bloomer, but becoming a woman at age fourteen had been a curse for Desire, a curse she'd had to endure for four long years, until she was legal in the eyes of the law.

"Who was that man, and what did he want?" Lori asked, pulling her back from the past. "He looked pissed."

Desire tucked her hair behind her ears, and her memories to the back of her mind. "He wants the bride to call off the wedding."

Lori inclined her head, her dark wavy hair brushing against her porcelain cheeks. "What? Why?"

"He claims he's in love with her."

"Ohhh. So why's he bringing his sorrow to you? Why not talk to the bride herself?"

He just did.

"Is he a friend, foe, or relative of the groom?"

"Half brother."

"Oooh, this is juicy," Lori crooned. "So which wedding is it? Gilford, Miller, Thompson, Lewis, Newman? Oh please tell me," she pleaded, naming off the weddings Desire had been hired to plan for the next two years.

Hunter. "I'd rather not say." *She couldn't say.* She was so grateful that no one but her and Chad's families knew about their engagement. It might have to stay that way for a while, at least until Chase went back to Iowa. "I hope he drops his stupid fantasies before he causes more trouble for that poor couple." *Poor* being the operative word, she thought, as tension knotted in her stomach.

"I doubt that," Lori said. "He doesn't look like the kind of man who would take *no* for an answer. But God, he's hot. Hot, hot, hot." Lori fanned her now scarlet face with her hand. "I never saw him before. Is he from around here? I've met all the grooms we're working with and none of them could compare to that hunk, not by a long shot. What woman would want his brother over him? The minute I saw him, I wanted to take my clothes off. Sex oozes out of every pore of his body. Wow!"

"Looks are deceiving," Desire said in an effort to justify her own body's treacherous reaction when she'd first spotted Chase walking across the parking lot.

"Then lead me to the table of deceit," Lori said with a chuckle. "I'll eat until I rupture, and then go back for more. Mmmm. I would love to have him for lunch." She smacked her lips.

Desire opened her mouth to warn Lori to keep her covetous eyes off her man when she remembered that Chase wasn't her man. She was engaged to his brother. The moment she'd accepted Chad's proposal, she'd declared open season on Chase Hunter, and there was not a darn thing she could do about it. She and Chad were meeting Derrick Browne, a news reporter from *Twin Town Times*, for lunch, and by the end of the day, everyone would know she was off the market.

She glanced at her bare ring finger. The ring Chad had given her, the one she'd forgotten to bring with her today, was still in its box at the back of her sock drawer where she'd stashed it the night he'd proposed.

She'd hoped to be able to give it back to Chad last night with an apology for accepting his proposal in the first place. But things hadn't gone as she'd hoped. The results of the tests her father's oncologist had ordered a week ago had come back. His PSA level had increased. He was not in remission anymore. He could be dead in a year.

"See, baby girl, if you want me to walk you down the aisle, you gotta do it soon. I'd love to be able to hold at least one of my grandbabies in my arms before I die."

Desire trembled now as she'd trembled at her father's words—his dying wish, so to speak. She's had no choice but to tell them about her and Chad's engagement. Her father had wept with joy as he'd hugged her and praised her for making such a wise decision.

It had been so long since Desire had seen her father happy. How could she tell him that she'd only agreed to marry Chad to make him happy, when he hadn't even asked her if Chad made her happy?

She'd made her bed. She had to go and lie down in it. There was no turning back now.

But there is, a little voice in her head said. *It's not public yet. You can still stop it. And hurt my father? No. I can't. I won't do it.*

"What are you doing here so early, anyway?"

Desire shook off the chill as Lori went to rearrange the stack of crackers that had become undone when she'd shoved Chase into the table.

"Opening and setting up is my job." Lori tilted her head and squinted her eyes at Desire. "Are you firing me? Are you trying to prove that you don't need me?"

Desire pushed to her feet. "I need you more than ever now, Lori. You have no idea."

"Good. 'Cause that's what I need to hear, boss." Lori pulled her tablet from her tote and booted it up. "I spoke with the caterers for the Miller wedding, and they are fine with the extra fifty guests, but because it's such short notice, it will cost them quite a bit more per plate. I checked with the groom and bride and they're fine with the price increase…"

And thus began the most twisted business day of Desire's life.

CHAPTER FIVE

He'd gone about it all wrong.

Chase flipped his signal and gunned his Yamaha, sending an unhealthy stream of exhaust into the atmosphere as he zipped past the traffic moving way too slow for him at seventy miles an hour. The machine vibrated under him as he opened it up to the road, forcing it to perform like it did in younger days.

Like the machine between his legs, his and Desire's first encounter was supposed to pulse to life. It was supposed to be one of anticipation, possibilities, illumination, and it wasn't supposed to happen at her place of business.

When Chase had finally decided to return to Evergreen, he'd scheduled the first week of his homecoming down to the last detail. He would take care of his professional business in the first couple days, and then on the third day, he would take care of his personal life—his wooing of Desire Summers.

Desire was to receive a bouquet of red roses, and an anonymous note to meet an admirer in the lobby of Hotel Andreas—the most luxurious venue in the area—and a very public place where she wouldn't have had reservations about meeting with a stranger. No matter the outcome of that first meeting, Chase had been prepared to date her, pamper her, spoil her, and convince her that they belonged together.

He'd imagined he would walk away from their reunion with a smile of elation on his face, his heart beating with the knowledge that Desire Summers loved him and wanted to be with him even after the years they'd spent apart.

Instead, here he was, madder than he'd been before he'd seen her, and speeding along Route 80 East toward Evergreen on his old bike that threatened to collapse from age and neglect at each mile he devoured.

If he'd followed his agenda, he would have gotten out of bed much earlier than he actually had, responded to the emails that had accumulated overnight from his European contacts, make some vital local calls over a cup of coffee, ridden over to the motorcycle shop on the east side of town, and while his bike was being tuned, scout out the areas around the Mannis River and Cedar Lake where construction of the new residential developments—the ones Chad had mentioned this morning—would begin in a few weeks.

Once he'd had a physical visual lay of the land, he would have headed over to Fontaine Enterprises to meet with Bryce and his team of real estate brokers, developers, surveyors, and engineers, and of course the representatives and architects from Carron Designs—the bid winners for most of the projects. Then he would have shown up at a very important meeting tomorrow morning where he would have finally flushed his enemy down the sewer.

Everything had been shot to hell. Chase flipped his signal, took the River Drive exit off the highway and cruised between row after row of red brick buildings and large granite mills that once powered factories along the Mannis River.

His plans had begun spiraling downward the moment he saw Lisa at the airport yesterday. If she hadn't been his limo driver, he wouldn't have had her card; he wouldn't have called her; they wouldn't have gotten wasted together; he wouldn't have slept with her; and Desire's contempt for him wouldn't have been revived.

Chase knew that it wasn't the idea of him sleeping with another woman that had Desire fuming, but the fact that it was her cousin and her best friend. He should have known better, he thought, as he turned into a narrow alleyway and slowed his speed to accommodate the crowds of pedestrians crossing the street, and walking along the sidewalks. He should have thought of the consequences of his actions instead of charging headfirst into a situation he knew would be revolting in the eyes of the woman whose heart he was trying to win back.

After the shame and stupidity of his blunder had worn off last night, Chase had realized that he needed to make a small detour in his plans. Instead of waiting a couple days, he'd decided to send Desire the flowers and the invitation to meet for brunch today. But with Lisa blabbing about their sexual encounter, and Chad's mention of his and Desire's lunch with the reporter, there was no time to waste before the engagement became public knowledge.

Ignoring the delicious aromas coming from his mother's kitchen, Chase had crept out of the house, hauled his old motorcycle from the garage, and dusted it off. Like a spurned lover, it had sputtered and groaned with his first attempts to start it, but it had eventually given in and had welcomed his attention, his touch to its contours, and eventually his weight when he'd climbed on and settled his ass on its leather seat and flanked its belly between his thighs.

On his way to Granite Falls, Chase had rehearsed a million ways to approach Desire once he saw her. He was supposed to convince her not to marry Chad. He was to show her in no uncertain terms that he was still in love with her, and make her admit that she still loved him, still wanted him after all these years.

He'd accomplished nothing. Well, not *nothing*. He had accomplished one thing. He'd reminded Desire of the passion they once shared. It was the tactless manner in which he'd reminded her that had ticked her off.

Chase parked in a space in front of Andy's Motorcycle and Bike Shop and climbed off. He looped his helmet over the handle bar, adjusted the satchel strapped across his body, and walked into the shop.

A few minutes later, he was back outside, discussing the tune-up with Will, the mechanic assigned to him.

"It needs a lot of work," Will said, scratching his head as his gaze combed the length and breadth of Chase's twenty-one-year-old navy blue Yamaha XJ600S. "It's gonna cost. Plus because it's so old, I'm not sure if we have all the parts in shop, which means it might take a few days."

"Money is no problem. But can we check for the parts so I'll know if I need to rent a car until she's ready to take the road again?"

Will's eyes lit up. "You know, it would be more economical in the long run to use the cost of a tune-up as a down payment on a newer model, or even a brand new bike." He pointed to a row of motorcycles in the parking lot—some new, some not so new. "We can give you a good deal and you'd be on your way in thirty minutes instead of waiting a couple of days."

"No, thank you. This bike and I go a long way back. I'm not abandoning her just because she's old and has a few hiccups. She's my first love." His heart somersaulted in his chest at the mention of first love.

"It's just a suggestion." Will wiped his greasy hands down the front of his navy blue overalls, adding to the stains that already lived there.

"Can you go back in and check for the parts now? I'll wait out here."

"Sure, Mr. Bennett."

Chase pulled his cell from his pocket. He had several missed calls from his mother. He speed dialed her number. "Hey, Mom," he said, when she answered on the third ring.

"Chase. Where are you? Please don't tell me you skipped town again."

His gut contracted at the hysteria in her voice. "No, I haven't skipped town, Mom. I just had a few things I had to take care of."

"So early? I made your favorite breakfast of western omelette with grits on the side, thinking we would have some time to sit and talk. But then I heard your old bike and knew you were gone."

"I'm sorry, Mom. I promise to make it up to you."

"I missed you, Chase. I just want to spend some time with my son. My firstborn, before you leave again."

"We'll have our time, Mom."

"How about today? I rearranged my schedule at the hospital."

I wish you hadn't done that. "You haven't told anyone that I'm home, have you?"

"No Chase, I haven't. I promised you I wouldn't, although I don't understand your reasons for secrecy."

"Everything will be explained soon. I promise. And I'll call you later?" he added, as he saw Will walking toward him. "I have to go. I love you, Mom." He hung up before she could do any more prying.

"We have all the parts," Will said. "But it will take a good while to get your bike in tip-top shape."

"I have time." *Time is all I have.*

"You sure you don't want to take one of our newer models for a test while you wait?"

"Yup."

"A man with time and money," Will said, giving Chase a sly smile.

Satisfied that the young man would follow his instructions, Chase handed over his key. "Take good care of my baby, Will," he said.

"I will, Mr. Bennett."

Chase crossed the street, jumped the railing, disappeared into the forest of trees, and followed the familiar path that would take him to the river, his mind once again infused with thoughts of his encounter with Desire.

He hoped that shakeup would be enough to at least give her pause before she made her engagement to his brother public. He knew it was awful to even entertain, but he hadn't missed the look of terror on her face when he'd pointed out the scandalous backlash of an affair between her and her brother-in-law.

Chase grimaced. He'd been with only one married woman in his entire life, and looking back now, he knew it was one too many. He'd just turned nineteen, and she was thirty-nine. He'd know she was married to a local politician, but he'd been too young and horny to let it deter him. Blame his raging hormones. They'd met at a restaurant in Evergreen where he'd been waiting tables the summer before he'd been shipped off to college. She'd shamelessly flirted with him and complained about her husband's inadequacies in the bedroom during Chase's one-too-many trips to her table to fill her water glass.

She'd left him a big fat tip, had returned for dinner two more nights in a row and asked to be seated in his section. On her fourth visit, they were making out in her car in a dark corner of the parking lot. A week later, she took him to a motel in a neighboring town where they began meeting three to four times a week during the rest of the summer. She'd given him his first taste of alcohol, and had taught him how to please her, and every other woman since her. Even to this day, and after being with countless faceless, nameless women, Chase's experience with Sophie Totten was high on the list of the best sex he ever had.

Then one afternoon when his bike refused to start, Sophie decided to make a house call.

His mother, who'd unexpectedly returned home from work, busted them in Chase's bedroom, right in the act.

Remorse slowed Chase's stride through the woods, as he recalled the look of horror on both his mother's and his lover's faces. After the shock of finding her baby boy in bed with a married woman old enough to be his mother had worn off, Azura had made *Mrs. Selectman* stand in the middle of the room—butt naked as she'd found her—while she laid into her. She'd told her that for a married woman in the public eye, she should have higher moral standards, and no wonder our young people were so out of control if it was women like her they had as role models. By the time Azura was done lecturing, Sophie Totten was shaking her head in agreement.

Then Azura had sat Chase down and told him that if she

ever heard he had lain in a married woman's bed again, it didn't matter to her how old he was, or where he was, she was going to find him and give him a good whooping.

Chase inhaled sharply. Screw-ups like that had made it easy for his mother, and everyone else in Evergreen, to believe that he'd deliberately publicized that X-rated clip the night of the talent show. He'd been charged with intent to distribute pornography, but because his stepuncle was the chief of police at the time, he'd avoided jail time and gotten away with just paying the fine—a fine that had wiped out all his savings.

Now, fifteen years later, Chase knew without a doubt that if Desire married Chad, she would be the second married woman whose bed he would visit time and time again. His mother would be meting out a whole lot of whoopings because he and Desire wouldn't be able to keep their hands off each other. Some things were just meant to be, and no amount of threats, obstacles, space, detours, or time could change their destiny.

He and Desire belonged together. He'd known it since the day fourteen-year-old Desire had matured into womanhood while snuggled up against him, holding on to him for dear life as they'd cruised through the back roads of Evergreen on his motorcycle.

He'd been seventeen, old enough and wise enough to realize that in order to protect her from himself, and protect himself from her father, who never hid his dislike for Chase, he had to stop hanging out with her.

Chase took a turn in the path and was immediately inundated with memories as the rushing sound of the river graced his ears. A few more yards along, the swift flow of the current rushing downstream, and a long abandoned one-story red brick building that had once been a boarding house sitting up on a gently sloping hill, filled his line of vision. Wheaton Boardinghouse had been home to the young women who'd moved to the area to work in the numerous mills along the river during the Industrial Revolution. On the other side of the river, traffic whipped by in a constant stream on their journey north.

As he walked toward the building, Chase's heart stirred with heated memories of making out with Desire in one of the rooms during the most exciting, enjoyable, passionate week of his life.

Desire had been eighteen, an adult in the eyes of the law, and old enough to make her own decisions. In effect, even if Gerald Summers hadn't been ready to accept the reality of his daughter's adult choices, his threats had no longer mattered to Chase. Nevertheless, Chase had played it safe and kept his and Desire's budding relationship a secret from the world.

If they hadn't hidden their love, at least from their families, maybe, just maybe, Chad would not have moved in on his girl, or at the minimum, he might have checked with Chase first to make sure there weren't any lingering feelings between him and Desire, and the threat of another scandal wouldn't be looming over their families again. Maybe, just maybe.

Chase took the flight of stone steps leading up from the river shore and strode along a cobbled path toward the front of the building. With the door to the main entrance missing, he stepped inside and removed his sunshades. He stood still for a moment, his eyes scaling the perimeter of the open space that had once served as a foyer, dining, and meeting room. To his right a long hallway, that used to separate two rows of bedrooms on each side, stretched the width of the building. The missing back door afforded him a partial glance of the Presidential Range rising majestically against a clear blue sky, peppered by an array of wispy clouds.

Pulling his camera from his satchel, Chase picked his way carefully through the debris scattered around the entire wing. He inspected, surveyed, and snapped photos of what remained of the interior—the concrete floor, the brick walls, and the exposed ceiling beams. Weather-beaten from a combination of wind, rain, snow, and fallen trees, the roof had been caved in, the interior fixtures gutted, and the windows shattered. The remaining doors barely hung on by their hinges, like stubborn fall leaves, clinging to their branches, refusing to accept the approach of winter and certain death.

The structure had gone from bad to worse in his absence, but what really mattered, the essential qualities, the backbone—rafters, walls, and support beams—were as strong and sturdy as when the foundation had first been laid, well over a hundred years ago. The skeleton of Wheaton Boardinghouse was as sure and sturdy as the majestic mountains behind it. All she needed was a little cosmetic work, a touch up here and there, new interior fixtures, and she would be thriving with life again.

Like Granite Falls, Evergreen had also been one of the most prosperous mill towns in New England. With most of the old buildings in Granite Falls restored and fashioned into thriving businesses, developers—both local and foreign—had set their sights on Evergreen. Because of its perfect location, with the White Mountains serving as a picturesque backdrop and its proximity to the Mannis River that made for some breathtaking views, Wheaton Boardinghouse had been earmarked to become Wheaton Estates, an exclusive assisted-living home for those who could afford to live out their lives in style.

Not a bad place to spend the last of your days, Chase thought as he picked his way along the hallway on the eastern and better preserved wing, also flanked by rows of bedrooms running the width of the building.

Chase's heart drummed in his ears as he came to a stop at the last room. The door was closed, but the visions of lying on the floor with smooth brown arms and legs wrapped around him wheeled across his mind. Age-old, soft feminine sighs, deep masculine groans, and the sounds of lips smacking intimately against lips and skin resonated in his ears. He'd burned for her, tortured himself by waiting to make love to her in the perfect setting, somewhere more romantic than the musty room of an abandoned building. He'd wanted it to be different with Desire, because she was different from the other girls he'd already been with up to that point—girls he'd taken in a hurry in all kinds of sleazy locations. He'd wanted Desire's first time to be special because she was special, and so he'd waited.

Chase's gaze fixated on the black doorknob. For his own peace of mind, the prudent thing would be to leave without going inside where the memories would be even more intense, but being a glutton for punishment, he turned the doorknob and crossed the threshold.

He was greeted by the warm scent of vanilla emitting from three candles on a small table in a corner. His gaze drifted to the floor where a foam mat was spread flat next to the table, a folded fleece blanket in the middle of it.

His stepfather's old army mat. Chase had provided the mat, and Desire had provided the candles when they had made this building, this room—the biggest and cleanest one on the wing—their temporary love nest.

As his vision lingered on the mat, steamy memories of love in the dark came down on Chase like a crushing waterfall. His skin tingling from Desire's soft caresses along his back, his buttocks, and his thighs. His heart racing as her lips trailed along his bare chest, her tongue licking his nipples, her mouth moving south to his belly and beyond until he stopped her, pulling her up, laying her along his body, his hard shaft pressing into her hot moist heat as he sucked on her succulent, firm young breasts while they rubbed up against each other, simulating licentious mating rituals until she sighed her climax into his mouth, shaking like a horse-drawn buggy over cobbled stones on top of him.

Chase knelt and ran his palms along the vinyl covering of the mat. No dust or debris from the broken windowpane, and the floor had been swept, he realized, taking a quick glance around the rest of the room. A blue folding card table and two matching folding chairs had been added to the sparse furniture, and a battery operated lamp hung from a nail driven into a block of wood on the wall. A boom box sat on a shelf above the table, with a stack of tapes beside it. Had Desire been visiting their love nest in his absence? Chase wondered. Or had some other love-struck couple found their intimate hiding place and made it theirs?

With a sigh and a mixture of conflicting emotions, Chase chose to go with the former as he stood to his feet, made his way to the door and closed it behind him.

Desire's love for him was as strong, as steady, and unwavering as it was before he left. If it weren't, she wouldn't have let him under her skin this morning. She would not have fought with him, kicked him out of her place of business. He'd felt her struggle to hide her feelings for him, her desire to cave in to the cravings of her heart and body. And he'd sensed her jealousy that he'd slept with Lisa. She still loved him. She just wasn't ready to admit it.

Chase hoped she came to her senses before her engagement to his brother became public knowledge. Neither the Hunters nor the Summerses could survive another scandal in this town.

He'd made his move. The ball was in her court.

***

Chase veered his newly tuned Yamaha into the underground garage of Fontaine Enterprises and cruised toward the area of Bryce's private elevator. He parked his bike in a space near the back of the garage and climbed off.

"Thanks for the ride, old girl," he muttered, running his fingers along the newly polished leather seat like it was a lover's voluptuous bottom, still warm from cuddling his body. He smiled, basking in the pleasure *she'd* given him on his way back to Granite Falls. Now, if he could only convince Desire to give him a chance, show her that they still fit together, his world would be complete.

Tucking his helmet under his arm, Chase adjusted the strap of the satchel across his shoulder, his heart dancing to another beat as he headed for the elevator. He'd never set foot on the grounds of the building, but he knew it like he knew the back of his hand.

He'd drawn up the designs long before he'd met Bryce Fontaine, one of Granite Falls' young emerging business moguls. Fontaine Enterprises was operating out of an old mill building by the Aiken River when Bryce had approached Carron Architecture Designs about constructing the headquarters for his company.

Chase was just a gardener at Carron, a college dropout, who—in the eyes of everyone around him—wasn't headed anywhere in particular. No one had any idea of the passion burning a hole in his heart. Chase had been fascinated with the stunning natural landscape around him ever since he'd had his first panoramic view of the area from a hot air balloon. Even at the age of twelve, his mind had been teeming with visions of large and esthetically designed structures that would enhance the twin towns' beauty and attract more visitors, residents, and businesses to the area.

And so when Bryce had commissioned the architects at Carron, Chase had begun sketching in secret. His designs—the ones Desire was supposed to display that night—had won the bid. But his name had been removed from the file and someone else's inserted in its place.

Chase stepped off the elevators into a commodious waiting area, and before he could decipher the merger of emotions that attacked him at being in this building for the first time, he found himself enveloped in a bear hug from Bryce Fontaine, founder and CEO of Fontaine Enterprises.

A giant at six feet four inches tall and a couple feet wide, Bryce was probably the tallest man in the region. They exchanged hearty pats on the backs as if they were best friends seeing each other after years of separation, when in fact they'd met only a few weeks ago in Casco Viejo, a beautiful old historic area of Panama City, Panama.

Bryce had purchased the two rows of dilapidated buildings on one entire street in Casco and had solicited Chase's architectural expertise to restore the buildings for both residential and business purposes.

"Chase. It's good to see you, man. In Granite Falls, that is." Bryce's grin was wide and bright as he led Chase into his office and closed the door.

"You too, Bryce." Unable to help himself, Chase scanned

the office, his fingers itching with the memory of months of sketching as he'd prepared for the night of the talent show.

"Does it feel strange?" Bryce asked, following his gaze.

Chase nodded. "Yeah, yeah it does."

"I'll give you a tour before the others arrive. The caterers are setting up one of the conference rooms down the hall."

There was a catch in Chase's voice as he removed his satchel from across his body and wrapped the strap around his wrist. "It might take a week to show me around. I'll probably want to take my time and thoroughly inspect every nook and cranny. Make sure it meets my initial specifications."

Bryce nodded. "Totally understand. But you need not worry about any inadequacies. This building has been voted the most esthetically beautiful in the area. The towers come in second and third, and—"

"Who's that, Daddy?"

Chase glanced to the other side of the room. He immediately recognized Eli, Bryce's four-year-old son, from the family pictures Bryce had shown him. The boy, a spitting image of his father, was dressed in a suit and tie, and was seated behind a small desk equipped with a laptop, a phone, and all the other supplies one would find on an office desk.

"Who are you around these parts?" Bryce asked Chase in a lowered voice.

"Mr. Bennett, a potential employee of Fontaine Enterprises. Just for today."

"Let's make it Mr. B. for Eli. He hasn't yet mastered the art of discretion. He thinks everything he hears should be shared with anyone who will listen."

Chase nodded his acquiescence. It wouldn't be fun to have his cover blown by a precocious four-year-old, he thought, as he watched Eli remove a pair of enormous headphones from his ears and set them on the desk.

Bryce turned to face his son. "This is Mr. B."

"Is he one of our employees?" Eli asked, as he climbed down from his chair and walked toward his father and Chase.

"No, Eli. He's not an employee." Bryce indicated for Chase

to follow him across the office.

"Is he an associate?" Eli asked, following them.

"Something like that," Bryce said with a grin, as they stopped in the seating area under the wall of glass that overlooked the White Mountains.

Eli held out his hand to Chase. "Hi, I'm Bryce Henry Eli Fontaine, but you can call me Eli. I'm four, and I have a sister named Elyse. She's four, too 'cause we are twins. But I'm older, and bigger. I also have three cousins: Jason, Alyssa, and Anastasia, but they're older than me. Do you have brothers and sisters and cousins, too, Mr. B?"

Whoa. Chase blinked in rapid successions. Bryce wasn't kidding about his son's proclivity to share information. "Hello, Eli, it's an honor to meet you. And yes, I have one brother, no sisters," he said, equally impressed with the child's firm grip.

"It's nice to meet you, too, Mr. B."

Now, this was the kind of son he'd fantasized about making with Desire, Chase thought. Handsome, smart, and cultured. His son or daughter would be about ten or eleven years now. But from his encounter with Desire this morning, his gut told him there was still hope.

"What kind of business are you in?" Eli asked. "Are you rich like my daddy? Are you a billionaire?"

"Okay, that's enough interrogation," Bryce interjected in a stern voice. "Go back to your movie, Eli. Mr. B and I have business to discuss."

"Okay, Daddy." Eli reluctantly returned to his desk and replaced his headphones.

"Wow, you've got him trained," Chase said, grinning. "I realize he's your son, and that he'll take over Fontaine Enterprises one day, but isn't he a little young for grooming? I mean, he has his own desk in your office. Aren't there child labor laws in this state?"

The roar of Bryce's laugh resounded around the room. "Don't you worry, Mr. B. I'm not breaking any laws where my son is concerned. Kaya is taking Eli and Elyse to Tashi's Photography for a sitting. They model for her. Well, all five of my kids do. Tashi is doing a piece on twins' fashion for some fancy New York magazine. Eli begged to come in with me this morning. Kaya's picking him up on her way to Tashi's studio."

"Tashi is, um—" Chase tapped his finger against his forehead and furrowed his brows. "Adam's wife, right?"

"Yes." Bryce indicated a club chair, and then sat in the one across from Chase.

Chase placed his satchel and his helmet on the floor at his feet. "And Erik is married to Michelle. They have four kids between them, and—"

"Soon to be five. They're adopting a little six-year-old boy from Columbia. Matthew."

"Good for them. And Massimo is married to Shaina. They have a daughter and a new son."

Bryce nodded. "Mass Jr."

"And you and Kaya are pregnant, again. Congratulations."

"Thank you," he said, his smile warm and affectionate as he obviously thought of his child growing inside his wife's belly. "You've been studying."

"I make a point of knowing the major details about my clients' lives, especially those who live in my hometown." As he observed Bryce's expression, Chase knew that he would also be beaming with pride and wonder when Desire's belly became swollen with his own child. He stretched his legs out in front of him as an indefinable feeling of rightness filled him. "Was *Baia Degli Amanti* to your satisfaction?" he asked Bryce.

"It exceeded it. We were all awed at the luxury and coziness of the cottages, the landscaping. It was spectacular."

"I'm not going to ask about the last-minute dance pole request. I can only imagine the lascivious acts that took place on that island."

Bryce laughed. "You can ask, but what happens in *Baia Degli Amanti* stays in *Baia Degli Amanti*. I can only tell you that those poles enhanced the honeymoon experience for all of us."

Now that was the kind of silly, elated expression one would expect from a man in love when he talked about his woman, Chase thought, as he watched Bryce's grin widen and deepen as he obviously recalled flashbacks of his honeymoon last year. "As long as my clients are satisfied."

"Oh, we were immensely satisfied with everything. Our time on the island brought us closer together as husbands and wives, as friends, and families. We shared information with each other that we'd never shared before." Bryce sobered up and leaned forward. "And speaking of sharing information, have you told your family who you really are?"

"No, not yet."

"What about Desire? Have you seen her?"

Bryce was the only other living soul who knew how he felt about Desire. "I saw her this morning. She wasn't happy to see me."

"No?" He quirked an eyebrow.

"She's engaged to be married to my brother."

Bryce sat up straight. "You don't say. Since when?"

"He proposed four days ago, and she accepted. But they haven't made it public yet."

"And, I assume that it won't be made public."

"Your assumption is correct, my friend. I just have to get this business with DC Designs taken care of first."

"When it comes to matters of the heart, you can't play around. You can't delay." Bryce admonished.

"Oh, I have no intentions of playing. As to delaying, twelve years is enough. Desire Summers will be mine by the end of the week," Chase stated with a pulse-pounding certainty.

"A man after my own heart. I'm so glad you're finally home, Chase."

"It *is* good to be home, Bryce." Chase smiled for a plethora of reasons.

CHAPTER SIX

"Excuse me a minute," Desire said as her office phone rang, breaking the silence of deep concentration in the display parlor.

Trinity, who'd been wearing a hole in the floor for the past ten minutes, didn't seem to hear her. With a smile, Desire hurried toward her office in the next room. Chad's name flashed on the Caller ID. He'd called her earlier to remind her of their meeting with the reporter from *Twin Town Times*. What could he possibly be calling about now? She picked up the receiver. "Hey, Chad."

"Hey, Desire."

His voice was as impassive as hers. *Definitely not the way two people who'd recently become engaged should be greeting each other.* There should be anxiety, anticipation, and... Desire perched on the edge of her desk and stared at her open calendar. God, she had so many weddings to plan in the next year. She would never have time for her own.

"You there still?"

She tensed. "Yes, I'm here. What's up?"

"Funny you should ask," he said with a nervous lilt to his voice.

Desire frowned. She'd never known Chad to be nervous

about anything. "What, you're still in court?"

"No. I'm at my office. As you know Judy is on vacation."

"Yeah." Desire twirled her finger around a lock of hair resting on her shoulder.

"Marilyn called in sick this morning, and the temp I hired never showed. So I have to take care of this—this thing that came up."

"You want to postpone the meeting with the reporter?" *Say yes.*

"No. Just delay it. I already called and asked Derrick to move the meeting down half an hour. He's fine with the change. Would that be a problem for you?"

"Nope. No problem at all."

"Perfect. See you in about an hour then."

Desire hung up and stared out the window at traffic going by on Main Street. Was this a foretaste of the way her life would be once she and Chad were married? No skip of her heartbeat, no jitters of her nerves, no tingling of her skin, no trembling of her bones when she heard his voice, when she saw him, or was near him for that matter?

You want to commit adultery with your brother-in-law? It's best if you end it now, rather than wait for this very thing to happen between us once you're married. Is this what you want, Desire?

"No!" Desire jumped at the sound of her own voice. She shook her head, as if she were trying to wake up her comatose brain. How dare he suggest she would commit adultery with him if she married Chad? He had no right. He didn't know her. She was not the naïve, trusting eighteen-year-old whose heart he'd broken. She'd grown up. She wasn't easily swayed anymore. *Really?* "Really."

Taking a deep breath, Desire pushed the questions, the threats, the thoughts, and the man who'd posed them out of her mind completely, and walked out of her office.

Back in the display room, Trinity was still pacing between the three tables Desire had set out. She probably didn't even realize that Desire had stepped away.

Watching the worry lines on her forehead, anyone would

think she was new to the whole bride-to-be scenario. Money really couldn't buy everything, Desire thought. It could buy expensive bone china dinnerware, crystal glasses, and silk and linen napkins and tablecloths. It could even buy romance, but it couldn't buy love, happiness, or any other of life's intangible blessings.

For Trinity's sake, Desire hoped this wedding would be her last. The press was already comparing the poor girl to Elizabeth Taylor, and a few meanies were making bets that this marriage would be much shorter than Trinity's fifteen-month second marriage.

"Still undecided, huh?" Desire asked, going to stand on the opposite side of the table. She leaned against the wall, watching Trinity closely.

"It's so hard to choose." Trinity said, flipping her long brown curls over her shoulder. "I need a little more time. I hope I'm not keeping you."

"Not at all. Take your time." *I have an extra forty-five minutes to spare.*

"Thank you, Desire."

Desire smiled as Trinity went back to her worrying. She'd had to reschedule her other morning appointment in order to meet with Chad and the reporter, so she did have time to kill, even more so now.

She, Lori, Jacques, and Gillian had spent the better half of the morning discussing floral arrangements, cake decorations, menu, and music with Trinity. The others had left, what seemed like eons ago, to take care of some changes and discuss another pre-wedding photo shoot with Tashi Andreas, the wife of one of the billionaires from last year's group wedding.

Trinity wasn't getting married until next May, but she wanted everything finalized before she went back to LA at the end of the summer. She didn't want to make a trip during the winter months, and Desire's schedule didn't leave room for travel out west anytime soon.

"Which one would you choose?" Trinity asked.

Desire inhaled sharply, her mind plummeting into total

lockdown. It wasn't the first time an indecisive bride had asked her that question, and her response had always been the same. She was yet to meet the bride who thought they'd made the wrong choice.

But today, the question hit home for Desire, especially because of her confrontation with Chase this morning. Ever since she was old enough to fantasize about waking up in the arms of the man of her dreams—her husband of one day—Chase's warm gray eyes were always the ones smiling back from the pillow next to hers. It hadn't changed, not even after Chad had proposed. When she closed her eyes and thought about love, marriage, and kids, Chad's image wasn't the one that popped to the forefront of her mind.

She wasn't going to lie. It *had* been hard for her to remain focused on work with the side effects of Chase's hands crawling up her stomach, his hot breath fanning her cheeks, his smooth, moist lips flittering against hers, his voice in her ears, his scent in her nostrils, his hard shaft pressing into her groin…

"Desire, which one?"

Desire snapped the lid on her fantasy box, and walked over to stand beside Trinity. "Just close your eyes and imagine you're waking up in your honeymoon suite in the arms of the man of your dreams—your husband of one day. You open your eyes, and across the room a table is laid before you. Which setting would bring you most joy as you sit down to share your first breakfast as husband and wife?"

"Then it's this one." Trinity stepped in front of the last of the three tables with four chairs—all draped with white silk covers and cobalt blue satin bows tied across the backs—strategically placed around it.

"I thought this would be your favorite," Desire responded, following her to the setting comprised of a cobalt blue and white silk tablecloth, and a Royal Worcester fine bone china dinner set that sported a blue cobalt border, heavy gold gilt, and a hand-painted floral centerpiece on each item. Baccarat crystal wine and water glasses, and a champagne flute completed the luxurious setting.

"I like what you did with these." Trinity ran her fingers over each of the six pieces of Christofle Malmaison sterling silverware tied together by a blue satin ribbon. "It's different from the norm of positioning the utensils around the plate."

"I thought of tying everything together because when we first met, you kept saying that you're 'tying the knot' instead of 'getting married.'"

Trinity chuckled. "I love the way you think, Desire, and I noticed you took your 'tying' theme to the limit," she added, pointing to the centerpiece.

Desire smiled as she stared at a plain, yet very expensive Baccarat bowl with a white unscented votive inside it and stalks of blue iris tied around the entire outside perimeter. "You mentioned that the blue iris is your favorite flower, and since it denotes faith, hope, wisdom, admiration, and courage, I thought it would make a great centerpiece. I wish you all this and more in your marriage, your tying of the knot," she added.

Trinity wiped a red-tipped finger across one eye, smearing black mascara and eyeliner on her cheek. "You're awesome, Desire. And thanks for not judging me. Even though this is my third marriage, you've treated me as if it were my first."

"It doesn't matter how many times a woman marries, Trinity, her wedding day should always be special."

"It's going to be different this time around. Frankie was my first love in high school, you know. We were friends for a long time before we became lovers."

"No, I didn't know that." Desire had met the groom last winter when he and Trinity had traveled east for some skiing. "Well, in that case, I'm glad I chose the iris since it also signifies cherished friendship. What happened to break you apart?" She was sure Trinity and Frank's reason was a children's Bible story compared to hers and Chase's. Nobody could top what went down between her and Chase.

"Life happened," Trinity said with a faraway look in her eyes. "His father died just before we graduated and after graduation his mother moved him and his two younger siblings to Arizona. We tried to make a long-distance relationship work, but it eventually faded as the months, then years, rolled by. He had to concentrate on a career and helping his mother raise his siblings. Theirs was a working family."

While yours was play. "How did you guys meet up again?" Desire's pulse raced at the similarities between her and Trinity's lives when it came to lost love and reunions, sans the scandal of course.

"At a mutual friend's wedding. We'd both just gotten divorced and he'd moved back to LA to work in a computer software company. We started hanging out, reminiscing, and rehashing old times. One thing led to another, and before long the friendship and the passion we once shared began to surface again. And now here we are, planning a wedding. Frankie would be happy to just head down to city hall and get it over with, but I wasn't having that. We're not going to hide our love from the world. I'm stressing over this wedding because I want the best for Frankie, for us."

"That is romantic."

"You think so?" Trinity giggled like a little girl. "Frankie is so different from all the men I've dated in the past. He isn't rich, just a regular white-collar worker. He isn't near as handsome as my previous two husbands. He's shorter than me, and a little overweight, but I have him on a diet," she added, laughing. "He's everything a girl like me shouldn't want, didn't want because my friends thought I was too good for him."

She pressed her hand to her chest, the expensive 24-carat diamond tennis bracelets on her wrist sparkling in the ray of sun coming through the window, while the modest half-carat diamond and white gold engagement ring on her finger tried to keep up, but failed miserably. "Frankie has a good heart. He loves me. I love him. I feel safe with him. I can be myself. I don't have to pretend to be someone I'm not, the *someone* everyone wants me to be."

"I've only met him once, but I do feel the love between the two of you," Desire said, her eyes tearing up for indiscernible reasons.

"My first two marriages were all about social status and prestige. I married men my family and friends approved of. I was a trophy wife, two times over. You know the one thing that I took from both marriages?"

Desire shook her head.

"Even if you aren't honest with anyone else in this world, you have to be honest with yourself or you'll never be happy. I wasn't in love with my previous husbands. I don't even know if I ever loved or liked either one of them. But I know without a doubt that I love and like Frank Dumas. This time, I'm marrying for love. That's how I know it will last. Love is all that counts, Desire. It's the only reason two people should get married."

But what if love eludes you? And what if one of those two people is a vile, narcissistic, two-timing jerk despite the fact that the mere thought of him makes your heart pound a mile a minute, your skin tingle, and your body turn to mush?

***

Desire took a left turn off Main Street onto Union Street and headed in the vicinity of the Fontaine Towers, Trinity's words echoing in her ears: *You have to be honest with yourself.* Like she didn't already know that, and like the sexy, low-down, dirty vagabond she loved hadn't preached that same message when he'd cornered her this morning.

Last year, after Victoria's lies about a sexual liaison with her employer, Bryce Fontaine, had come to light—lies her father had believed for eleven years because he loved his daughter and trusted her judgment, character, and choices, lies that had plunged the Summers and the Fontaine families into a war of silent antagonism—her father had hung his head in disgrace and had gone through another period of self-deprecation, blaming himself for providing the gun that Victoria had used to kill Pilar Fontaine.

Even though Bryce had assured her father that it was not his fault and that he, Bryce, had forgiven Victoria after realizing that it was her battle with self-esteem and her unstable mental condition that had driven her to commit her ghastly crime, her father still wallowed in guilt.

Discovering that her sister had been a delusional liar had caused Desire to begin questioning her twelve-year-old decision to believe the worst of Chase. There were truly two sides to every story. She'd been wrong about her sister. Dead wrong.

When she'd learned that Trinity had been married twice before, Desire had judged her, thinking the rich socialite knew nothing about real love. Trinity had proved her wrong a short while ago and had even opened her eyes to the possibility of second chances.

Could she have been wrong about Chase, too? Desire wondered. She'd tried, convicted, and condemned him without giving him the chance to tell his side of the story. Driven by anger, hurt, and humiliation the first few days after that embarrassing night, she'd ignored his calls, his text messages, and had refused to see him when he'd come to her house to explain his side. What could he have possibly told her to make her pain go away, to redeem himself in her eyes?

Consequently, she'd begun to believe everything everybody had been saying about Chase Hunter. He was a bad seed, a troublemaker, an unethical, irresponsible manwhore.

Once she'd cooled off, Desire had realized that she still loved Chase, no matter what. He was *her Chase,* had been since the day she first saw him when they were both children. Ready to forgive, she'd waited for him to show up at her house again, to apologize, and make his case. But he never returned to her doorstep.

Not long after the humiliating night, she'd learned from Chad and Azura that Chase had disappeared without even saying goodbye to them. At that point, she's had no other option than to write Chase Hunter off as dead. She'd deleted him from her contact list and her life.

With a shiver of vivid recollection, Desire reflected on the day Chad had told her that Chase was gone. Her life had felt so empty. Her heart had been crushed all over again. Chase had always been there for her, protecting her like the big brother she never had, watching over her at the playground, picking her up and soothing her every time she'd fallen off her bike or stumbled over an obstacle in her path. He'd kept the neighborhood children from bothering her, from pulling her hair, making fun of her, or making racially slurred comments because she was one of the few African-American children in the town. How would she live without him in her life? she'd wondered then.

In her anger, she should have remembered how kind and gentle and loving Chase had always been with her. She should have remembered that he'd always treated her like a princess, put her above everyone and everything else in his life. He'd been there for her even when she'd messed up, and the one time he'd needed her to believe in him, or at least give him the benefit of the doubt, she'd turned her back on him. She'd allowed others' opinions to influence her decisions, her heart's true desires, which were to trust Chase, understand him, believe in him.

A tear slid down Desire's cheek as she pulled her car into the underground garage of Fontaine Towers #2. She'd been so wrong about Chase, just as her entire family had been wrong about Victoria. If she'd only known that he hadn't returned to her house because her father had threatened him, she might have been a bit more forbearing, probably wouldn't have deleted him altogether, but kept hope and the love they had for each other alive. Had he tried to call her only to realize that she'd blocked him, cut him out of her life?

Desire exited her car and walked toward the elevator, offering perfunctory smiles to the three women and two men who were waiting to go up into the tower.

As soon as she'd learned that Chase had returned home this morning—despite the fact that he'd slept with her cousin—she'd known that her plan to marry Chad would go up in smoke. She just didn't know that it would be so soon. She'd thought that Chase would need some time to absorb the shock, analyze the situation, and set his own plan of sabotage into motion. But she should have known better, remembered that Chase was not the kind of man to wait out any situation. He was spontaneous, a man who attacked a problem as soon as it raised its ugly head.

And this was ugly, she thought as she stepped on to the elevator and pushed the button for her desired floor. Knowing Chase would take action, could she have subconsciously decided to marry Chad in order to get Chase's attention?

Well, whether consciously or subconsciously, she'd gotten it.

Desire bit down on her bottom lip as the elevator stopped on the eighth floor and the women stepped off. Why had Chase come home? Had he somehow found out about her engagement to Chad, or was it something else? She might be kidding herself into thinking that Chase still cared enough to keep her from making a bad mistake. Maybe he'd returned for some other reason and had stumbled on the information by accident.

Chad had asked that they keep the engagement quiet for three days, and she'd gone along with it for her own practical, yet selfish reasons. She wondered now about Chad's reasons. What did he have to gain by not telling the world that they were engaged?

Yesterday was three days. Yesterday, Chase had come home to learn about the engagement. His anger might have nothing to do with their feelings for each other. He might just be pissed off that his little brother had moved in on his girl while his back was turned.

"Have a nice day, ma'am," one of the two men in suits said, as the elevator doors opened on the fourteenth floor.

Desire's hand tightened around the straps of her Kate Spade handbag. *Have a nice day?* Her day had started out horribly, and it was about to get worse. "Thank you," she said on a nod before stepping off.

Taking slow, deep breaths, Desire walked down the corridor, passing several doors that opened up into offices. Her steps faltered as she drew nearer to the backside of the building that overlooked the Aiken River. She stopped at the last door on the right, her heart fluttering erratically in her chest.

Even if you aren't honest with anyone else in this world, you have to be honest with yourself or you'll never be happy.

At least let's be honest and truthful about our feelings. That has never been a problem for us.

Her epiphany had come from two very unlikely sources today.

Here was her moment of truth and honesty. What she was about to do might bring her more embarrassment, but she was used to it. At least she would be honest with herself. Without giving herself time to back down, Desire opened the door.

The outer area was empty. She crossed the room and listened for voices behind the closed door of the inner office. Except for the sound of Bach's Symphony #5 coming from inside, all was quiet. He was alone. With the ease of custom, she turned the knob and opened the door.

Desire stared across the room, speechless, as wave after wave of shock slapped at her.

CHAPTER SEVEN

Chase adjusted his sunglasses and stared unimpressed as Tomas Taylor, one of the representatives from Carron Architectural Designs presented his plan for River's Edge, the first phase of residential homes slated to be built along the Mannis River in Evergreen.

"As you can see from the position of the roads," Tom said, pointing to the models on the giant projector screen, "most of the homes will have access to the waterfront, especially along the southern edge of the river. The lots with direct beachfront access all went within the first week of advertising. I'm confident that the others will be sold soon…"

Chase honestly could not tell if the man had been running his mouth for five minutes or fifty. His mind was elsewhere—on Desire and the sexual magnetism still sizzling between them. God, he'd been one heartbeat away from locking her door and taking her right there up against the wall of her business establishment. It was only the information—now facts—surrounding his family history that had tempered his cravings.

Ever since he'd learned the macabre truth about his biological father, Chase had been on a mission not to become him, especially because it was his own *ménage à trois* indiscretion that had been the catalyst for all his pain and his troubles. It had been hard for him to give up his womanizing, bed hopping, and one-night stands, but he'd finally settled into the art of exclusive, monogamous relationships, which were all short-lived since Chase diplomatically called it quits when the women began acting as if they owned him.

He might have shared his body, and maybe some of his affections with a string of countless, faceless, and sometimes nameless women, but his heart had only ever belonged to one. *His Tender Roni.* And making love to her while she was engaged to his brother would have been counterproductive to his new and improved character. Maybe if he weren't aware of the facts about his father, it would not have mattered so much. But he was aware. It did matter.

But you slept with her cousin, his annoying conscience proclaimed.

That was a mistake, poor judgment in the heat of anger and hurt. I'm not my no-good-for-nothing-rotten father. I'm…

"Mr. Bennett!"

Chase jumped at the sound of Bryce's voice. He sat up in his chair and looked around at the team of men comprised of commercial and residential real estate brokers and developers, engineers, aerial photographers, surveyors, zoning and chamber of commerce directors, and Marcus Spencer, Fontaine Construction's main engineer, sitting around a conference table at Fontaine Enterprises.

Fourteen pairs of eyes were trained on him, all with waiting expectation. He also noticed that Tomas had reclaimed his seat on the right side of the table. How long had they been trying to get his attention?

"Your thoughts," Bryce said from the head of the table, directly in Chase's line of vision, his lips pressed closely together as if he were holding in a chortle.

Chase adjusted his glasses again, wishing he could remove the damn things, but he needed to maintain anonymity, just for a little while longer. He'd asked his family and Lisa to keep his presence a secret. He hadn't asked Desire, but he was almost certain that she would be the last person to broadcast the news that the infamous Chase Hunter who'd embarrassed her beyond repair had returned to town.

Nope. Desire's lips were sealed.

Chase cleared his throat and glanced at the models still on the screen. "I strongly propose moving the first row of houses at least half a mile up the hill away from the riverbank where the soil is most susceptible to bank volatility."

"And on what exactly is your proposal based?" Tomas asked in rapid defense as if he'd anticipated the criticism and had come prepared to fight.

Chase straightened his back and planted his elbows on the table. "A load of reasons. Pun intended. The weight from these massive waterfront mansions, the irrigation systems, and septic drain fields you're installing will easily exceed the sediments, causing increased soil hydration. And your decision to replace the deep-rooted native vegetation of the riverbank with a fancier shallow-rooted grass is even more troubling. We'll be on a collision course with geotechnical riverbank failure—slumping, as we know it—in no time at all."

"I don't think we need to worry about slumping for the next hundred years or so." Tomas sent Chase a grinding stare. "The rate of erosion is still very low. We haven't had any problems with the residential communities we built around the Aiken River several years ago."

"You haven't had any problems, *yet*. I've checked out the layout of those properties. It's only a matter of time. Riverbanks are as different and varied as women's backsides. You have to be conscious of the weight you apply to each. Some can sustain heavier loads than others."

The men laughed, and Chase waited until it was quiet before he continued. "Wouldn't you rather there be no slumping, ever, than have it become someone else's problem in a hundred years? The sediments around the Mannis River are a lot less stable than that of the Aiken. You would have known that if your engineers had done their jobs before you signed on the dotted lines. The retaining wall, riprap, concrete, soil and fill usually used to stay slumping will only exaggerate the problem. Frankly, I'm surprised Granite Falls' zoning board allowed you to build so close to the bank."

"Are you trying to say something?" Hansel, the other Carron representative, asked. "Are you accusing us of bribery, Mr. Bennett? If you're going to accuse us of something, at least stop being a coward, take off your sunglasses, and look me in the eye."

"My sentiments, exactly." Tom took up frontline defense again. "You're an out-of-town agent of a developer. Where is your boss, the one who should be giving orders?"

"Probably doing the same thing yours is. Hiding in the shadows, waiting to see how the fighting turns out."

"At least my boss is local and well known." Hansel picked up the banner again. "I fail to understand why Mr. Fontaine is asking the opinion of a stranger, or why he has allowed you to lead this meeting. If you—"

The Chamber of Commerce representative raised his hand to speak, but quickly dropped it when Bryce's fist came down on the table with a resounding thud. The occupants of the room jumped and immediately trained their focus on him like elementary school children in a disruptive classroom.

"I asked his opinion," Bryce stated, his voice sharp with defiance, "and I'm allowing him to run the meeting because I believe he has excellent vision, Mr. Taylor. It's always good to have fresh eyes on projects of this scale, especially when they are still in the preliminary stages when everything needs to be thoroughly thought out to the minutest detail. If you can't handle a few constructive criticisms and judicious suggestions, you are free to join forces with the second-highest bidder—the next in line."

Chase smiled inwardly at the scathing glance Bryce sent down the table at both Hansel and Tom. Except for the night he'd met him for the first time, in the several years they'd shared a friendship, this was the first time Chase had witnessed Bryce's temper. He was indeed the ruthless, giant mogul he'd been dubbed in the business world—fiercely loyal to his friends and severely destructive to his enemies. Chase was grateful that he was the man's friend and not his enemy. He knew Bryce had only come to his defense because Chase was not at liberty to do so without giving away his position and stake in the whole affair. He hoped he'd be able to drop all acts by tomorrow evening.

"I'm sorry, Mr. Fontaine. I never meant to offend you." Tomas ducked his head into his chest, the same way a dog tucked his tail between his legs.

"I'm not offended," Bryce stated imperiously. "But I think you owe Mr. Bennett an apology."

Chase raised his hand to stay the apologies from Tomas and Hansel, which he knew were anything but sincere. He didn't blame them. Carron was on the verge of bankruptcy. Their construction company had gone out of business years ago, but Carron Architectural Designs had miraculously won all the bids on all of the impending real estate projects—thanks to Bryce's astute business scheming on Chase's behalf. Carron Architects were fighting for their lives. It didn't help that Chase had been taking shots at most of the designs and proposals they presented.

Although his involvement with the projects had begun months ago, Chase hadn't even bothered to look at Carron's designs until a few minutes before the meeting was called to order. His own designs—those that would be executed—were already drafted. They would be presented to the town and the prospective landowners in a few days. He had no doubt that the future residents of River's Edge and the other development would be delighted with his vision.

It must be humiliating to be called to heel in front of men with whom you had to live and work side by side, and especially if that calling to heel had been done by an outsider whose opinions were unequivocally lauded by the most important man in the room, and one of the most influential men in the region. "No need to apologize, Mr. Taylor, nor you, Mr. Chapman. I am an outsider. I would react the same way if the situation were reversed. Forgive my effrontery."

"In spite of the fact that Mr. Bennett is a newcomer," Bryce said, apparently not letting Carron's men off the hook so easily, "his concerns, nonetheless, are disconcerting to me. I'm commissioning my team of engineers to inspect the areas along the Mannis' riverbank. Fontaine Construction will not be moving forward until I have a satisfactory report. In addition, we will be following Mr. Bennett's suggestions to build farther up the hill away from the river."

Chase's cell phone buzzed in his back pocket. Ignoring it, he cleared his throat and glanced at Tomas and Hansel. "Well, gentlemen, now that we've discussed your plans for River's Edge, let's see what you have for the Sandy Point development on Cedar Lake. If—"

His cell phone vibrated again. "Excuse me one minute," he said. Reaching into his back pocket, and holding it under the table, he glanced at the screen: *Urgent message from Chad.* Chase sighed inwardly. *So damn dramatic.* "I'm sorry, but I have to take this outside," he said rising. "Urgent business of another nature," he added, walking toward the door.

"We'll discuss Fonandt Energies supplying energy to the communities until your return," Bryce said.

Chase nodded, then closed the door behind him. *What's so urgent? Is something wrong with Mom?* he typed as he walked to the end of the corridor and looked out on the town below.

Chad: *Mom is fine. Where are you?*

Chase: *In a meeting.*

Chad: *What kind of meeting?*

Chase: *What do you want, Chad?*

Chad: *We need to talk.*

Chase: *Can't it wait? I'll be done in about an hour.*

Chad: *No. It's about Desire.*

Chase's heart fluttered inside his chest: *What about Desire? Is she hurt, in trouble?*

Chad: *I don't think so, but I think you had something to do with it.*

Chase frowned: *Do with what?*

Chad: *I'll tell you when I see you. I need to see you. NOW!!! Where are you?*

Chase cursed aloud. He would love to tell his brother to go to hell, and return to his meeting, but he knew Chad would continue texting and calling until he got what he wanted—whatever the heck that was. It was better he dealt with him now. He glanced up and down Evergreen Drive: *I'm in Granite Falls. Meet me at Bean Time Café on the corner of Evergreen Dr. and Oak St.*

Chad: *Be there in ten.*

As he walked down Evergreen Drive, Chase spotted his brother pacing back and forth in front of the café. Tension was ripe in his lean frame. They clearly weren't going inside to sit down and have a calm conversation over a glass of iced coffee.

Chad had said that the urgent matter had to do with Desire. Only one thing could have his brother so riled up. Desire must have broken off the engagement. But why the hell would Chad think he had anything to do with Desire's decisions to end their engagement if that was indeed the case? He was certain Desire would not have told Chad that she'd seen Chase this morning.

Perhaps this call to meeting was just like old times when Chad would take pleasure in blaming Chase when things fell apart in his own life. If the urgency was that Desire had broken off the engagement, this would be the first time his little brother had rightly placed the blame.

Chase braced himself as Chad turned and spotted him a few yards away. They met under the flashing neon *Open* sign at the end of the block.

"What did you say to her?" Chad bellowed as soon as they were face-to-face.

"To whom? What are you accusing me of this time, little brother?"

"Desire and I were supposed to meet the reporter at Mountainview Café for lunch but she never showed. I've called her and called her to no avail. Nobody knows where she is. Not even her parents and her employees. It's like she disappeared into thin air."

So he had gotten through to her this morning. "And how the hell is that my fault?" Chase tried hard to hide the exclamation of joy that threatened to spill from inside him. He honestly felt bad that his little brother was in obvious pain, but it was nothing compared to the agony he would have felt if this ridiculous unholy matrimony had taken place.

"You saw her this morning."

Chase was bemused for a minute. "Did she tell you that?"

"I said I haven't seen her all day. Gill told me."

"Who's *Jill?*"

"Her marketing and advertising specialist. Gillian. We call her Gill for short."

Chase did not know how to process that bit of information. Was Gillian the one he'd run into on his way out of Weddings by Desire this morning? And why would one of Desire's employees be taking information back to Chad? Was Chad having her followed? Well, if he had, he would know where she was. Chase shrugged. "So what if I went to see her? You did suggest that I welcome her into the family this morning. Remember?"

"Drop the act, Chase!"

"Would you keep your voice down?" Chase said as a couple of pedestrians stopped to toss curious stares in their direction. He grabbed Chad's arm and dragged him into the alleyway, to the back of the building and the parking area where traffic was essentially nonexistent.

Chad shrugged his arm away, just as he used to when Chase would drag him about when they were kids. His eyes were two blazing spheres of sapphire. "Did you tell Desire that she wasn't good enough for me, that her family was cursed? Is that why you went to see her this morning? I don't need you protecting me, Chase. I'm not a kid and—"

"What the hell, Chad? Why would I tell Desire that her family is cursed?"

Chad swallowed and looked off into the distance before meeting Chase's gaze again. "Her reputation and character took a downward swirl that night at the country club," he said in a less vociferous voice.

Chase pressed his fingertips to his temples. He was starting to get a headache. "I can imagine. The people in these twin towns aren't very nice or forgiving."

"It might not have been so bad if her crazy sister hadn't gone and committed coldblooded murder a few months after you pulled your stunt at the country club."

Chase chose to ignore Chad's jab at him. "I wish I'd been here for Desire. I could have helped her—"

Chad waved his hand, dismissively. "You weren't. You dropped your pile of crap and then you bailed on all of us. You left Desire here to be mocked and scorned. She lost all her friends. She became the black sheep of the town. She suffered, Chase. She was miserable for so long. She wanted to leave, but couldn't because of her father's heart attack, and then his being diagnosed with prostate cancer seven years ago. She had to change her life, give up her dream college to take care of her parents. You destroyed her, Chase."

Chase had nothing to do with Desire not attending the college of her dreams because she had to take care of her parents, but the fact that she'd suffered as a result of that sickening video would forever be a steel weight around his neck. He clenched his jaws so tightly, excruciating pain shot into his brain.

"With two strikes against the Summers family name," Chad continued, oblivious to Chase's pain, "no family around here wants Desire with their son. She's good enough to—well, you know what—" he said, with a snarl, "but not good enough for anything permanent. The three boyfriends she'd had over the years dumped her when they found out who she is. Why do you think she's marrying me? She can't do any better. I'm her best offer. Her only offer."

You self-righteous prick.

"So you can understand my concern that you might have driven a nail in her coffin when you went to see her this morning. You must have said something unkind to her. You could have destroyed her only chance of marriage."

Chase took a deep steadying breath. "I did no such thing."

"You didn't say anything derogatory about her family?"

"Nope. Not a word."

"Then I don't understand why she didn't show for lunch with the reporter."

"You haven't spoken to her all day?"

"Just before lunch, I called to tell her that I would be running late for the meeting. I was held up at my office. My…"

His voice trailed off. He slumped against the side of a jeep, a faint glint of panic in his eyes.

"You were held up in your office and…" Chase asked with a hint of impatience.

Chad dropped his gaze to the pavement, his face turning a shade of pink, but then he immediately caught Chase's gaze again, his apparent flash of panic gone. "It doesn't matter. She didn't show for lunch." He pushed off the jeep, as if the thought of being too comfortable unnerved him.

"You said no one knows where she is?"

"Right after our text exchange, her mother called and said that she'd finally heard from her."

"And?"

"She said Desire wanted to be alone, but she didn't tell her where she was. She asked her to tell me that she would call later."

"That's good. See, you have nothing to worry about. She's probably just overwhelmed. Marriage is a big step, enough to scare any blushing bride. Broadcasting the news of your engagement is a huge commitment. She might just need a little more time for it to sink in."

"You would think she's immune to wedding jitters seeing she makes a living planning weddings."

Chase's mind flashed back to the night in the garden maze when Desire had shared her fantasy of her own wedding ceremony with him. That was a lifetime ago, long before Desire… He shook the memories way. "She's the bride now, so I can see her having jitters."

"You think so?"

You poor, sad puppy. "Sure."

Chad nodded his head. "She has this secret place where she goes to when she wants to be alone. She won't tell me where it is. Hopefully, once we're married she won't need to go off like that anymore. Or maybe we can go off together for some private moments."

"Maybe."

"It was shortly after you left that she began taking off to her secret hideout. You were close before that night. Did the two of you go there together? Do you know where she is, Chase?"

Chase looked his brother straight in the eye. "Nope. Have no idea." He placed his hand on Chad's shoulder. "Listen, little brother, I'm sure Desire will surface when she's good and ready. But I need to—"

"Go back to your meeting."

"Yep."

Chad gave him a curious stare. "What kind of meeting?"

"A job." *That was true.*

"So you're planning on sticking around? You're not going back to Iowa?"

"Nope. No plans for that in the foreseeable future. I've been gone for way too long. I'm home to stay." *Home is where my heart is, has always been.*

Chad hugged him. "I'm really glad you're home, Chase. I really did miss you. You can help me plan my wedding, throw me a bachelor party, and be my best man. It will be like the old days when we were growing up."

Chase felt like the prick he'd just mentally called his little brother. His guilt mounted by the second. "Yeah. Sure."

In spite of Chad's warped, selfish reasons for marrying Desire, Chase knew that he and Chad would probably be exchanging blows once Chase and Desire surrendered to their passion and made their feelings for each public. It was just a matter of time before some psychological slumping began for the Summers and Hunter families.

In the meantime, he needed to find Desire. And he knew exactly where to look for her.

CHAPTER EIGHT

When he spotted Desire's car in the clearing where the road was too narrow to accommodate larger vehicles, Chase gassed his motorcycle—dirt, gravel, dead leaves, and twigs flying in all directions.

Adrenaline rushed to his brain, jamming all fear of skidding and colliding headfirst into a tree trunk. A quarter mile in, he brought his bike to a halt, applied the brake pedal, kicked the rest stand into place, and jumped off, all in one fluid motion.

He pulled off his helmet and sprinted toward the rear of the boarding house and the entrance with the missing door. The resounding tenderness he'd felt at the realization that it *was* Desire who'd been visiting their secret lair was tempered by concern as he flew up the stone steps. Evergreen was a fairly safe town, but one could never be too careful.

Years ago, he and Desire had come here under the cloak of night with only the stars and his motorcycle's headlight to guide them, but that was different. A defenseless woman alone in an abandoned building in the woods was a magnet for trouble, especially this late in the day when dusk would soon descend. Desire could so easily have fallen victim to a vicious attack.

Chase was out of breath when he finally stopped at the

door to their old secret hideaway. His blood curdled at the muffled sobs over Al Green's "How Can You Mend This Broken Heart," coming from the boom box inside. He opened the door to the sight of Desire curled up on the mat, her face buried in the fleece blanket clutched in her hands.

"Desire." Chase dropped his sunglasses and helmet next to her bag on the card table, and in the next instant, he was on the mat, his arms about her, pulling her close.

Her body stiffened momentarily, and then she relaxed as if accepting the comforting maleness of him. "Chase—My—My Chase. You're here," she whispered between sobs.

A lump formed in Chase's throat. Her sobs, Al's tear-jerking vocals, the lyrics and the beat of the song tore away at Chase's gut. "Yes, baby. Your Chase is here." He pulled her closer, curling his body into hers, cradling her head into the crook of his arm, and fitting her perfectly against him.

The carnal hunger that had surged between them this morning was now supplanted by a deep soulful intimacy—the kind that remained when you took away the passion and the romance, the kind two people who were deeply connected to each other shared.

This morning, Desire had had a thousand reasons to pretend she didn't want him sexually, but there was no need for her to pretend she didn't need his comfort this very moment. He'd always been her *person*, showering her with TLC as a little girl when the neighborhood kids said mean things to her or excluded her from their playtime and birthday parties. She'd come running to him, expecting him to be her hero, to dry her tears, to put her smile back on her face.

In spite of the years of separation and silence between them, there was no doubt that Desire still needed him to soothe her hurts away, take on the boogieman for her, Chase thought, as her body racked with her sobs and her hot tears soaked the sleeves of his white cotton shirt.

Back then, he was the protective big brother she never had. Today, he was her all-encompassing man.

"I'm here, Desire, darling. I'm here, baby," he whispered,

kissing the back of her head and caressing her forehead, even as he wondered about the reason she had blown off lunch with Chad and the reporter. The Desire he knew wasn't a cop-out. She saw things through. She never bailed. She was honest and straightforward. And that stick-to-itiveness, that honesty and loyalty, were the reasons she hadn't given in to her feelings and kissed him this morning.

He'd read the longing in her eyes, just as he was certain she'd read it in his. The old Chase Hunter would have gone for it—and then dealt with the consequences later. But he wasn't the old Chase Hunter. He'd changed—hopefully into the kind of man Desire could be proud of, the kind of man she need not fear would embarrass, abandon, or hurt her, ever again. Well, that is, if she could forgive him for sleeping with Lisa—his latest, and absolute last transgression where other women were concerned, he swore.

The music stopped, then Desire abruptly ceased crying as if she'd suddenly decided that she'd wept enough. She nestled deeper into him, pressing her shoulders into his chest, her back into his belly, and her derrière into his groin like it was the most natural thing in the world for her to do.

The rushing sounds of the river flowing downstream, the heat radiating from her slender body, and the floral scent of her hair, inundated Chase with fervent memories of their week on the mat. He cursed inwardly as his shaft responded to the wiggle of her backside against him.

Oh well. He wasn't a saint or a monk. He was a man. A man in love with the woman lying in his arms. He tightened his hold, his love for her flowing as freely as the river outside.

"How did you know where to find me?" she finally asked in a hoarse voice.

"I came by here earlier today and I saw the mat, the candles, and the additional furniture. At first I thought someone else was making use of our secret lair, and it kind of pissed me off, if you must know. But after I spoke with Chad—"

She went rigid at the mention of Chad's name. "You spoke

with—*him*?"

Chase frowned at her avoidance of saying Chad's name, and her harsh emphasis on *him*. What the hell had Chad done to her?

"What did he say?"

That was an odd question, Chase thought. He stared at the tree branches bobbing outside the window as he stroked his fingers through her hair, loving the silky feel of her tresses. He'd missed these simple acts of tenderness. "*He* told me you were missing, that no one knew where you were. He said you stood him up for lunch." Chase waited for her to explain why she'd gone MIA, but when she didn't, he asked. "What happened, Desire? Why have you been crying?"

With one deft move, she twisted out of his arms and knelt with her back to him.

Chase's arms felt empty without her to fill them.

Involuntarily, his gaze slid over the slender curves of her shoulders, her tangled curls cascading down her back to the tiny span of her waist. He drank in the provocative swell of her hips under the skirt she'd worn to work this morning—the skirt he'd lifted up her thighs, ever so slowly. "What did Chad do to upset you so much?" he asked to keep his mind from trudging down dangerous, lustful paths. This wasn't the time.

"Why do you think *he* did something?" she asked, as she reached for the lighter on the table and lit the three candles.

Chase watched the wicks flicker to life, sending miniature shadows dancing on the wall behind the table. "Because you tense up when I say Chad's name. See, just like that," he added when her back went ramrod straight. "Desire. Talk to me. You've always been able to talk to me about things that bothered you. I'm hoping that hasn't changed. I'm here for you. Whatever it is that's bothering you, just tell me."

She turned and stared at him, as if she were assessing his declaration that he was there for her. Her gaze traveled up and down his body. "Why are you all dressed up? What happened to your Carver Farm T-shirt and jeans?"

"I had an appointment," he said, wishing he'd had the time

and luxury to change back into comfortable clothes. "But that's not important at the moment."

His chest tightened at the exhaustion in her eyes, the puffy bags under her lids. Yet despite the sadness, her beautiful brown eyes dazzled in the candlelight that had now spread to the rest of the small room. Disappointment washed over him when instead of returning to his arms, she sat on the mattress, folded her legs under her, and spread the blanket across her knees.

"Did you know *he's* gay?" she asked bluntly.

Definitely not the question he was expecting. Chase pondered on his response while he pushed to a sitting position. "Well, since he's had his share of girlfriends, I don't think he's gay. I would say he's bi."

Accusation was livid in her eyes. "You knew all this time. Didn't you? You were going to let me marry him knowing—"

"First of all, I would not have let you marry him, Desire, and second," he added when her eyes sparked in defiance and her mouth opened in protest, "I didn't know all this time. I haven't been around to keep an eye on Chad's sexual preferences and escapades."

She leaned her back against the wall. "But he's one of the most macho men I know. He never exhibited any of the stereotypical mannerisms that would indicate he was anything but straight."

"Sometimes there aren't, especially if you're trying to stay in the closet as Chad obviously is." He shrugged. "I thought he'd outgrown his curiosity, but I guess I was wrong."

"What curiosity?" She narrowed her eyes.

Chase planted his palms on the roughened floor behind him and leaned back, supporting his weight on his arms. He was tempted to tell Desire that she should wait to get all her answers from Chad, but since Chad clearly had no intentions of coming clean with her, Chase decided that she deserved to know. "I walked in on Chad and another boy when he was younger," he said.

"Oh my God! What did you do? Did you tell Azura?"

He shook his head. "I was just a kid myself. I wasn't going to have that kind of discussion with my mother." *Especially not after I got blamed for the incident with Susie Connor.* He was sure Chad would have found a way to pin the blame for that incidence on him, too.

"So she doesn't know that her son is gay, or bi, or whatever?" She flared her hands.

"I'm pretty sure that if she knew or even suspected, she would not have approved of your engagement to Chad. My mother is honest, that much I can say." *Well most of the time.* He wished she'd been honest and open with him about her past, about his father. If she had, that jerk wouldn't have been able to chase him out of town. He wouldn't have had to leave Desire behind. He was more than certain that Desire would have forgiven him eventually and that they would be married and have had a couple babies by now.

"Who was it? The other boy with Chad?" Desire asked.

Chase cleared his throat. "I'd rather not say." The boy, now a man, was still living in Evergreen and was married with children—whether happily or unhappily, Chase hadn't a clue. But he was not one to stir up trouble for anyone, especially since he himself had fallen victim to blackmail to keep family secrets buried.

Whether or not that man had grown out of his curiosity, or was playing both ends behind his wife's back, Chase didn't know, and he didn't care. It wasn't his business. His business— the only business he wanted to be concerned about—was sitting right in front of him.

"What were they doing?" Desire asked him, her eyes wide with interest.

"Fondling each other. He told me it was a one-time thing."

She brought her legs up under the blanket and wrapped her arms about them. "Obviously, it wasn't."

Obviously. Chad had lied to him as recently as this morning when he'd told him that it never happened again. "I know lots of girls experiment with each other during their adolescent years. I guess boys do, too."

"Have you?" she asked, watching him warily.

"No. Never. What about you? Did you experiment with your girlfriends when you were younger?"

"I didn't need to experiment. I knew what..."

"You wanted," he finished when her voice trailed off and she looked past his shoulder out the window behind him. He was sure it still pained her to think of them as a couple, much less speak about it, even though, like him, she knew they belonged together and would be together, especially now that her engagement to his brother had ended even before it began. *Or had it?*

Could she still be thinking of marrying Chad with this new revelation about him in the open? She hadn't said the engagement was off. His brother deserved a punch in the face for asking Desire to marry him when he had no intention to honor their vows, another punch for the political reasons he was marrying her, and one more for saying that she couldn't do any better than him. Chase ached to deliver those punches.

A look of tired sadness passed over her face. "You must have been laughing inside this morning when I told you he was a good man."

"No, Desire. I would never laugh at you. And like I said, I didn't know that Chad was bisexual. How did you find out?"

She squeezed her lids as if trying to block out some unpleasant image. "I went to his office to tell him that the engagement was off. I saw them."

So he had gotten through to her. He inhaled deeply, suppressing the urge to pull her into his arms and kiss her until the sun came up. "So you were breaking off your engagement with Chad?" he asked, as casually as he could.

"After you cornered me this morning, I was going to ask him to postpone making it public. I needed time to deal with your unexpected and inopportune return to town. But then, I decided to end it once and for all after what Trinity said."

His head dipped to one side "Trinity?"

"The client I saw this morning. She told me that I had to be honest with myself or I would never be happy. She said love was the only reason you should marry someone."

Chase grinned. "Did you tell her about me, about us?"

She shot him a withering glance. "Not everything is about you Chase Hunter. I didn't tell her about you or us. There's no *you* or *us*. Trinity was talking about her own life. Despite the fact that her father is a successful Hollywood producer, and that she was practically born with an Oscar in her hand, she has lived a very unhappy life, especially when it comes to love. This is her third marriage."

Chase chose not to comment on her statement that there was nothing to discuss about the two of them. He wanted to hear her say that she still loved him and that she wanted them to pick up where they had left off. But he wasn't kidding himself into thinking it would happen before the misunderstandings between them had been cleared up. Desire was evidently still in denial where her feelings for him were concerned. He would have to wait a while longer for that kind of admission from her. He hoped it wouldn't be too long.

"Since we have established that you don't love my brother in that way, I would think you'd be relieved that you have a reason to call off the engagement. But you're obviously in a lot of pain over what you saw."

Desire tossed the blanket aside and got off the mat. She paced the small room as her mind reeled back to the scene in Chad's office. That low-down dirty rat had told her that he was stuck at the office because something had come up. *Something had come up indeed. Two things, to be exact.*

Chad and his partner had been so engrossed with each other, they hadn't the slightest idea that someone else had entered the room. After the shock had worn off, Desire had swallowed the bile that had collected in her throat and backed out into the main office. To avoid running into anyone on the elevator and having to smile and pretend that her world was all right when it wasn't, she'd taken the stairs.

She'd felt so stupid as she'd stumbled down the fourteen floors, even more stupid than that night at the country club when Chase's sex tape had popped up on the screen. What was wrong with Azura's boys? One was a man whore, the other was in the closet, and both had fidelity issues.

She came to a stop in front of the only window in the room and wrapped her arms around her belly. "My tears weren't tears of pain and sorrow, Chase. I was angry. Angry at myself. At you for sleeping with Lisa last night and then coming to my work this morning, making a mockery of my engagement to your brother and reminding me of what we once meant to each other."

"Desire, that was poor judgment," Chase said behind her. "I was—"

"I don't want to hear your excuses for sleeping with my cousin, Chase, any more than I want to hear Chad's for cheating on me." A dry skittish laugh escaped her throat. "I'm furious that Chad had the nerve to propose when he clearly had no intention to be faithful. I've heard enough lies, had enough of people hiding things from me, people influencing me, telling me how I should feel, how I should react to situations."

Her anger rose to a fever pitch as she thought of all she'd given up in order to please those around her. "I've spent most of my adult life hating Bryce Fontaine for having an affair with my sister which consequently led to his wife's death, only to find out last year that the affair was all in Victoria's head. I spent the last eleven years paying for her crime—being a good girl for my parents instead of following my own heart, my dreams, my desires. That's why I was crying." Desire beat the air with her fists, and bit her lips. She would not fall apart again. "I'm done being manipulated. I'm done being a good girl."

"That's the Desire I used to know. The girl with her own dreams and aspirations, the girl who followed her heart, the girl I grew into love with, many years ago."

Desire turned to find Chase standing inches away from her. His warmth, the scent of his cologne, and the shadows dancing in his sensual eyes all worked together to amplify his appealing virility that had always attracted her. Since he'd come to her rescue, she'd been trying not to think about the delight she'd experienced in his arms night after night in this very room for that one glorious week. The intoxicating warmth of Chase's touch that still lingered in her blood, that still made her flesh tingle, was making her lightheaded.

She blinked and took a step back from him. "I shouldn't have accepted Chad's proposal. I was caught off guard, and then caught up in the idea of marriage. My parents love Chad. Azura loves me. And my dad—he—isn't well," she stammered on a sniffle. "His cancer is back. He could die in as little as six months." Her throat hurt with the thought of losing her father. "He talks about nothing but walking me down the aisle and holding at least one of his grandchildren before he dies. I'm the only child he has left." Despite her determination to stay strong, tears slid from beneath her lids. "He has been so sick and sad for so long, I just—I just wanted to make him happy again before he goes."

"I'm sorry to hear that." His voice was laced with genuine concern. "I wasn't here for you with Victoria, but I'm here now. I'll be at your side, no matter what happens with your dad." He paused, his eyes clouding with sadness for her. "I know how much you love your dad, but it's not your job to make your parents happy, Desire, even if they're sick and dying."

"I know, but it doesn't make me feel any less obligated. And face it, I'm thirty years old. If I'm going to produce children, I need to start now. Most of the girls I grew up with are married, some on their second time around. After your sex tape and Victoria's crime, the eligible men in this town treated me like a leper."

The muscles in his jaws tightened and his eyes shone like shreds of murky glass. "So Chad was right. He told me he was your last hope of marriage in this town. I didn't want to believe him, believe that you would marry for any reason other than love, Desire. I knew it that night you kissed me in the garden and described your wedding day, walking along the maze in a white dress with a long train, and butterflies and doves flying overhead."

"You remember all that?" She lowered her gaze, feeling utterly stupid. She'd been so young and naïve about the realities of life and love. She'd thought love was a garden path she would stroll leisurely down, hand-in-hand with Chase. She hadn't foreseen the thorns and briars popping up to prick her and make her bleed. Her sheltered upbringing hadn't prepared her for that sort of pain. She'd had no idea such hurdles existed.

A low moan escaped her throat when Chase hooked a finger under her chin and raised her face, forcing her to meet his gaze. His piercing gray eyes seemed to reach deep into her soul, searching out the truths she'd buried at age eighteen because she was too scared to embrace them.

"Of course, I remember, Desire. I remember everything about that night. The air was warm and perfumed with a blend of summer flowers. The moon and the stars were out. Bobby Brown's "Tender Roni" was blasting from the museum speakers. You were wearing a yellow sundress, a pair of pearl earrings and a matching necklace your sister had given you for your birthday, and white sandals. Your hair was parted in the middle and fell on either side of your face, and you had a French manicure and pedicure. You smelled of *Heavenly* from Victoria's Secret. Your mouth tasted like chocolate and peppermint. I remember that night and the week we spent in this room, the passion, the heat, the moans of ecstasy. Everything, Desire. *Everything.*"

The low, husky tenor of his voice as he recounted that night made Desire ache for the fulfillment of his lovemaking that had begun eons ago. Her knees buckled and she hastily pulled out a folding chair from under the table and dropped wearily down into it. "Those foolish childhood fantasies flew out the window when the stark reality of adulthood set in," she said, astutely avoiding his gaze by staring at a tear in the vinyl tabletop. One look in his eyes and she was sure her heart would explode with the love she still felt for him. "Plus—"

"Plus, what?" he asked, as he sat down in the chair on the other side of the table.

"Plus, I didn't know if I'd ever see you again. So much time had passed, I didn't know if you even still—"

"Loved you?" he asked when she stopped, too scared to utter the *L* word around him.

CHAPTER NINE

"Look at me, Desire," he prompted softly.

Desire swallowed, and kept her focus on the rip in the vinyl. The air around them was charged with electricity, yet it seemed that neither of them was ready to be swept away by the undercurrents. There was still so much to be discussed and explained between them. They couldn't move forward until the past had been resolved.

She was a wedding planner who'd seen a few marriages fail in less than a year because the bride and groom had buried unresolved issues instead of facing them before exchanging their vows. Apparently, they'd hoped the issues would resolve themselves, but it was never the case. Desire truly believed that love conquered all things. If she didn't, she wouldn't be so passionate about her work. But she'd come to learn that what many people thought was love was sometimes merely a strong dose of lust.

"Desire, look at me," he repeated, still with that measure of gentleness in his voice.

Desire raised her head, and her entire body tingled at the heartrending tenderness she saw in his gaze.

"If you wanted to get married and make babies, all you had to do was call me. I told you that I would be here when you were ready to hear my explanation about what happened that night. Didn't you get the note I left for you, *Tender Roni?*"

Desire pressed her lips together to keep from crying out at his endearing nickname. Chase had begun calling her his *Tender Roni* when she was ten. She missed that. "No." her voice cracked on that single syllable. "I didn't get any note from you. When did you leave it? Where did you leave it?"

"The day I left town. You weren't answering my calls, so that morning, I staked out your home, waiting for your parents to leave so I could talk with you. When they finally did, I knocked on the door, only to find that you weren't home either. The little girl next door told me that she saw you and Victoria leaving before I got there. I texted and called her, but she wasn't answering me either."

"I forbade her to answer. I couldn't talk to you, Chase. I didn't know what to feel, think, or say." She ran her finger along the tear in the vinyl, massaging it like an old scar that remained after a wound had healed.

"I figured as much," he said without malice. "I waited for you to come back. You never did. I'd run out of time, so I wrote you a letter, climbed through your bedroom window, and left it on your dresser."

"You did what? Suppose my father had caught you in his house?"

"He probably would have shot me like he'd threatened when I tried to see you. I honestly hoped he would have caught me, because then he would have either permanently put me out of my misery, or wounded me, so every time I looked at my scar, I would remember how much I hurt you. If he'd known what we'd been doing the week leading up to the night of the show, he probably would have shot me the first time I showed up at your door."

"Don't say that." The image of Chase lying on the lawn with a bullet hole in his chest and his blood seeping from his heart sent chills coursing up and down Desire's spine. She shuddered.

Chase covered her left hand with his right. "If he'd

wounded me, you would have come to see me in the hospital, wouldn't you, *Roni*?"

Desire closed her eyes, allowing his comforting touch to soothe the aching in her heart, still her troubled mind. She laid her right hand over his and he instantly added his left. "I would have come to see you, Chase." She could feel her throat closing up. "What—what did the note say?"

"I told you that I was sorry, that I had been set up, and that I would explain everything when you were ready to forgive me. I told you to call me when you were ready to talk. I didn't care how long it took. I wrote that my heart belonged to you, and that I would always love you. I waited months for you to call, Desire, and in that time, I never gave another woman a second glance, much less a thought. I was waiting for you, honoring our love."

He paused, glanced past her shoulder while his Adam's apple moved up and down as he swallowed. Finally, he brought his gaze back to her, pain and regret livid in his eyes. "When you began dating other men, I knew that it was over between us. I'd lost you."

Tears slid from Desire's eyes and splashed on their hands still clasped together on the table. "I never got your note, Chase. My dad must have found it. I think my mother would have given it to me if she knew how we felt about each other. She's a lot more forgiving than he is. She has always told me that I should follow my heart when it comes to love. My dad never liked you. He thought you were a wild child from the day you moved next door to us. He thought even less of you as a teenager when your reputation with the girls in the neighborhood began circulating. I think that's why he moved us to Granite Falls. He wanted to put space between you and me."

He made no effort to hide the mist that appeared in his eyes. "I'm sorry I was such a bastard. Maybe if I didn't have such a bad reputation, you would have given me a chance to explain what had happened." One of his thumbs moved gently back and forth across the back of her wrist. "That *thing* with those women happened long before that night, Desire. I wasn't unfaithful to you, or to our pledge of love for each other. I meant it when I said I loved you, and that I belonged to you. I still do. But I could also understand what seeing that tape did to you."

Jagged and painful emotions swirled through Desire as she tried to deal with her love for her father, and for the man he despised. She pulled her hands from beneath Chase's and laid them on her lap. "It wasn't just me, Chase. It was my entire family. You have to understand where my father was coming from. He ran for mayor two times before he was elected. He won by default the third time because his opponent was brought up on charges for abusing city funds. He was the first black mayor in a town with less than one percent black population."

"I know. I voted for him when I turned eighteen."

"He took great pride in the fact that the Summers family name would go down in history. I'm a Summers, so when I clicked that button and your sex tape popped up, he—" She paused, her vision still darkly colored with the memory. "He blamed you for putting a stain on our family name. His feelings about you turned to hate that night."

"I understand, Desire. I told you this morning that I don't blame your father for threatening me, but—" He paused, obviously struggling with some inner pain.

"But what, Chase?" she asked as a chill black silence enveloped them.

"The thought of you with other men almost killed me. You were *my* Roni. Mine."

"You didn't wait around for me to move past the hurt. You just took off without even saying goodbye."

"I did say goodbye. You just never got it."

"It doesn't matter. My father would never have accepted us as a couple after that. You were scum to him. And that's probably why he destroyed your note before I could find it." Her throat felt parched. She'd cried herself into a dehydrated state. She wished she'd thought to bring some water with her.

"I thought the best way to get over you was to date other men."

He winced as if she'd shoved a knife into his chest. "Did they help you forget me?"

Desire shook her head as she stared into his eyes. Like Chase had pointed out this morning, honesty was the one thing they'd always had between them. He was the only person in the world with whom she'd ever felt safe and secure enough to bare her heart. "I missed you more because each time a man held me, I wished it was your arms around me. Each time one kissed me, I ached for your lips. That aching fed my unhappiness and kept my anger alive, but everything changed last year."

"How?"

Desire wondered if she would ever have been able to let go of her anger if fate hadn't intervened. "I'm sure you heard about the group wedding I planned last year for the four most powerful men in Granite Falls. The LaCrosses, Fontaines, Andrettis, and the Andreases."

"The entire world heard about that." His smile was wide and animated, his even white teeth sparkling against the candlelight. "It put you and your business on the map. I hear you're in demand now—celebrities and politicians alike are standing in line for your services. I'm very proud of you, Desire."

Desire reveled in his open admiration of her. Her family and the few close friends she cherished had expressed their pride and congratulations at her accomplishments many times, but it was extra special coming from Chase. "It kind of fell into my lap when the wedding planner the brides had initially hired was injured and couldn't finish the job."

"They were foolish not to hire you in the first place," he said with conviction.

"I can't blame them, seeing that my family and the Fontaines weren't on speaking terms."

"Are you on speaking terms now?"

Desire nodded. "I refused to take the job until Kaya—that's

Bryce's second wife," she said to clarify, "spoke with him. I didn't need him sabotaging everything in the middle of my planning. Time and effort, you know."

"That makes good business sense. Kaya must have been very convincing," he said on a smile.

"I guess, because the next thing I knew, Bryce was at my parents' home trying to mend the rift between our families. That's when my father found out that Victoria had lied to him. She'd told Dad that Bryce had forced her into a sexual relationship while she was working for him, and that he tossed her aside for Pilar. She said that Bryce fired her when she threatened to sue him for sexual harassment. It was easy for Dad to believe because of Bryce's reputation back then, you know."

He shook his head, causing a lock of dark hair to fall across his forehead. "It must have been shocking for your father to learn that his little angel wasn't an angel after all."

"It was a shock for all of us. My family had condemned Bryce without hearing his side of the story—even blaming him for both his wife's and Victoria's deaths. It got me thinking that there were really two sides to every story. I didn't give you a chance to tell yours before I condemned you. I was wrong, Chase. And I'm sorry. I should have given you the benefit of the doubt before cutting you out of my life."

"It's okay, Desire." He wiped at the tears that had slid from her eyes to her cheeks.

The warmth of his touch took her back to happier times—happy times she craved again.

He offered her a forgiving smile. "We all make mistakes, but the important thing is that we learn from them. It took us twelve years, but we're here now, mending the rift between us. I'm sorry about Victoria, about your dad's stroke, his cancer, and failing health. I regret not being here for you during that painful and difficult period of your life."

Desire's chest felt as if it would burst from the lingering anxiety. "I needed you so much, Chase. I knew that if you were here, you would have made me feel better, just like you used to do when I was a little girl. It had gotten so bad that I finally broke and asked Azura for you. She didn't know where you were. No one knew if you were dead or alive."

His expression darkened with an unreadable emotion and the muscles of his jaws flinched. "I wanted to be here. You have to believe that, *Roni*, but I couldn't come back."

"Why? What happened that night, Chase? You said you were set up? Who set you up? Why would someone do such a mean, vile thing to you?"

CHAPTER TEN

Jealousy. Greed.

Chase wanted to speak out loud, but he couldn't.

"I used to think that it was Susie Connor," she said. "I even asked her, and she swore she had nothing to do with it."

The chair creaked under his weight as he leaned back and folded his arms across his chest. "Why do you think it was Susie?"

"Because you broke your date with her to meet me that night. I thought she'd found out that you were in love with me and wanted to get back at me."

Chase had had that very same thought for a minute, but he'd quickly abandoned it for a multitude of reasons. First, Susie wasn't that calculating to mastermind such a devious plot, and definitely not in such a small window of time. Second, she wasn't that techno savvy to change the time stamp on a video when she didn't even know how to use the one on her phone, even after he'd shown her several times. Third, she'd had no idea about his passion for architecture or about his thumb drive. Fourth, he and Desire had been very careful about being seen together as a couple, so he doubted Susie knew about them. He could go on and on about why it couldn't have been Susie.

In hindsight, Chase had realized that his exile had also protected Desire. He'd had no doubt that she would have become a pawn in his nemesis's nasty game to destroy him. That bastard would have offered her a shoulder to cry on, seduced her, used her, and then discarded her—just to hurt Chase. He might have even threatened to harm her physically to make sure that Chase stayed away.

Eight years ago, when Chase began investigating his archenemy, he had been horrified at the lengths that man had gone to in order to get his way in both his professional and personal lives. Chase had been his first victim, and his inability to fight back had empowered the bastard to go after other defenseless targets. Many lives and families had been ruined. A familiar chill settled in Chase's stomach at the thought of Desire standing in that man's line of fire.

As victim after victim was discovered, Chase had recognized and embraced the fact that the covert nature of his and Desire's short affair was indeed a blessing.

"Do you think that she lied to my face, Chase?" Desire asked, breaking into his thoughts.

"No, Susie didn't lie to you. It wasn't her, and it wasn't about you." That much he could reveal to set her mind at ease.

"Then who was it? Who hated you that much?" Rancor sharpened her voice.

Chase shot to his feet and walked the length of the room and back in ten agitated strides as he tried to figure out just how much to reveal to Desire. He trusted Desire, even when she had given up on him. But telling her about the bastard who had stolen twelve years of their lives—years they could never get back—might lessen the impact of his revenge.

Knowing her, she might try to talk him out of it, tell him to let bygones be bygones, let go of the past, and concentrate on the future like her father and Bryce had done. It would be sound advice, but the wheels of justice had already begun turning, and it wasn't in Chase's power to stop them, not that he had any intention to back off.

Businesswise, it wasn't just the survival of DC Designs that he had to worry about. Bryce had put his reputation and his company's integrity on the line, too. And then there was the personal issue that hadn't been resolved. If the news of his return to Evergreen got out before the plan was enacted, that son of a bitch might carry out his threat to make his mother's past public knowledge.

No, he had to see his plan through to the end, or he might very well end up right back where he was chased out of town.

"Chase! Why can't you tell me? Was it my Dad? Did he find out about us? Could he have done something this disgusting? Could he have embarrassed me just to run you out of town? I wouldn't put it past him."

The despair in Desire's voice tugged at Chase's heartstrings. He came to a stop in front of her and held out a hand. His heart somersaulted when she placed hers in his. He tugged her gently to her feet. "It wasn't your father. He might hate me, but he wouldn't have used you to destroy me. He loves you, and he wants the best for you like any good father does."

She let out a harsh breath through her mouth, and squeezed his hands in relief.

"Do you trust me?" He stroked the inside of her wrists with his thumbs.

"I—I don't know—if—"

"Please. I know it's a lot to ask after the long silence between us. But I need you to trust me, just this one last time. I promise to tell you everything very soon."

"Okay. I do trust you, but I don't understand why you wouldn't tell me who set you up. I have a right to know since they used me to get to you."

Her insightful statement was like a stake through Chase's heart. "You're absolutely correct. And that's one of the reasons I need to take care of him before I reveal his identity, or my return to Evergreen. I left to protect you, Desire." *And my brother and mother*, he wanted to add.

"Did this person threaten me?" Fear, stark and vivid, glittered in her eyes.

113

"He couldn't, since no one knew about us. And I want to keep it that way."

"For how long? How long do we have to wait to let the world know we're together? We can't move forward until we settle the past, Chase. I want to move forward with you. I love you. I never stopped loving you. I want to be with you." She clasped his face in her hands. "I couldn't admit my true feelings this morning because of my commitment to Chad and my promise to my father, but now...now...everything is changed, and you're telling me that we have to wait."

He placed his hands over hers and brought them to his chest, pressing her palms against his heart. "Do you feel this? It beats for you, only for you. I, too, long to be with you, my love. More than anything I've ever wanted in this world. The chance of us reconnecting like this, here, in our special place, talking, making plans for the future like we did a lifetime ago is the only thing that gave me hope all these years." He kissed her palms.

She dropped her gaze to his chest. "You want to know the real reason I said yes to Chad's proposal?"

"There's another reason other than giving your father grandchildren before he dies?"

A sheepish smile parted her lips. "It was subconscious; nevertheless, it was there. Maybe that's why I can't stay angry at Chad. I was using him as much as he was using me."

He placed a finger under her chin and lifted her face. "What is it?"

She trembled and wet her lips. "I was kind of hoping that when you heard the news of our engagement, you'd come running home to stop it. But I guess it wasn't necessary. You're here, and not because of it—or is it? Did Chad call to tell you before our three days were up?"

He dropped his hands to his sides. "Nope. I snuck into the house last night to surprise my mother and Chad and overheard them talking about the engagement. My little brother honored that agreement. And judging from what you saw today, I'm pretty sure it worked out to his advantage.

However, you can imagine how the news made me feel."

"Mad. Devastated. Like your world had finally come to an end. That's how I would have felt if it were the other way around."

"Hopeless. Angry. Hopeless mostly. That's when I called Lisa and things got out of hand. Can you forgive me for that horrible mistake? I promise it's the last stupid thing I will ever do. I will never hurt you like that again."

"I forgive you, Chase, and I'm sorry you had to find out that way. No wonder you ran to Lisa. I created that mess by not being honest with myself. Would you have returned?" she asked after a short pause. "I mean, if you hadn't already decided to come home? Why did you come home anyway if it wasn't to stop me from marrying Chad?"

"Truthfully, I was waiting for a sign, for the right time, and when I saw the photo of you in the garden, I felt as if you were sending me a message."

Her eyes grew wide and curious. "You read the article about me in Granite Falls People News?"

"You sound surprised."

"Well, yes. I wouldn't think *Granite Falls People News* is the kind of magazine you would be reading down on an Iowa farm."

"What do you think a farm boy reads?" he asked with mild curiosity. "I mean, we have dreams of becoming billionaires one day, too."

"The *Farmer's Almanac* for one," she said on a chuckle.

Her laughter sent warmth racing from Chase's head all the way to his toes. He hadn't heard her laugh in forever. God, he'd missed her. Missed her laugh, her smile. Her everything.

The growing restriction in his crotch warned him that the sexual tension they'd experienced this morning was brewing again. Involuntarily, his hands slipped up her arms, bringing her closer until there was no space between them. She trembled as the soft contours of her body melted into his. As if in a trance, Chase watched her tongue dart across her lips—those moist, voluptuous lips that had haunted his sleep for four thousand, three hundred and ninety-seven nights.

The sound of his heart beating in his ears was like a drum beating at a mating ceremony. He dipped his head until his lips were centimeters from hers. He inhaled the flowery scent of her skin, the sweetness of her dewy breath as he waited—giving her the chance to pull away, to stop him, to protest what she must know was about to happen between them.

Sharing their first kiss after what felt like a lifetime. Their kiss of reconciliation. The first kiss of many to come for the rest of their lives.

She whimpered, and her tongue came out to wet her lips again. This time the moist, warm tip grazed his bottom lip sending a sudden bolt of electricity washing over Chase. He groaned in a heated response and, locking his hands against her spine, he pulled her upward and inward as his mouth opened over hers. When she wrapped her arms around his neck, Chase gave himself completely over to the ecstasy of being in Desire's arms again.

Fire coiled in his belly as she parted her lips, thrust her tongue into his mouth, and curled it around his with a hunger that superseded any Chase had ever experienced.

"Desire," he whispered her name, loving the raspy sound of it in his own ears as he backed her against the wall. Bending his knees, he pulled her skirt up above her waist, and pressed the bulge in his crotch into the sweetness between her thighs. He instantaneously felt the heat and the moisture pass between them.

She trembled and moaned as they began a simulated dance of mating. "Make love to me, Chase. I need you so much. I want you. I want you now. I don't want to wait."

"Yes, baby, yes." Chase crooned, forgetting that anything or anyone else existed beyond the four walls of the small room. He kissed her deeply, devouring her essence, savoring her sweetness as she offered it all up to him.

There was no reason to deny themselves the joy of each other anymore. They were in their own secret place that no one knew existed. She was safe with him here and, judging from the moans and groans, the heavy sighs, the labored breaths, and the passion swirling around them, the years of separation had only intensified their need and love for each other.

"I love you so much," he whispered against her mouth as his hands reached for the buttons of her blouse. "So much. I need you. I need—"

Chase swore as his phone began to ring between their tangled bodies, reminding him that there was, indeed, a world of issues outside these four walls—issues that both he and Desire had to resolve before they could be together.

With a groan, he reluctantly disengaged their mouths and gazed at her pouting lips, wet and swollen from his kisses. Even though he was annoyed at the interruption, Chase was glad for it. Desire was still engaged to his brother. Until she told Chad that the engagement was off, she remained off limits to Chase. He wanted to do things right between them this time. The ringing stopped and his voicemail ringtone sounded.

She tightened her hold when he tried to step back. "It stopped ringing," she said, her eyes flickering with love and passion. "Just ignore it."

Chase's shaft pulsed against her in total contradiction to his logic. "We got carried away, but we both known it would be unethical if we made love. The fact is, in spite of what my brother did, you're still engaged to him."

"Don't remind me." Her mouth took on a sour twist. "If he hadn't cheated on me, you and I wouldn't be in this position. That's a fact."

"Are you sure about that, Desire?" Chase asked, glancing down their bodies to where his still impressive erection was pressed into her groin.

She tensed at the question, but made no attempt to respond. She didn't need to since they both knew they would have ended up in this very position eventually. Thank God it was way before she'd married with his brother. Nevertheless...

"Two wrongs don't make a right," he said, stepping back to give her room to pull down her skirt and tuck her blouse in. He tried not to think of the vision of her sexy brown thighs and legs, the moist outline of her mound against her black silk thong. He swallowed. "The old Chase would have had you naked and under me by now. But I've grown up since you last saw me. I'm trying not to be that selfish, narcissistic degenerate you once called me."

"I don't think of you that way anymore."

"But I would be that jerk if I made love to you before you ended things between you and Chad. Which reminds me," he added, pulling an envelope from his back pocket. "I have something for you. I picked it up from my post office box this afternoon. I was going to give it to you later, but now's as good a time as any." He placed it in her hand.

"What is it?" she asked, staring at the unopened envelope addressed to him.

"Eight months ago, my decision to come home coincided with the end of my last relationship. I hadn't been with a woman since, until—well, the other night."

"I have already told you that I've forgiven you for sleeping with Lisa."

"I know, but I still regret that it even happened. Anyway, although I've always, always used protection, I had myself tested. I'm clean. This is my bill of health. It's unopened so you'll know I haven't tampered with the results."

"Chase, I believe you. You've never lied to me about anything, so if you tell me you're clean, I don't need to read this." She handed it back to him. "I'm also clean," she added, avoiding her gaze for a second. "But I don't have a bill of health to prove it. The thing is—"

"Your word is good enough for me, too," he said, returning the envelope to his pocket. "But in case you're not using any other form of birth control, although I'll hate it, I am willing to use condoms when we do make love. Thank God I don't have any on me right now, or else we probably would have gone the distance, despite my declaration of morality a few minutes ago."

She laughed. "I don't want to use condoms when we do make love. Let's make my father's wish come true. Let's make a baby for him, soon. He shouldn't care if it's conceived out of wedlock."

"Desire—"

Her phone buzzed in her purse. She walked over to the table and retrieved it. "It's Chad again. He left thirty messages," she said, scrolling through them.

"He's desperate."

"I'll call him and end it right now."

"You need to do it in person. You have to confront him face-to-face and let him know you know what you know. Neither of you will have closure any other way."

Her chest rose and fell on a deep sigh, drawing Chase's attention to the full swell of her breasts. He almost choked on the saliva that backed up into his throat. "We have to do this right if it's going to work out for us. No more sneaking around, no lying to our families."

"I agree, but it's an unpleasant conversation. One I don't want to have."

"We all do things we don't want to do."

"You should answer that," she said, when his phone began ringing again. "It's probably Chad wanting to know if you found me. Or maybe you shouldn't answer if you don't want to lie about being with me." She tossed her phone back into her purse and walked over to the window.

"Touché. Challenging me to take my own advice, are you?" Chase laughed as he pulled his phone from his pocket and looked at the screen. "Damn!"

"What is it?" she asked, turning toward him.

"It's my mother. I promised to have dinner with her tonight after I skipped out on the elaborate breakfast she made for me this morning. I had to see you, stop you—you know. She wants to know when I'll be home."

"Then you should go."

"*We* should go. It'll be dark soon, and I'm not leaving you here alone. Why don't you have dinner with us?" He knew he was stalling. As much as he loved her and missed her cooking, he wasn't looking forward to dinner with his mother.

"Azura wants to spend time with you, not me."

She'll probably regret it by the time the evening is over. "Azura loves you. I doubt she'll be upset that I brought a guest to dinner. It's not like you've never unexpectedly dropped in for dinner before." *Still stalling.* "I believe you ate more meals at our house than you did at your own back then."

His statement brought a smile to her face. "The aromas coming from Azura's kitchen used to make my mouth water. My mother wasn't the greatest cook. We ate a lot of processed food. Boxed macaroni and cheese was a staple in our home."

Chase laughed out loud as he closed the distance between them. "Yep, you were around ten the first time you cooked me mac and cheese with boiled hot dogs on the side. I was helping you with your math homework when Mom called to say she was delayed at work and dinner would be late. You ran next door and came back with a box of macaroni and cheese and a package of hot dogs."

"Aghh!" She grimaced in good humor. "That was awful. The macaroni was hard and lumpy, and the hot dogs were half cooked."

"Lumpy and runny at the same time, actually. I still don't understand how that was possible, but I ate it all with a smile on my face even though I almost choked in the process. The ketchup was good though. I ate a lot of that."

"And then you had a stomachache all night, and the next morning Azura was at our house wanting to know what I fed her son for dinner. She begged me not to cook for you again." She brought her hand to her mouth to stifle her giggles.

Her laughter reached deep inside Chase, rooting out a host of memories he'd almost forgotten existed. "Those were the good old days."

Flashes of candlelight twinkled in her brown eyes. "That's when you started calling me *Tender Roni.*"

"You were tender to me, even if the *roni* you fed me was hard." He chuckled heartily. "And like Bobby Brown sings, you do stand out in a crowd. Always did."

"Of course I stand out in a crowd. I'm one of the very few

black women around here."

"No, sweetheart. You stand out because you are the most beautiful woman around here, and in the world. You would stand out, no matter your ethnic makeup."

"You're saying that because you want to get into my panties." She sent him a twisted look.

"I don't think I need to say anything to get into your panties, Desire. We have chemistry and passion between us, darling. And it's deadly explosive. All we need to do is think of each other. You'll get wet, and I'll get hard." His cock swelled and strained against his pants.

A tremor touched her smooth wet lips, and she shifted from one foot to another. "And that's exactly why you shouldn't be inviting me to dine with you and Azura. It would seem strange that you, and not her other son, my fiancé, is bringing me to dinner."

"I suppose it would raise questions."

"Questions you're not ready to answer," she reminded him. "Besides I have to prepare for my confrontation with Chad."

"Are you going to talk with him tonight?"

"I don't have a choice. He's probably camping on my doorstep waiting for me to come home."

"Probably. He was pretty upset when I saw him. I've never seen my brother in such a panic."

"Good," she said, forcefully. "He knows what he did, and I'm sure once I let him know that I know, he'll try to talk his way out of it. You know how he gets when he's backed into a corner."

"It's why he's such a damned good lawyer."

"And a liar."

Her eyes and voice were laced with the kind of contempt Chase had witnessed only once before. He hoped never to be on the receiving end of Desire's wrath ever again. The pain he had caused her was unintentional, brought on by the malicious acts of another. But what Chad had done was deliberate, cold, and dishonest.

"I'm more concerned about how to break the news to my

parents," she added, her voice softening.

"Are you seeing them tonight, too?"

She shook her head. "I can't. I have to sleep on that one and figure out the best way to—" She glanced down at her hands, clasped against her stomach. "It will upset them, especially my father. I don't—"

He pulled her close, placing her head into the hollow between his shoulder and his neck. It fitted perfectly. "Tell them the truth, that you never loved Chad and that you only agreed to marry him because they pressured you into getting married and spitting out babies. If you're really brave, you can tell them that you still intend to get married and spit out babies—my babies instead of my brother's." He felt her smile against his skin as her arms went around his waist, holding him tightly.

"I wish it were that easy."

He stroked his fingers through her hair. "Love should be easy, Desire. It's when we try to manipulate it, abuse it, hide it, deny it, dishonor it, and run from it that it becomes difficult and causes us pain."

She lifted her head and smiled at him. "I forgot how philosophical you are. You're nothing like Chad when it comes to honesty. You've never, ever tried to deceive me. I should have taken it into consideration that night. I should have—"

He placed a finger on her lips. "There's no need to rehash the past anymore. You've forgiven me for hurting you, and I've forgiven you for not trusting in my love for you."

"I wish you would just explain it to me tonight. Now. If I know what happened, it might help when I talk to my parents."

"It's a long story and we don't have the time tonight. Plus, I think it's better if I show you."

"Show me what?"

"Would you have dinner with me tomorrow? That is, if you're free."

Excitement bubbled in her eyes. "It's Saturday. I'm free. Freer than I've been in years."

"Then it's a date—a very informative date."

"Where are we going?"

Revealing the venue would open up the gate for a flood of questions. "It's a surprise. But wear something really nice."

"How nice?"

"Elegant. We're dining in style in a very prestigious restaurant. In fact, we'll be driven there in a limo. I promised you a special evening long ago, and I plan to keep that promise."

"You don't need to take me to an expensive restaurant, Chase. If I wanted that kind of lifestyle, I would have it. I've had several would-be suitors since the billionaires' wedding last year."

"Do you have something against wealthy men?" he asked, causally.

"Not really. But you know me. I'm a low-key girl. I can cook us dinner at my place. Or better still, order in. We'll be completely alone."

"Not a good idea," Chase said.

She took a step back. "You don't want to be alone with me?"

He pulled her back in. "Oh I do, but if we were alone, we'd be making love instead of talking, and I do need to explain everything before we take the next step."

"What's the next step?"

Marriage in a couple days and our first baby in nine months. "It can be whatever you want it to be."

She drew in her lips thoughtfully. "Are you going back to Iowa?"

"I'm home to stay, Desire."

Relief washed over her face. "Okay, but limos are very expensive around here. They charge by the hour and even the cheapest ones could cost more an hour than you make in a week as a farm hand. I can drive us."

Chase suppressed his amusement. "I'm touched at your concern about my financial well-being, but the limo is already ordered and paid for."

Her brows furrowed into a frown. "You paid for a limo to take me to a dinner you hadn't yet invited me to? I don't get it."

"I planned it all before I came home."

"You did? Why?"

Chase sighed. He was tired of living in the dark where his family and now Desire were concerned, but he couldn't let the cat out of the bag prematurely. He tucked a curl behind her ear. His fingers lingered on her skin—soft and warm. "I promise you'll learn the whole truth during dinner tomorrow evening."

"But—"

He placed a finger on her lips. "No buts, my sweet." Before she had time to question him further, and before he gave in to his ache to lay her down on the mat and make love to her until sunrise, he added, "Come on. I'll give you a ride to your car."

"On your old bike? I'm surprised it still runs," she said with a skeptical twist of her lips. "It left a black plume of smoke in its wake this morning."

"Yeah, it did, didn't it? Well, I had her tuned. She's as good as new again."

"I don't know. I think you should sell it and use the proceeds for a down payment on a good used car."

He leaned his head to the side. "I can never get rid of her, and you know why."

"Because I became a woman on her."

"Yes. Now, come on. She'll be happy to feel your weight on her again."

Chase's heart did a jig when she placed her hand in his. And as they walked hand in hand out of the boarding house, images of Desire at different stages of her life skipping happily beside him flashed across Chase's mind. She'd trusted him, as a child, until he'd inadvertently broken that trust.

She was trusting him again, as a woman.

Chase swore in his heart never to let anyone or anything cause her to lose faith in him again—not even her father.

They had a second chance. It was more than most people got.

CHAPTER ELEVEN

Night had fallen by the time Desire pulled into her driveway, and just as she'd predicted, Chad was sitting on her swing porch waiting for her. As soon as her headlights hit him, he jumped up, sprang down the steps, and was knocking on her window even before she could turn off her engine. With a heavy sigh, she rolled down the window.

"Desire, where have you been? I've been worried sick about you. I thought something had happened to you."

"As you can see, I'm perfectly well." As he stood there, his hands on his hips, a scowl on his face as if he were chastising a teenager who'd broken curfew, and acting as if she was the one who was at fault, Desire longed to have this particular talk over.

She wished she'd confronted Chad when she'd caught him with his pants down, but she'd been too scared. She'd always been scared of conflict. She'd run from them as a child, and avoided them as an adult.

As she observed Chad's domineering stance, memories of Victoria cowering on the sofa while their father reprimanded her flashed across Desire's mind. She shivered at the alarming realization that her fear of conflict had arisen from her father and half sister's volatile relationship. Several times, Desire had seen her father cry after a heated argument with Victoria. She'd never told him, but she'd vowed in her little heart never to make her Daddy cry.

She'd been a good girl long before she'd even realized it. She'd spent her life trying to please her father because she didn't want to make him cry. She'd agreed to marry one brother and had given up on the other for him.

She should have fought for Chase instead of running away. She'd wanted to forgive him, be with him, but she didn't want to defy her father. She'd been a coward and allowed her father to control her. Chase was so right when he'd said that it wasn't her job to make her father happy. It was the other way around. Her father had never asked her how she felt about Chase, even though he'd had proof that Chase loved her, that there was an explanation behind the incident at the country club. He hadn't given Chase a chance. He hadn't given her a chance. He hadn't given *them* a chance. Instead, he'd destroyed Chase's letter before she had a chance to read it, never told her about it, and thus consequently destroyed her life as well. Well, almost.

Desire swiped at her tears and then picked up her tote from the front seat. She glanced at two other totes filled with work that was now four hours overdue, but decided to leave them in her car since she knew she wouldn't be able to concentrate on any work tonight.

"Baby, what's wrong? Have I done something to upset you?"

Don't call me baby. I'm not crying over you. She pushed her window button and once it was up, she turned off her car.

Chad opened her door and reached out a hand to help her out.

"Don't touch me. Stand back."

"Desire, what's the matter with you?" He stared at her as if she had two heads. "You didn't show up for our lunch with the reporter. You ignored my calls and disappeared for hours, and now you're acting like—"

"Like what, Chad? What am I acting like?" she asked, as she closed and locked her car.

"Like you hate me."

Desire set her tote on the hood of her car and glanced at her dark house, then over at Azura's. Chase's bedroom light was on and his motorcycle was parked in the driveway behind Chad's car. He'd gotten home before her. They'd decided that they shouldn't arrive at the same time, and since he was late for dinner with his mother, Desire had taken the long way home along the road by the Mannis River.

She glanced at her house again, wanting to escape inside it, without Chad. Again, she wished she'd confronted him in his office. If she had it would have been over and she and Chase probably would still be in their secret hideaway, making love. Her body ached for his touch.

"Desire, where is this attitude coming from? The last time we spoke, everything was fine. You were going to meet me at the restaurant. We were going to make our engagement public. But now, a few hours later, it seems as if everything we talked about, everything we planned is unraveling."

"I saw you, Chad. I saw you in your office with John. I saw the two of you. Together." She couldn't keep it in any longer.

His face flushed with humiliation in the dim lights from the lamppost as silence loomed between them. Finally, he found his voice, deflated though it was. "Desire, it's not what it looked like."

"It's not what it looked like? Then what was it, Chad? I think you're both a little too old to play doctor, don't you? Just admit that you're gay."

"I'm not gay. I'm not!" he repeated on a defiant shrug as if he needed to convince himself.

"What you were doing seemed very gay to me. You asked me to marry you and three days later, you're having sex with a man. These plans you just mentioned, what were they? To marry me and pretend to love me while you carried on behind my back?"

"No. I called John and asked him to meet me at my office. I wanted to tell him before we met with the reporter. I didn't want him to find out that way. But when I saw him—"

"The truth slapped you in the face," she said, when he broke off in midsentence and averted his gaze. "Is he the reason for the three-day wait to announce our engagement?"

He nodded "It was goodbye. I was saying goodbye to John."

"That was some goodbye." Desire leaned against her car as the laughter erupted from her throat. She should have known. She should have seen it. All the signs were there in plain sight. Chad and John, a science teacher at a local parochial school, were always together. They went to the movies together, vacationed together, attended the ballet and symphony together, dined together, and even double-dated until last fall when John married Teresa, another science teacher from a neighboring town.

As she thought about it now, Desire recalled how quiet and distant Chad had been at John and Teresa's wedding. He was the gloomiest best man she'd ever seen, and she'd seen a lot of them. At the time, she'd thought it was due to the fact that John wouldn't be able to spend as much time with his buddy, which was quite understandable, since they'd been friends since high school. It wasn't unusual for a man to have a male best friend, just as it wasn't unusual for women. Never in a million years would Desire have guessed that John and Chad were in the closet.

Was she now supposed to suspect that all men who spent too much time together had something to hide? How many of them were married, engaged, or dating members of the opposite sex? How many wives, fiancées, and lovers knew what their partners were doing? How many accepted it because they were too ashamed or scared of the embarrassment, the pain, if the truth came to light? What about those who hadn't a clue, those like herself who'd happened on the truth by chance? If she hadn't made the decision to end it with Chad, come clean with the reason she'd agreed to marry him, she would still be in the dark. "Has John been cheating on his wife with you all this time?" she asked, her heart heavy with the pain she knew was headed in poor Teresa's direction.

A momentary look of discomfort crossed Chad's face. "We broke it off after he got married, but then we—"

"But then you couldn't stay away from each other. How long have the two of you been lovers? Is he the only man you've ever been with?" she asked, wondering if John was the boy Chase had found Chad with all those years ago. If he were, they were both masters of deceit.

"I um—"

Desire pushed off the car. "You know what, on second thought, I don't want to know. I don't care."

"I'm sorry, Desire."

"What are you sorry about? That I caught you with your pants down? That I found out that you're a lying, cheating bastard?"

"I told you it's over."

"It might be over between you and John, but it's not over for you. You're gay. You're in the closet, and in denial."

His face turned a bright red. "I'm not gay. I'm bisexual. I like women, too."

"That's what you keep telling yourself. You date women to hide your true sexual orientation. This is the twenty-first century, Chad. You don't need to stay in the closet."

"It may be the twenty-first century, but there are a lot of folks walking around with eighteenth-century ideology when it comes to people like me. Even my mother."

"Azura is not like that. She's not a bigot. She judges people by the contents of their hearts, not by their color, or creed, or sexual orientation. You should know your mother better than that, Chad. She's the only person who stood by my family when everyone else deserted us. I understand that she might have a hard time accepting it because of her faith, but she's not going to disown you. You are her son. Like any good mother, she wants you to be happy. Have you ever been in love with any of the women you've dated?" she asked, watching him closely.

"No."

"Do you love John?"

He nodded. "You can't tell anyone. He teaches at a religious institution and he would lose his job if his employers found out. He would lose his family, too. Teresa would leave him and take their son with her."

"Don't you think she deserves to know? If it were me, I would want to hang my husband by the balls for lying to me and cheating on me." *Dear God, it could have been me.* If Chase hadn't come home last night, Desire would have had no reason to break it off with Chad. She would not have gone to his office and caught him in the act.

Desire had never put much faith in fate. Why should she when the lady seemed to have been working against her for years, starting with the night at the country club, Chase's disappearance, Victoria, her father's heart attack, his fight against cancer, and then her having to give up her dreams of leaving home and attending a prestigious college?

The tides had finally turned in her favor last year when the billionaire brides had approached her about taking over the planning of their wedding. She'd been understandably reluctant at first. She hadn't been looking forward to a confrontation with Bryce Fontaine and his friends, whom she'd been certain were in mutual agreement with his opinions of her family.

But in the end, it seemed that her planning that wedding was a part of some grand design Lady Fate had cooked up for the Summers and Fontaine families. It was Chad who had encouraged her to take the job. Now, she understood why. He'd seen an opportunity to use her to his benefit and grabbed it without blinking an eye.

But then again, Lady Fate had stepped in on her behalf by bringing Chase home at the precise moment, and then sending her to Chad's office. And where had she ended up? Right in Chase's arms where she'd known she always belonged. Chase had made her feel like that breathless girl of eighteen again.

If being separated from Chase had taught her anything, it was that they were meant to be. If theirs wasn't true love, it would not have lasted all these years, and they would not have been able to pick up where they'd left off so easily. So yeah, she now believed in fate.

Her heart hammered foolishly at the memories of spending time with him today. Her lips still tingled from his kisses, her skin from his touch.

"You hate me," Chad said in a doleful voice.

Desire took a deep breath. She didn't hate Chad. How could she when *she* had had her own selfish reasons to marry him? The only difference between them was that she would have remained true to their vows. *Would you have, now that Chase is back?*

Desire slammed the lid on the critical voice. "Out of all the women you've dated, why did you ask *me* to marry you, Chad? You're obviously not physically attracted to me since you've never made a pass at me in all the years we've been friends. Actually, the first time you ever showed interest in me was right after Michelle LaCrosse and her friends approached me about planning their wedding. When I initially turned her down because of the war going on between my family and the Fontaines, you encouraged me to take the job. Why?" Chase had already explained Chad's agenda to her, but she wanted to hear it from him, see if he could be honest about anything.

"I thought it was a good business move. And it was. Weddings by Desire exploded after that. Now, you're thinking about expanding."

"And…" she prompted when he grew silent, pushed his hands into his pockets, and drooped his shoulders like a beaten dog. She'd never seen him at a loss for words like this. Then maybe, he'd never been caught red-handed before. "Just say it, Chad. Get it all out."

"Okay. Yes, you were making some serious contacts in the entertainment, political, and business world. I met some important politicians in Washington at Senator Wilson's daughter's wedding last November, and I overheard the First Lady tell you that she'll be in touch when her children are ready to settle down. My long-term goal is to be a federal judge. These are connections I could never make on my own, Desire. I saw an opportunity to align myself with the most important people in the country and I took it."

"So I was just a means to an end?"

"Not entirely. I like you. I like your family." He shrugged. "I thought we'd make a dynamic couple."

"And how long do you think it would have lasted when you're in love with someone else? That speech you gave me about not being controlled by love and romance was just an act. I went along because it was an act for me too. I was using *you*, Chad. I'm in love with someone else, too. I've always been in love with him."

"Who is it? One of your former lovers?"

Telling him about her and Chase would just add insult to injury and open up the gateway to a whole other topic of conversation. She didn't have the energy. "I'm not at liberty to say, yet."

"Why, is he married? See, we're not so different."

Desire balked at his rude suggestion. "I'm not you, Chadwick Hunter. I'm not a cheater. If we'd gone through with the marriage, God forbid, I would have honored our vows."

"Then why did you accept my proposal when you just admitted to being in love with someone else, someone who is obviously unavailable to you?"

"Because of my father. His cancer is back. He might only have a year or so left. I wanted to make him happy, give him at least one grandchild before he dies."

"Oh, Desire. I'm so sorry. We can still give him what he wants. I told you I was saying goodbye to John."

In spite of the heaviness talking about her father brought to her heart, Desire uttered a skittish laugh. "Are you out of your freaking mind? I saw you making love with another man. You're gay. You think I would let you touch me after that? No! Not even for my father."

"There are other ways to make babies, Desire. Artificial insemination for one. I know couples who've gone down that route, as I'm sure you do. One of the billionaires from the wedding—Erik LaCrosse—was a test tube baby. He turned out fine."

Desire stared at him open mouthed. The Chad she knew had finally arrived. The attorney was arguing his case, presenting evidence to try to sway the jury. And it was now time for Desire to close this case.

"It's been a long day, Chad. I'm really tired and hungry. I just want to go inside, eat something, take a hot bath, and relax." She picked up her bag from the hood of her car and began walking toward her porch.

"Can we at least talk about it?" Chad asked, following behind her. "I can go pick up some takeout while you shower, and then we can discuss our options while we eat."

"Look, Chad," Desire said, standing on the bottom step, "neither one of us is perfect. We both decided to enter this marriage for our own self-serving reasons. There is no need for us to hash this out any further. There's nothing to talk about. Let's just be grateful that we never made our engagement public. At least that way we have saved face."

He dropped his head for a second. "Can we at least remain friends? I value your friendship, Desire. You were the first friend I ever had in this world. I'm sorry that I disappointed you."

Desire finally felt something. *Sadness.* "I don't know, Chad. You're a liar and a cheat of the worst kind. What you and John are doing to Teresa is dishonorable. You both need to fix it. In the meantime, I need space and time from you." She hurried up the steps and jammed her key into the lock.

Once inside, she dropped to the floor and let the tears flow. Apart from Chase and Lisa, Chad had been the only other true friend she ever had. He'd stayed true when everyone else had deserted her. She knew what it felt like to hide your true nature from the rest of the world. She'd been doing it for twelve long years. For Chad, it was even longer. Like her, he'd been afraid to let anyone know about the conflict raging inside him, afraid of being judged.

Desire ached at the thought of not having Chad in her life. He was family, even more so now that she and Chase had been reunited. You didn't abandon family, no matter what.

Desire shot to her feet and opened the door. Chad was sitting on her swing porch, his head in his hands. She rushed to his side and when she saw the tears streaming down his face, she threw her arms about him.

"Yes, Chad. We can be friends. We'll always be friends."

He dropped his head on her shoulder and wept, clinging to her in the dark as night swirled about them.

***

"Good, huh?"

Chase nodded as he swallowed the last delicious mouthful of his dessert. "It's the best peach cobbler this side of the Mississippi." He smiled at his mother seated across the table from him. She'd obviously spent most of the day in the kitchen preparing one of his favorite meals: rosemary roasted chicken, red skin potato salad with dill, sautéed garlic spinach, and a grilled peach cobbler for dessert.

"It's good to see you haven't lost your appetite. Up for thirds?" She reached for the serving spoon in the baking dish that now held only half the pie.

He raised his hand in protest. "As scrumptious as everything was, Mom, my stomach would burst open if I sent another morsel its way," he said, sitting back in his chair. "Makes me realize how much I missed home, missed you. It was nice catching up on Evergreen gossip and all the changes happening around here. And about you and Chad and life without me," he added, realizing that his absence had caused hardship for his mother and his little brother—not financially, since he'd been sending money back home every month to help with expenses—but emotionally.

Maybe Chad would have been out of the closet by now if Chase had been home to guide and support him. As annoying as Chad had been as a kid, he'd always looked up to his big brother. Even though he was only six years older than Chad, Chase always felt like the father figure Chad needed. Azura had named Chase 'man of the house' when she'd placed an infant Chad in his arms. He'd thought he was honoring that title when he'd left home to protect his family.

"Why did you leave, Chase? You broke my heart, you know."

Chase glanced at his mother's hands clasping and unclasping on the tablemat. Here was the moment he'd been dreading. During dinner, he and his mother had talked about everything except his sudden disappearance, and now his just-as-sudden reappearance.

"Why were you hiding out down on Carver Farm all these years? And why Iowa?" Her voice raised an octave.

Chase pushed his bowl to the side and laid his arms across the table. "I was born there, Mom. I thought I had some roots there, but I found nothing. You moved there when you were pregnant with me, and then you left for New Hampshire when I was three. I chose Iowa because it was the only other home I knew, *and* I didn't want you to know what I was doing."

"What do you mean? What *were* you doing?"

"I was looking for answers, Mom. Arizona answers."

Her hands flew to her chest as she straightened up and stared at him. "What kind of answers were you looking for?"

"Answers about my father. My original birth certificate listed him as *Unknown.* When I asked about him, you told me you didn't know who he was. It's not easy for a child not to know the identity of his father. Then after Chadwick died, you replaced *Unknown* with a name. When I asked about the change, you said it was because he was dead. I was puzzled, but I was a child, and it wasn't my place to question you. He isn't dead. He's alive, Mom."

His mother's lips tightened and she dropped her hands on the table. Her voice shook. "I'm sorry for lying to you, and for the confusion I caused you, but if you wanted to know about him, why didn't you just ask me? He never knew you existed. My aunt sent me away before anyone knew I was pregnant. She didn't want his family making any claims on you, and that's why he was *Unknown.*

"But after Chadwick died, I thought you should at least have a name if anything should happen to me. I told you he was dead to protect you. But I guess you don't need protection from him anymore. You're a man now. Nonetheless, he's an evil psychopath. He has no conscience, no empathy," she added, swinging her head from side to side. "He would take great delight in cutting your throat in front of me and laughing while you bleed to death. He's been up for parole a few times over the years. It's only a matter of time before the courts grant his release."

Chase reached across the table and covered her trembling hands. "You don't need to be afraid of him anymore, Mom. He's in jail for the rest of his miserable life. I made sure of it."

"How?"

CHAPTER TWELVE

Chase got up and walked around the table. This was a conversation he'd rather have in a more comfortable setting. It was going to be long and painful. Taking his mother's hand, he led her into the living room and sat her down on the sofa and then switched on a floor lamp.

"I have a story to tell you, Mom," he said, after he took one of the chairs on the other side of the coffee table. But before I do, I want you to tell me about my father, about what happened in Phoenix thirty-four years ago."

"I thought you already knew."

"He gave me one version, but from what you just told me about him, it probably isn't the true one. I didn't go digging through records because I didn't want to draw unneeded attention to you or me, for that matter. The fewer people who know of my existence, and the less they know about us, the better off we are."

She leaned back and settled into the black leather cushions of the sofa as if she was already weary of the conversation. "I don't know where to begin."

"Like they say, the beginning is a good place to start."

She cleared her throat. "The beginning. Okay. Um—I was engaged to be married to a man named Troy Williams."

"The name on my birth certificate."

She nodded. "We met on a back road one night. I worked in a fast food restaurant in Scottsdale and was on my way home to Phoenix when I got a flat tire. I was sixteen and had just gotten my license." A smile flittered across her face. "Troy was on his way to work in Phoenix, and stopped to help me put on the spare. It was my aunt's car." Her brows flickered a little. "As you know, my parents, your grandparents, died in a house fire when I was two. My father's elderly aunt—my only living relative at the time—raised me." She waved a hand as if brushing the painful memory away. "Troy followed me to his friend's repair shop and asked him to patch up the tire. He was sweet and kind, and he had this charming smile that could make a girl's heart leap ten feet into the air." A blush crept into her cheeks and she pressed both hands against her heart as if it was jumping from talking about Troy after all these years. "You remind me of him, Chase."

Him, or his identical twin brother? Chase wanted to ask, but he kept quiet. He'd never seen his mother blush before and he didn't want to ruin her memories any more than they already were. If she'd once been this much in love, how could she have not noticed that Chad and Desire weren't in love with each other? She should have known what love looked like.

"I was flattered when Troy asked if he could see me again. Then I met his twin brother, Roy."

"My father," Chase spat, his voice mirroring the antipathy he'd detected in his mother's at the mention of his father's name.

Azura held his gaze. "Yes, Chase, your father. There was something about him that disturbed me from the moment I met him. Troy said I was being paranoid because they looked so much alike. I let it go to keep the peace."

Her shoulders heaved and she stared blankly across the room as if she still carried the thirty-four-year old burden. Chase wished he could spare her the pain of reliving the most painful time of her life, but he needed to hear the truth. All of it. "Mom," he prompted softly.

She shivered as if someone had poured a bucket of ice water over her. "I'm sorry, son," she said, giving him a wry smile.

"I can see that it's painful for you to talk about it, but I promise that after tonight, you will never have to speak of it again. I just need to know."

She nodded. "Troy had just graduated high school. We were in love and he wanted to marry me right away. Of course that wasn't possible since I was still a minor, but my aunt gave her consent to an engagement. She liked Troy, and she was thrilled that I wouldn't be alone after she passed on. Anyway, Troy and I decided to get married immediately after I graduated high school. We were poor, all of us. The word "college" wasn't part of our vocabularies. In my neighborhood, a girl's biggest dream was to find a nice boy, marry him, settle down, and raise kids with the hope that one of them would make it out, be successful."

"That's why you were so adamant about Chad and me attending college."

"Yes."

"I'm sorry to have disappointed you, Mom."

She gave him a wan smile before rising to stare out the sliders that overlooked the back of the house. "Troy and I had a date one night, but he called at the last minute to say that he couldn't make it. His boss had ordered him to cover the night shift for another employee who'd called out sick. He said that since I was already dressed up and my heart was set on going out, he'd asked Roy to take me. He said it would give us a chance to get to know each other better. He wanted us to get along since we would be family someday."

She leaned against the slider and recaptured Chase's gaze. Her voice now held an ominous quality when she continued. "I didn't want to go anywhere with Roy. I didn't trust him, but I knew I had to make the effort to get along with him for Troy's sake. He loved his brother, but I knew in my heart that he was evil." She swallowed. "I had no intention of being alone in a car with Roy, so I told him to meet me at the restaurant, thinking he couldn't possible harm me if we were in a public place. Dinner was surprisingly pleasant. He told me stories about him and Troy growing up together, the shenanigans they used to get into, the pranks they used to play on their parents and their teachers."

Now I know where I got my propensity for misbehavior, Chase thought.

"I dropped my guard." Azura shook her head from side to side, a cynical snicker escaping her as if she blamed herself. "I relaxed. I began thinking that I'd misjudged him, that my misgivings were all in my head. How could I have been so stupid?"

"You weren't stupid, Mom. You were young, in love, and trusting."

"I remember going to the ladies' room," she continued as if he hadn't even spoken, "and when I returned, Roy had ordered me another soda."

Chase shifted in the chair, pain and anger brewing in his gut as he anticipated the conclusion of his mother's horror story.

"Halfway through it, I started feeling dizzy. I told him that I wanted to go home. He followed me to my car, but my hands were shaking so hard, I couldn't even unlock my door. I was in no shape to drive, so he offered to take me home. By that time, I was so out of it, I would have followed Satan into hell if he'd invited me." Her next statement was a suffocated whisper. "The next morning, I woke up in Roy's bed."

"That sick bastard!" Chase's fists curled on his thighs. Everything that bastard had told him was a lie.

"Roy was already up, and I could hear him moving around in the kitchen while I lay crying and wondering how to explain what had happened to Troy. I wanted to go home but I didn't have my car, and Roy's parents had left on a weekend hunting trip the day before, so I couldn't get a ride from them. What was I going to tell them, anyway?" she asked derisively. "'Mr. and Mrs. Williams, I'm engaged to one of your sons and just spent the night with the other.' I felt so ashamed."

"It wasn't your fault, Mom. You have nothing to feel

ashamed of." Chase went to his mother's side. She was trembling and tears were running in rivulets from her eyes. He wrapped his arms about her, his own eyes stinging.

She sniffled into his chest, holding him for a few seconds as if drawing strength from his closeness before she withdrew. She glanced up at him, her eyes murky with dread and pain. "I heard Troy's truck pull into the driveway. I heard the kitchen door slam behind him, then I heard them arguing. I didn't know it until later, but Roy had taken pictures of us, and sent them to Troy."

"Oh, Mom."

"I sneaked quietly into the kitchen and stood by the door. I heard Roy tell Troy that I seduced him. He called me a whore and said that he'd broken me in real good for him. Troy had a temper that burned hotter than the Arizona desert sun when he was provoked, and while Roy stood there taunting him, he lost it. He slammed Roy against the counter and punched him bloody. Roy reached into the sink for a knife, and stabbed Troy repeatedly in the stomach until he fell to the floor. I screamed and rushed to his side while Roy stood over us laughing and telling me that it was my fault, that if I hadn't fallen in love, Troy would still be alive."

Chase made no attempt to wipe away the tears slipping from his eyes. His poor, poor mother...

"I sat there holding Troy. I told him Roy had raped me. I begged him not to die. But his eyes—his eyes," she stuttered and swallowed, "when they last looked at me were filled with so much reproach, so much disappointment." She wiped a hand across her nose. "I have no idea where I got the strength, but I charged at Roy, knocking him to the floor. I picked up the knife he'd used on Troy and I started stabbing him. When he stopped moving, I dropped the knife and ran. I just ran and ran and ran. I've been running ever since." She dropped her head on his chest and sobbed.

As he wrapped his arms about her, Chase knew for certain that his mother had never repeated the details of that morning to anyone in the last thirty-four years. "You don't have to run anymore, Mom. You are safe now," he said when she lifted her head. This time he detected a hint of relief in her eyes. She finally had someone with whom to share the darkest day of her life. She finally had the chance to unload the burden of guilt she'd been carrying around for way too long. Chase hated himself for the question he was about to ask, but he needed to know. "How do you know Troy wasn't my father?"

She rested her hand against his chest. "I was a virgin, Chase. Troy and I were waiting until our wedding night. When Roy raped me, violated me, and killed the man I loved, I had nothing else to lose. I wanted to kill him. I tried to kill him. I thought I'd killed him."

I will kill him. Chase never thought he could despise anyone more than he despised the man who'd set him up and sent him looking for the truth in the first place. He never thought that a son could have murderous intention toward the man who'd sired him. "How did you escape going to prison for stabbing him?"

"My aunt mortgaged her house to hire the best lawyer she could find. He worked tirelessly to keep the case from going to trial after I told him that I was pregnant. I couldn't bear the thought of you being taken away from me. That would have killed me for sure."

"He lied to me. But what else should I expect from a hardened criminal?"

She frowned in confusion. "You said you went to see Roy. What story did he give you?"

"He told me that you were engaged to his brother but that you'd been messing around with him on the side," Chase said, trying to be as delicate as possible. The picture Roy had painted of his mother wasn't a good one. The names he'd called her were horrible. "He said Troy found the two of you in bed and you attacked him with a knife, and that when he intervened, you stabbed him too."

"You believed him? Is that why you stayed away so long? You were embarrassed to have me as a mother. You resented me?"

"Oh, Mom, no. I never resented you. It was the other way around. I thought you might resent me every time you looked at me. I must remind you of that darkest period of your life. You must have wished I'd never been born."

"Oh, Chase, my darling baby boy." She clasped his face in her hands. "Yes, when I found out I was pregnant, I wanted to abort you. But as time passed and you began moving around inside me, I started falling in love with you. You were mine. Mine, and as crazy as it may sound, you are part of Troy, too. I see Troy when I look at you. God was kind to me in that aspect."

"I wish He'd been kinder. Prevented the rape and the murder."

"Then I wouldn't have had you."

"How can you say that?"

"I believe that everything happens for a reason, Chase. Good or bad. Despite the gruesome circumstance under which you were conceived, you were born for a purpose. You may not know what it is yet, but you keep looking. That's why I named you 'Chase'. I wanted you to chase after your dreams, chase after your purpose in life until you find it."

I already know my purpose in life. I've known it for two decades.

She furrowed her brows. "Why did you go looking for your fa—for *him*?" she asked.

Taking his mother's hand, Chase led her back to the sofa, and this time, he sat down next to her. "Someone here in Evergreen found out about Troy and Roy."

"What? How? My case was sealed. I was a minor. No one was supposed to have access to that information."

"Well, I'm sure you know what people will do when they're jealous of you."

"Who's jealous of you? Is this person, this information, the reason you left home?"

He nodded. "I left to protect your secret. This person would have aired your dirty laundry. He told me that you were a fugitive from the law, that you were wanted for murdering my father. I didn't know what to believe, but when he threw the names out at me, I knew there was some validity to his claim. Troy Williams is the father you named on my birth certificate. He *is* deceased, and since you've never told me the story, I didn't know what to believe."

"I should have told you a long time ago."

"Yes, you should have."

"But that's not the kind of conversation a mother has with her young son. You weren't old enough, mature enough to deal with that kind of truth, Chase. And I didn't want you blaming yourself for something you had no control over. I didn't want you thinking that you were the cause every time you thought I seemed sad, or was even upset with you. I didn't want you carrying around that kind of guilt. It would have been totally misplaced."

"Perhaps not." *But if you had told me, I wouldn't have wasted a decade of my life. I would have been a successful architect right here in my hometown, been married to Desire and have had a couple of babies by now—my three purposes in life. Chickens always come home to roost, Mom. They always do.*

"Did you love Chadwick?"

She dropped her gaze to her hands, twisting on her lap. "I did in my own way, but you never forget your one true love, especially if you never had a chance to express that love physically. It's like a wound that never heals, no matter how much salve you put on it. Have you ever loved anyone like that, Chase?"

"Yes. Desire." It felt so good to be able to tell someone.

Her head shot upward, and he detected the stark fear and concern in her eyes. "Your brother's fiancée? Chase, how could—"

"It's not like that, Mom," he said quickly, knowing exactly where her thoughts were headed. "I'm nothing like him. Desire and Chad aren't engaged anymore."

"They're not?"

"She's probably breaking up with him as we speak."

"Because of you?"

Because of Chad. But that was Chad's story to tell. "You

know Desire and I have always been close."

"Ever since you were kids. I knew she had a big crush on you."

"Were you worried because of Roy?"

"Never. You got in a lot of trouble, but I always knew you had a good heart, Chase. I knew you would never do anything to hurt Desire, or any girl for that matter."

Chase's love for his mother spiraled, both for her trust in him and the fact that she could love the child of the man who'd raped her. She was indeed a remarkable woman. "I would never hurt Desire. Not intentionally. In fact, I went out of my way to avoid her as much as possible, but when she turned eighteen, she told me how she felt and all those feelings I'd bottled up came gushing out. We pledged ourselves to each other."

"But then you messed up the night at the country club."

"Yes," he said, avoiding her gaze by staring out the sliders. His mother had never seen the video, but he was sure that hearing about it was just as appalling to her. "I apologize for the embarrassment that stunt caused you," he said, recapturing her gaze. "But you have to know that it wasn't my doing. I would not have done something so disgusting, especially after I'd pledged my heart and love to Desire."

"Like I said, I know you would never do anything to hurt Desire. So what happened that night? Does it have something to do with the story you said you would tell me? Is that why you left?"

Chase took his mother's hand. "Yes, Mom. It has everything to do with it."

***

The next morning, Chase gazed at the sandstone and glass structure on the opposite side of Airport Road in Granite Falls. It was a boring building or perhaps it was just plain ugly. However, its proximity to the airport made it the perfect location for a global architecture company to set up shop.

Once it was expanded to at least seven stories, instead of the current four, one would be able to enjoy panoramic river, lake, and mountain views. He wouldn't even mind a view of Fonandt Wind Farm's turbines at the base of the mountain range to remind him that it always paid to have friends in high places.

He couldn't wait for the demolition to begin. It was going to be a very busy and interesting summer, Chase thought, swinging one leg over his motorcycle seat. He opened the storage compartment, pulled out a large white envelope, tucked it under his arm, and crossed the street.

Thoughts of his upcoming night with Desire set off a throbbing deep in his groin as he climbed the steps to the building. He hadn't spoken to her since yesterday afternoon, but when Chad had come home last night carrying the ring he'd given Desire, Chase knew she'd officially broken it off with his little brother.

The fact that Chad had said nothing about Chase and Desire's afternoon together meant that Desire hadn't told him about them. She could have used their love as retaliation for Chad's indiscretions, but she hadn't. Desire was kindhearted and sensitive to others' sorrows, even her enemies. She would suffer in silence before she took revenge on those who'd hurt her. It was one of the many reasons Chase loved her so much. The world would be a much more pleasant and tolerable place if there were more people like her. If he'd given her the explanations she needed yesterday, she would have talked him out of his revenge. And having his revenge was vitally important to Chase. He would never be able to live with himself if he allowed that bastard's crimes to go unpunished.

"Hell *has* to be paid," he vocalized the phrase that had driven him along all those years. It was finally judgment day.

The lobby was empty, except for a young brunette behind a circular receptionist desk, a yellow highlighter in one hand and a frown of concentration on her forehead as she stared into an open book on her desk. Chase felt a hint of guilt that the poor girl had been ordered to come in on her day off, just to greet him. She was a single mother of a two-year-old. She worked days and attended Evergreen's Community College at nights as she worked on gaining her Associate's Degree in Business Administration, he'd learned during his covert investigation of each and every employee of this company.

It was dedicated and hardworking employees like her that had caused Chase to change his revenge strategy. Too many innocents already paid for the guilty. He would not add to the injustice pool. Chase mentally promised to make it up to her once she both pledged and proved her allegiance to him.

As he drew closer to her desk, she glanced up, immediately closed her book, and gawked at him as all women did when they encountered him for the first time. Chase knew the effect he had on women. Heck, they used to have the same effect on him, especially the pretty ones, like this one. *Used to*, he thought as the most recent heated memories of kissing Desire sent a tingling into the pit of his belly.

He sucked in his breath as he stopped at the receptionist's desk. "Good Morning."

"Good Morning, Mr. Bennett, I assume." She gave him a warm and friendly, yet nervous smile.

"Except you're expecting someone else."

"No. You're the only person we're expecting, sir. We're closed on weekends, but I came in to…" Her voice trailed off as she glanced at his left hand resting near a notebook on her desk. When she noticed his bare ring finger, her blue eyes sparkled with interest.

"Has your boss arrived yet?" Chase asked, breaking the awkward silence.

"Yes, Mr. Bennett. He's waiting for you in the conference room on the fourth floor. It's the third door on your right."

"Thank you, Rosalind," Chase made a point to say her name with emphasis. She appeared to almost swoon in response. "You can leave now." He didn't want any witnesses hanging around once the meeting was over.

"But, Mr.—"

"Thank you for coming in just to meet and greet me. It's

your day off. Go enjoy it." He tapped the cover of her *Fundamentals of Business Process Management* text. "Seems you have homework to finish. I'll explain your absence to your boss."

A smile settled on her face. "Thank you, Mr. Bennett. I actually have a test on Monday night and I do need to study for it." She picked up a backpack from the floor and shoved her text, notebook, pen, and highlighter into it. "Thank you so much. It was nice meeting you, Mr. Bennett."

When she exited the building, Chase headed for the elevators. In less than a minute, he stepped off onto the fourth floor and strode toward the conference room. He'd requested that the meeting take place today, Saturday, a day when the company was closed for business, as Rosalind had pointed out.

He could have held the meeting anywhere in Granite Falls, but he'd chosen this building and this day for three specific reasons. First, to minimize the chances of someone overhearing the conversation and reporting it to the local news media. Bryce had already warned Chase that his life would not be the same after today. It was easy to be the CEO of a billion-dollar company when no one knew who you were, but the minute the word got out, he would be in the spotlight for who knew how long. Secondly, he knew how the bastard's mind worked and he wanted the entire conversation recorded. Thirdly, Chase needed to spend one peaceful night with Desire before the press began hounding them.

He wondered how Desire would take the news once he told her tonight. He hoped she'd handle it well and not hold it against him for keeping her in the dark.

Chase astutely pushed all thoughts of Desire to the back of his mind as he came to a stop at the door of the conference room.

For a moment, he vacillated between knocking and simply walking in, catching the man behind the door by surprise. Deciding that the former would give him the greatest satisfaction, he knocked.

Within a few seconds, the door opened, and Chase was staring down at Lewis Carron, the son of a bitch who'd chased him out of town.

Yep, this was totally better. *Awesome.* Chase reveled in Lewis' expression of absolute shock—gaping mouth, wide bulging blue eyes, and ash-white face as if his brain had been short-circuited. Chase grinned as he surveyed Lewis' five-foot, ten-inch stature dressed in an expensive gray suit, white shirt, striped tie, and shiny black leather Italian loafers. He was only a few years older than Chase, yet his wheat-gold hair was already besieged with strands of gray—probably from the stress of keeping his victims in check.

"You!" he finally said with open scorn.

"Nice to see you too, Lewis. But is that all you can say to me after twelve long years?"

His contemptuous smirk deepened as he took in Chase's attire—worn, torn, and slightly soiled jeans, a Carver Farm T-shirt, and sandals. He chuckled. "Still a field hand huh, Hunter? Couldn't make it down on the farm? Here to beg for your old job back?"

"Actually, I was—"

"The answer is no." He squared his shoulders and fluffed his chest in an attempt to assert some form of authority, Chase surmised. "I don't have time for you, boy." He glanced down the hall in the direction of the elevator. "I have an important meeting in a few minutes. I will deal with you later. So scram, boy." He made a shooing motion with his hand and attempted to close the door.

"Can't do that," Chase said, bracing his foot against the bottom part of the door. "The thing is, Carron, I *am* your meeting."

Carron staggered backwards, his bony fingers at his mouth. "You—You're Mr. Bennett?"

Chase flashed his teeth, surprised that he could remain this calm. He'd always thought he'd be jumping with rage when he came face-to-face with Lewis Carron again, that the first thing he'd do was punch the dirtbag in the nose. But looking at him now, Chase realized that it wouldn't be a fair fight. There was no victory in an unmatched brawl. Besides, striking Lewis would indicate that they were at war. They weren't. V-Day had arrived the moment Chase had made the decision to return home. The sweet taste of revenge he'd been feasting on for more than a decade was gone. "Yep, that's me," he finally said, entering the small room to tower over Lewis. "Bennett, as you know—since you went digging into her past—is my mother's maiden name."

Lewis' shoulders drooped significantly as the reality concerning the fate of his company finally came full circle. "That means you—you're the CEO of DC Architectural Designs." Another backward step brought him up against the conference table. He plopped down on its edge. "You're the company that offered to bail out Carron to keep it from going into bankruptcy?"

"Very good, Lewis. I *am* DC Architectural Designs."

"But why?" Lewis shrugged defiantly. "Why bail me out? Why not just let me sink into financial ruin?"

Chase released a cynical laugh. "Because that won't be enough. It couldn't make up for the years of my life you stole from me. It couldn't make up for the pain, embarrassment, and financial hardship you caused my family. Also, although some of your executives and employees *will* go down with you, there are a few who are really good and hardworking. I don't want to put them out of work and ruin their lives. Last, I wanted to see the look on your face when I finally stuck it to you."

The color returned to Lewis' face and a callous laugh erupted from his belly. "You think I'm just going to roll over and let you usurp me, boy? I'd rather see Carron Designs in the ground than hand it over to the likes of you. I haven't signed on the dotted lines yet. You should have waited until the ink was dried, just like you should have waited until after the talent show to tell me about your designs. I began putting my plan in place the moment I saw them. I wasn't going to let some washed-up college dropout walk away with that fifty-thousand-dollar grand prize, and the chance to start his own company. I had to take you down, boy. And I had to make sure you didn't rise again, not around here, at least." He looked Chase up and down. "You were a hound, so it was easy to get that bitch and her daughter to screw you and to videotape it. And boy did they screw you. You haven't learned a damn thing, boy."

Chase's fists curled at his sides, but he killed the urge to strike the bastard. Lewis Carron wasn't worth the effort. "You see, that's where you're wrong, Lewis. You underestimate me, which is understandable since you don't know me. I've learned many things since I've been gone. I learned not to trust anyone who hasn't proven he can be trusted. I learned to be wary of people who flash their teeth at me. I learned that in this world of business, it doesn't matter how big and bad you think you are, there is always someone bigger and badder who's gunning to kick you in the ass. And, I've learned never to let your enemy know when you're coming. I've been in town for two days and you didn't even know."

Chase slapped the envelope down on the table, grateful that this scum didn't have a family. If he'd had a wife and children, Chase would have been forced to consider them. This made it so much easier. "I brought these for you. I suggest you read them over carefully before signing. You can leave them right here, in this room, on this desk. I will pick them up on Tuesday night when I officially take full control of Carron & Son Architectural Designs."

"Are you deaf as well as stupid, Hunter?" Hatred blazed in Carron's eyes. "I told you I'm not signing my company over to you. In fact, I'll give you a couple days to spend some time with your family since you haven't seen them for so long. But come Wednesday morning, I want you gone. You set foot in Evergreen again, and the world will know your mother is an attempted murderer."

His eyes hardened as he snickered. "You have a lot more to lose now. Let's see how long your company survives after everyone knows about your mother. Maybe then *I'll* do you the courtesy of bailing out your DC Designs. I've brought bigger giants than you to their knees. And all I had to do was make a few calls, prey on their weaknesses, and use vital secret information against them. When that doesn't work, I threaten their families."

"You know all dances do come to an end, right? The music eventually stops. And once it does, and whether or not you enjoyed the dance, you do have to pay the piper. Those are the rules of the game. Hell must be paid."

He snorted. "Your song and dance is over, Hunter. I've been in the game of extortion long before you. I *made* the rules."

Funny he should use the word "extortion" so freely and blatantly, Chase thought. "Are you done?" he asked, quirking an eyebrow, as if he were dealing with a temperamental child.

"Oh I'm done. And so is your DC Designs. What the hell kind of name is that? What does DC mean? 'Dumb Chase?' That's it, isn't it?" He cackled at his own joke.

Anxious to excrete this venom from his life forever, Chase tapped the envelope with his finger. "Before you go making promises you can't keep this time, I suggest you check the contents of this envelope. You'll be surprised at my offer. I bet my firstborn child that you won't be able to refuse it. You'd be a fool to. It's that good. And one more thing, you will not breathe a word of my return or the fact that I'm the true owner of DC Designs to anyone, or else you will be arrested and probably spend the rest of your life behind bars. See you around, Lewis. Then again, maybe not," he added on a nonchalant shrug of his shoulders as he turned and walked out the door.

God, that was good. Liberating. The smirk on Chase's face turned into a full-blown grin that eventually erupted into laughter as he reached the elevator. Just before the doors closed, he had a glimpse of a red-faced Lewis running down the hall like a madman, shaking a handful of papers at him.

Back on the main floor, Chase left the building. He stood on the steps and breathed in the cool morning air. Finally, he was at liberty to give his full attention to Desire, to concentrate on his date with her tonight, and plan the rest of their lives together.

CHAPTER THIRTEEN

Desire pulled into the driveway at the side of her parents' home, turned off her engine, exited her car, and walked across the lawn toward the back of the house.

It was early on Saturday morning, but her parents, Gerald and Ruth Summers, had always been early risers, as was she this morning. She was still astonished that she'd been able to sleep last night after the day she'd had juggling her time and emotions between the two Hunter brothers. Nevertheless, she'd slept more peacefully than she had for a long time.

She knew without a doubt that her serenity was due to the fact that Chase was back in her life and still as much in love with her as she was with him. The only anxiety Desire felt now was that of seeing Chase tonight, being with him in the most intimate way a man and woman could be together. Finally, they would be able to express their love for each other—openly and freely.

The anticipation sent waves of excitement through her as she opened the door. The kitchen was empty, but the smell of eggs, pancakes, and maple syrup, and the used plates on the table told her that her parents had already eaten breakfast and were probably in the living room watching CNN over coffee. It was a ritual they'd developed after her mother had retired from her job as principal of Evergreen Elementary School.

During good or at least tolerable weather, they would end their morning ritual by walking the trails behind their development. In inclement weather, they would drive to the mall and take their walk inside.

As Desire strolled through the kitchen and dining room, she prayed that she and Chase would still love each other and want to spend time together when they were her parents' age. Theirs was a love that grew stronger and stronger with time, just as hers and Chase's would, she thought, happiness springing from deep within her as she entered the living room.

"Now that's the smile of a woman in love," her father said from the recliner—his favorite spot on the sectional. He flashed his pearly whites at her, his brown eyes twinkling with merriment, as he immediately opened his arms wide.

Desire placed her keys on the mantel over the fireplace and, walking across the room, she sat beside her father and wrapped her arms about him. Once a medium-built man of average height, her father had lost a few pounds over the past few months. He would diminish even more once his chemo began. She swallowed the lump in her throat as the faint scent of musk from his cologne tickled her nose. "Hi, Daddy." She splayed her hands over his short, curly salt-and-pepper hair, knowing that in a few months, maybe weeks, it would all be gone. *Again.*

"Hi, baby." He squeezed her a little bit longer and harder than usual, making her heart pound with love and guilt. "What are you doing here so early?" he asked, releasing her.

"I was just about to ask the same question," her mother said. She muted the TV before giving Desire a quick hug and a kiss on the cheek. "If you'd called, we would have held breakfast for you. It's been a while since we had breakfast together. Do you want me to make you something?"

"No." Desire placed a restraining hand on her mother's arms as she attempted to get up. "I'm fine." She smiled at her mother, a slender woman with brown eyes, high cheekbones and a mouth that always seemed to be on the verge of smiling.

Desire had always been told that she had her mother's mouth and her father's eyes.

"So what brings you by so early? Not that we don't love having you drop by anytime," her mother said.

"I need to talk to both of you." She looked from one to the other.

Her father's grin widened over his coffee mug. "About the wedding?"

"Actually, yes. But—" A faint thread of hysteria fluttered in Desire's belly. Anxious to get her life going in the right direction for once, she'd stopped by on her way to the spa to inform her parents that her engagement to Chad was off. But looking at her father now, she realized that it was going to be even more difficult than she'd thought. No matter how gentle she tried to be, she would break his heart.

"Did you and Chad set a date? You're not planning on a long engagement, I hope. You know I may not have a lot of time."

"No, Daddy, we haven't set a date."

"Well, let us know as soon as you do, Desire," her mother piped in. "And like your father said, don't wait too long. I'll have to plan a dinner party for the Hunters and us, but I would like to do it before your father begins his treatments. You know how sick he was the first time."

Desire nodded, too choked to speak. She stared blindly at the CNN news reporter on the TV. The reporter's mouth was going a mile a second, but her message was falling on deaf, impassive ears. She didn't need any reminders of her father's impending doom, and although her parents were only being pragmatic, the truth of that reality pricked her to the core.

She glanced at her father, his smile cutting into her like shards of glass. She loved him, and although she knew he was trying to protect her, she was nevertheless angry with him for destroying Chase's letter.

"So if it's not about the date, what did you want to talk to us about?" Her mother pulled her feet up under her like a little girl, and turned sideways to look at Desire. "You want me to help you pick out a wedding dress, a cake, shop for your honeymoon wardrobe?" she asked excitedly.

"I would love for you to help me with all that Mom, but the truth of the matter is, I'm not—"

"Aunt Ruth? Uncle Gerry?"

Desire closed her eyes at the sound of Lisa's voice coming from the kitchen. *What was she doing here?* All of a sudden, her parents' house had become Grand Central Station.

"In here, Lisa," Ruth responded to her niece.

Lisa walked in, but as soon as she spotted Desire, surprise siphoned the cheery smile from her face. "Hey, cuz. I didn't know you were here."

"I guess my car didn't give me away, huh?" Desire forced herself to breathe normally. She hadn't talked to Lisa since yesterday morning when Lisa had told her about her night with Chase. There was no need for Desire to be upset with Lisa. When Lisa had slept with Chase, she didn't have all the facts about Chase and Desire's relationship, just as Desire didn't have all the facts about Chase when she'd agreed to marry Chad. She was certain that if her cousin knew that she still loved Chase, she would not have slept with him. They'd always been close and would never intentionally hurt each other. "What are you doing here?" she asked Lisa.

"You haven't told her yet, Aunt Ruth?" Lisa asked as she sat on a chair on the other side of the recliner.

"Tell me what?" Desire frowned at the awkward look that her parents and Lisa exchanged.

Her father cleared his throat. "Your mother asked Lisa to move in with us."

"Why?"

"To help me with your dad. You remember how difficult it was the first time. Well, I'm not as young anymore and I will need someone here, especially at night."

"I can do that. I can help." She looked at her parents. "I helped out the last time."

"Yes, Desire," Lisa said, "but you're getting married. You have a wedding to plan. You and Chad. Who would have guessed? I like him. I think you make a cute couple. Maybe me and—"

"Lisa." From the look on her face and the tone of her voice, Desire could just imagine what was going on in Lisa's mind. *Two cousins marrying two brothers.*

Lisa pursed her lips, indicating she'd gotten the message. "The thing is, you should be concentrating on your wedding. Aunt Ruth and Uncle Gerry were there for me when my mom died and my dad remarried and moved out west. It's my turn to give back. I don't mind. We're family, and family look out for each other, especially in the time of need."

"I don't want anything to distract you from your wedding plans," her father said. "I want to walk you down the aisle while I still have strength in my body, and look halfway decent doing it. Can you give me that, baby?" he asked, taking her hand and squeezing it in his.

Tears stung Desire's eyes. "Yes, Daddy, I can, and I will give you that. I'll set a date soon, but the thing is—" Desire glanced over at Lisa. She wanted so much to tell her father that he would be walking her down the aisle sooner than he thought, and hopefully hold his first grandchild in his arms before he died, but throwing her rekindled happiness in her cousin's face in front of her parents would be cruel. She had no wish to hurt Lisa, even though Lisa had been quick and all too anxious to share the details of her one night of sex with Chase, and had also almost just broadcast it to her parents. The last thing she wanted was for her father to find out that Chase had slept with Lisa. It would just give him one more reason to hate Chase.

Desire took a deep, calming breath and blanketed the images that rose to her mind. It was in the past, even though recent. She and Chase were starting over. That meant forgiving and forgetting all the hurt and pain they'd caused each other before yesterday. All she wanted now was for her family and the Hunters to band together as one.

"What were you going to say, Desire?" her mother asked.

"I'm hosting a dinner party tomorrow night."

"For whom?" her father asked.

"For our family, you included, Lisa, and the Hunters, Chad and Azura."

"What about—"

"I will be making the announcement of my wedding date," she said, cutting Lisa off for the second time. Didn't her cousin get it?

Lisa sat back, clamped her mouth shut, and twisted a strand of her bleached blond hair around her finger.

"That's a wonderful idea, Desire," her mother said, smiling happily. "We should all be told at the same time, so we can all be on the same page from beginning to end."

"So you're really getting married?" her father asked with tears in his eyes.

Desire hugged him. "Yes, Daddy." Tomorrow night, she would kill all her birds with one stone. She hoped that after the surprise had worn off, the two families would be able to settle down, forgive, heal, and band together as one family, wanting the same thing—for their children to be happy.

Although, she thought, it wouldn't be a surprise for her father since he already knew—had known for years—how Chase felt about her. But Desire chose not to dwell on her father's shortcomings. It was in the past.

"By the way, am I your maid of honor?" Lisa asked.

"Of course. You're my best friend."

"Sweet. Girl, we will have so much fun planning this wedding. I can't wait."

I hope you'll still feel the same way when you hear that I'm marrying Chase.

* * *

The sun was high in the sky when Chase walked out of Joanne's Boutique. Yet he decided not to don his sunglasses. There was no reason for him to hide anymore. He was back, *for real*, and he wanted the whole world to know.

As he crossed the street, he pulled his phone from his

pocket. He needed to hear Desire's voice, to tell her that he loved her, and that he was looking forward to seeing her tonight. But before he could dial, his phone rang.

He stopped short as he recognized the number. His first reaction was to ignore it, but past experiences had taught him that it was better to deal with a molehill before it grew into a mountain.

He raised the phone to his ear. "Hi, Lisa."

"Hey, Chase," she said in a distinctly provocative voice. "How have you been? I hope you're settling in nicely."

"I am. Thank you."

"No! Thank *you*. That was some homecoming, huh?" She giggled.

Chase swallowed. He'd opened the door when he'd slept with her. He had to close it before she advanced any farther. "Lisa, I—"

"If you're up to it, there's more where all of that came from. I'm working today, but if you're free tonight, we can—"

"I'm not free, Lisa," Chase said, as he reached his bike. He cradled his phone on his shoulder and unlocked the chain to his helmet.

"Okay, then maybe tomorrow? I'm off. We can spend the whole day having at each other."

"I'm sorry, Lisa, but what happened between us shouldn't have happened. I apologize for—" He stopped, not wishing to make her feel used, which she was. "I shouldn't have called you."

"Chase, come on, I'm a big girl. If you're worried that I'm going to stake some kind of claim on you, I won't. We're just having fun. Right?" She paused. "I mean, if you want more out of the relationship, I'm open." She giggled again at the double entendre. "You know what I mean."

A stab of guilt ripped through his chest. "It was fun." He could give her that much satisfaction. "I like you, Lisa, and I don't want to hurt you."

"Oh my God, you saw Desire. She told you that I told her about us. Are you mad?"

There's no us. "I'm not mad at you. I'm mad at myself for allowing it to happen. And no, Desire didn't tell me anything. When I saw the two of you on her porch yesterday morning, I figured out what you were talking about from the looks on your faces." *You told her, even though I asked you not to.*

"I'm sorry, Chase. I knew she was crushing on you when she was a kid, but when you told me she was engaged to Chad, I figured she'd gotten over her childhood infatuation."

"Quite understandable. The thing is…" He paused, remembering that Lisa had difficulty keeping her mouth shut. She'd probably only kept his return a secret because she wanted to stay on his good side to get a few more slices of him. He should definitely not tell her that he and Desire were in love. The public should hear it from him and Desire when they were ready to announce it, not from her cousin.

"The thing is what, Chase?"

He cleared his throat. "The thing is, what happened between us will never happen again. I'm not *that* Chase from the past. Casual sex isn't gratifying for me anymore. The next time I make love to a woman, it has to mean something. It would be because I'm in love with her. I know that's not what you want to hear, Lisa, but—"

"No problem, Chase. I understand. But if you ask me, you haven't changed. You're still a hound. I consider myself used," she said, and immediately hung up.

A queasy feeling settled in Chase's belly as he mounted his bike. *This* mountain was never a molehill. It had appeared, fully-grown, the moment he'd picked up the phone and called Lisa two nights ago.

Damn! Damn! Damn!

***

Desire beamed with excitement, anticipation, and curiosity as the white limo transported her to the still undisclosed location of her rendezvous with Chase.

"I might as well be blindfolded," she muttered, staring at

the black shutters locked into place across the heavily tinted windows. The privacy partition was up, sealing her off from her driver and the rest of the world. She was alone, cocooned in a chamber of leather, glass, chrome and polished wood trim, with water, and Miguel singing "Coffee in the Morning."

Yep, it will be *coffee* in the morning, she thought, smiling wantonly at the edited version of the song. She glanced down at her attire, still awed at the splendor and intricate details of her Monique Lhullier Off-the-Shoulder Ruched Mikado Gown, Dark Red—as the tag had stated. In layman's terms, the nylon, spandex, and silk gown had an off-the-shoulder sweetheart neckline, a V-back, cap sleeves, a pleated full skirt with tulle details at the sides, and a rounded hem that swept the floor when she walked. Silver stilettoes, decorated with rhinestones and a silver satin clutch completed her wardrobe.

Desire had never felt so beautiful, so attractive, so feminine, so sophisticated before. It was even more special because the man she loved had obviously gone to great lengths to plan this night. He'd picked out the perfect dress and shoes, the perfect size, just to prove how much he loved, cherished, and adored her. This was the kind of date Bryce and his friends, and other wealthy, and not-so-wealthy husbands who worshipped their wives planned for them. She'd seen them around town, and although she'd been bitten with the little jealous bug, Desire had always been happy to see that true love did exist. Now, it was her turn to experience that kind of devotion. Chase was giving her the royal experience.

Desire's heart fluttered wildly. Tonight, she was Cinderella, Belle, Aurora, and all the other princesses in the fairy tales her mother used to read to her when she was a little girl. Then when she was too old for fairy tales, Chase had read her a different kind of story.

Her eyes grew misty at the memory of sitting next to him on their porch swing sipping hot cocoa in the fall and spring, and lemonade in the summer while he read to her about great African and Egyptians queens, like Nefertiti of Egypt, Candace of Ethiopia, and Makeda of Sheba with whom King Solomon had fallen in love. She'd loved the Queen of Sheba most, because even at a young age, she was already fantasizing about Chase falling in love with, and marrying her. Chase was King Solomon and she was Makeda. And here she was, on her way to the ball, where her king, the man of her dreams, awaited her.

Desire bit her lips as she tried to guess their dinner venue. She could count on one hand the number of restaurants in Granite Falls that would warrant such elegance and sophistication: Hotel Andreas, Ristorante Andreas, The Odyssey, The Iliad, and Whisperwind—Hotel Andreas being the most sophisticated and Whisperwind the least. She could rule out The Odyssey. Chase would never take her there tonight of all nights when he knew it was where Chad had proposed to her.

Curiosity gnawed at Desire as her fingers toyed with the heart-shaped diamond pendant at the base of her neck and the matching studs in her ears. Her dress, her shoes, her accessories, and her jewelry had all arrived by special delivery this afternoon. The card inside had simply read, *Forever Yours.*

She didn't have to guess who had sent them. The question that had been hammering at her since the delivery was where had Chase gotten this kind of money to lavish on her? She'd seen this gown in Joanne's Boutique, and knew that it cost more than a field hand on an Iowa farm made in six months. She knew enough about jewelry to know that the set she wore cost more than most people made in five years—herself included.

So what was up with Chase? Who was he, really?

Desire took a sip of water and leaned back into the leather sofa, her forehead furrowing as she reflected on their time in their hideaway yesterday. Chase's hands were manicured, the tips rounded, his palms smooth and strong as he'd caressed her. They weren't the hands of a farm worker. His skin was tanned, a little darker than it was before he left, but he wasn't sunburnt. He was olive toned like Massimo Andretti and Adam Andreas—billionaires who spent time in the sun because they desired to, not because they had to.

As she thought about it now, Desire realized that she'd had her first clue the morning Chase had shown up at her business, smelling delightfully irresistible. *Straight to Heaven* wasn't the kind of cologne a farm worker could afford. And then the silk shirt and dress pants and expensive Italian leather shoes he'd been wearing yesterday...

Desire shuddered on a breath as she came to terms with the only explanation. *Chase was rich.* Filthy rich. When he'd told her that he'd changed, that he wasn't the same man who'd left Evergreen, he'd been hinting at much more than his character. Why was he hiding behind his jeans and Carver Farm T-shirt? Why was he riding around on his old bike instead of in a car? How could she not have put two and two together before now?

Because you were preoccupied with Chad's cheating and your father's illness.

Right on cue, she thought as her intercom buzzed. She pressed the button on the side of the door. "Yes."

"We have arrived at our destination, Ms. Summer. I trust your ride was pleasant," her chauffeur said.

Desire cleared her throat as her heart began to pound. She couldn't believe how giddy she felt, like this was her first date, ever. "Yes, it was pleasant, although it probably would have been even more so if I were allowed to enjoy the scenery."

"I'm sorry. I'm just following orders."

"It's okay. I understand."

"Have a wonderful evening, ma'am."

"Thank you." She pulled out the compact mirror from a compartment in the door and glanced at her reflection. Her makeup was still fresh—her lip gloss and her updo hairstyle still in place. She touched the few tendrils of black curls brushing her cheeks and shoulders before picking up her clutch.

A few seconds later, the limo door opened, and her heart went into lockdown at the sight of Chase standing in the courtyard of—yep, as she'd guessed—Hotel Andreas.

He looked dashing, elegant, in a black tux, white shirt, and a black bow tie. His luscious dark hair fell like a silk curtain from his crown to frame the outline of his chiseled, shaven face and brush against his wide shoulders. Behind him, the wall of water fountains with light bulbs floating through the streams added a hint of mystique to his lure. Chase Hunter was irresistible in jeans and T-shirt, but dressed like this, he possessed the unequivocal power to send a woman into cardiac arrest.

Desire's heart lurched madly in her chest.

He seemed to understand exactly what was going on inside her and smiled wickedly as his gaze traveled slowly and appreciatively down her body, then back up to her face. As their gazes tangled, a powerful flood of lust settled between Desire's thighs.

He hadn't touched her physically, yet, but the heat from his gaze generated wanton images of their naked bodies fused together in intimate combat. Never in her entire life had Desire ever wanted anything more than she wanted to make love with Chase. *Now.* Forget about *coffee* in the morning. She wanted *coffee* now. How was she going to get through dinner?

"Queen Desire. Welcome," he said, holding his hand out to her.

"King Chase." Tingles spread to all parts of her body as she placed her hand in his and stepped out of the limo on unsteady legs.

"You look absolutely ravishing." He brought her hand to his lips, his warm gray eyes twinkling in the numerous lights from the waterfall.

"As do you." Her heart raced at the warm touch of his lips against her skin. She was sure that like her, he wanted nothing more than to bypass dinner and go straight to bed, but last night he'd stated that he wanted to tell his side of the story that had ripped them apart before they made love. She had to agree with his decision. It was best that she learned everything about the man to whom she was about to give her heart, mind, soul, and body forever this time.

She'd always been in love with the old Chase Hunter—the first-born son of Azura Hunter, the boy next door, the juvenile troublemaker, the devil-may-care college dropout. The Chase Hunter standing before her was someone she didn't know, someone to whom she hadn't been introduced. Rushing into bed with a stranger was never a wise thing to do.

She had to give herself the chance to meet him, get to known him, see if she liked him, and when all was said and done, hopefully fall deeply in love with him, even more deeply than she loved the old Chase.

She swooned a little as the evening breeze sent a whiff of his *Straight to Heaven* up her nostrils.

His hold on her hand tightened. "You okay, baby?" the old Chase asked.

She nodded on a smile. "I'm fine, I'm still trying to take in all this," she said, waving her hand about and glancing around at the throng of people filing in and out of vehicles, some in casual and some in elegant attire, and entering and exiting the hotel. She'd almost forgotten how crazy Granite Falls could be in the summer. It was *the* place to be in the Northeast.

"Someone has exceptional taste in women's clothes, and shoes, and jewelry," Desire said, as the limo drove away. "And he got the sizes right, too," she added, smiling indulgently up at Chase, and brushing her knuckles along his smooth cheeks.

"Someone has been paying attention," he drawled in a deep sexy voice, capturing her hand and kissing the palm.

She swallowed the moan that rose in her throat. There would be plenty of time to yield to his seduction later. She cleared her throat and narrowed her eyes at him. "And who is this someone? Chase, this is the most expensive venue in all of New England, not to mention that you need to make reservations with a nonrefundable down payment months in advance. The only way to get a table at short notice is to have an inside connection." She placed her hand against his chest and trembled at the powerful beat of his heart under her palm. "Who *are you*, this new Chase in a tux?" The Chase I knew, the one I loved hated, "monkey suits," as he used to call them. He was right at home in jeans and T-shirts."

His grin was disarming, but still unrevealing. "Let's go find out. I only hope that you'll love "monkey suit" Chase as much as you love T-shirt and jeans Chase." He emitted a low groan as he placed his hand on the small of her back and led her toward the hotel's entrance. "You smell delicious too, by the way. I can't wait to enjoy you, eat you, lick you until there is nothing left of you, but me."

If he weren't holding her against his side, Desire would have fallen flat on her face as they entered the very glamorous lobby decorated with water fountains, glitzy chandeliers, polished marble floors, white orchids hugging marble Corinthian columns, and enormous potted plants strewn throughout.

"Every time I enter this hotel, I feel like I'm walking into heaven," Desire said as she looked around at the clusters of guest reclining on elegant sofas and chairs, and sipping wine as they enjoyed the sweet melodies coming from the live piano player.

"It is something, isn't it? You get your money's worth for sure."

A young concierge approached them. "Good evening, sir. Madam," he said with a slight bow. "Your room will be ready shortly."

"Room?" Desire asked, gazing quizzically up at Chase.

"Private dining room."

"We've reserved a waiting area for you." The concierge led the way toward a cozy arrangement of four chairs near an enclosed water fountain. "A waiter will be over with complimentary drinks and antipasto." He bowed again and left.

From the corner of her eye, Desire saw a little boy running toward them, shouting, "Mr. B. Mr. B."

Desire immediately recognized the kid as Eli Fontaine, Bryce's four-year-old son. Surely, he was mistaken, she thought as he stopped in front of Chase, grinning up at him. All too quickly, she realized that Eli wasn't mistaken, when Chase released her and crouched down to the boy's level.

"Hi, Eli. How are you, little buddy?"

Little buddy? Desire frowned as Chase hugged the child as if they were old acquaintances.

"Are you here to do business with my daddy again? Are you still his colleague?"

"Not tonight, Eli," he said, rising to his full stature. "Tonight, I'm here to have fun." He winked at Desire as if they were part of some secret association.

Uh-uh, they weren't, not in this capacity. Desire wasn't surprised at Eli's use of the word "colleague." He was an exceptionally intelligent child—a prodigy—only four years old, but already fluent in three languages, and could carry on a conversation as well as any teenager she knew. Everyone perceived Eli as a young Bryce in training, who would probably be ready to run Fontaine Enterprises with his father in a few years. The fact that he had the features and giant-like physique of his father made the speculations even more convincing.

It was the *again* that had taken her aback. She stared down at Chase. *Who the heck was he?* And since when was he a colleague of the business mogul, Bryce Fontaine?

She waved away the waiter coming their way. This little forum right here required her undivided attention.

CHAPTER FOURTEEN

"Eli!" a male voice called.

Desire turned to her left as the rest of the Fontaines emerged from a cluster of couches under a window overlooking Crystal Lake—Bryce at the front, followed by his lovely petite and very pregnant wife, her fourteen-year old nephew, Jason, her nieces, eight-year-old Alyssa and five-year-old Anastasia, and Elyse, Eli's twin sister.

A young couple approached Bryce and Kaya, stopping their progress, and while the adults conversed, the three younger children ran ahead of their parents. Jason continued his leisure stroll, looking around the restaurant as if he were expecting someone. Haley, their nanny, trailed behind them, but kept a watchful eye on the youngest children.

Desire returned her attention to Chase as the girls sped past her to him. They paid her no mind at all. It was as if she wasn't even there. She was old news. Mr. B was new. New to her too, she conceded as the mystery of Chase Hunter skyrocketed to a whole new level in Desire's world.

"What's your name?" Alyssa asked, smiling sweetly up at Chase through a pair of brown eyes.

"He's Mr. B," Eli said. "He's Daddy's friend."

So, he'd graduated from colleague to friend, Desire thought, gazing down at the group of children gathered around Chase. She didn't miss the animated grin on his face as he interacted with them. Her pulse quickened at a vision of Chase on the floor romping with their own future children.

"You must be Alyssa," he said, grinning at her.

"Yes, I'm Alyssa." Her smile widened as she twirled a finger around a strand of her long curly brown hair. "How do you know my name?"

"A little birdie told me."

She snickered, brazenly. "I'm eight. How old are you?"

Way too old for you. Desire smiled, remembering how at that age *she* had been crushing on a then eleven-year-old Chase. *Run along, little girl. This catch is mine.*

"A gentleman never reveals his age," Chase said, giving Alyssa a wink before turning to Anastasia. He pinched her nose. "And you must be Anastasia."

She giggled shyly and held on to her sister's hand as she stared at Chase through bright hazel eyes.

"Elyse, right?" Chase said, ruffling the curly black hair of the youngest Fontaine. "You have your daddy's black eyes and your mother's lovely smile."

Unlike her gregarious, garrulous twin, Eli, Elyse was quiet, sweet, and shy. She was usually in her father's arms when Desire had run into them in public—a true daddy's little girl. And true to her nature, Anastasia ran back to her parents and right into her father's arms.

"Hi, Miss Desire," Jason said, joining them. "You look really nice."

"At last, someone noticed me," Desire said, grinning at the teenage boy. "Thank you, Jason."

"Is he your date?" he asked, pointing at Chase.

"Um, yes. Ch—Mr. B, this is Jason Rogers. Jason, my date."

Chase shook Jason's hand. "It's nice to meet you, Jason. You look a lot like your father, Michael."

"You knew my dad, my real dad?"

"Yes. I had my first ski lesson from him."

"He taught me, too. But I don't ski as much anymore. It reminds me of him too much and it still hurts that he and my mom aren't around anymore. Maybe when it doesn't hurt as much, I'll start skiing again."

Desire's arm automatically went around the boy's shoulders. Although she said nothing, she could feel the tension in his body subside at her hug. She was a grown woman, and yet the anticipation of losing her father was already sending her into depression. She could only imagine what it was like for Jason and his sisters to lose both of their parents in one day, before they even had the chance to really know them. "It will get better, Jason," she said, for her benefit as much as for his.

"Bryce told me that you're excellent at martial arts," Chase said. "You're on your green belt now, and the star student in the region? That's quite an accomplishment."

The sparkle returned to his eyes. "Thank you. I'm going to a camp in New York next month. Then it's down to Washington DC for the East Coast tournament. I'm excited about camp but a little nervous about the tournament. I'll be up against some of the best."

"I'm sure you'll do well," Chase said.

"Daddy, look. It's Mr. B," Eli shouted as his parents joined them.

"Yes, Eli, I see that." Bryce placed Elyse on the floor. "So you've met my children, Mr. B," he said to Chase. "Sorry about Eli waylaying you like that."

Desire didn't miss the wary glances between Bryce and Chase, but before she could analyze them, his two youngest daughters were tugging Bryce's hands.

"Can we go to the playroom, Daddy?" Anastasia asked, as a burst of laughter came from the room next door. "I want to see the fishes in the aquarium."

"Yeah, Daddy, can we, please, please, please?" Elyse chimed in. "I want to ride the train."

"Okay, just for a minute. We have to leave soon." He signaled Haley over, and after quickly introducing her to Chase, he instructed her to take the three youngest children next door.

Eli raced ahead of his sisters. He was definitely not a follower, but a born leader like his father, Desire thought.

Kaya glanced at the two older children. "You, too. Go."

"The novelty of that room, the fishes, and the trains wore off a long time ago for me, Mom." Jason said.

"Me, too," Alyssa added. "It's boring. I'm a big girl now." She flipped her curls over her shoulder, and smiled up at Chase.

"Okay, then, Charlie and the car are up front. You can go wait with him. We'll be out soon."

"But, Mommy, I—"

"Alyssa, you heard your mom." Bryce's voice was uncompromising, yet gentle. "Say your goodbyes, both of you. You'll see Mr. B and Miss Desire again soon."

Alyssa folded her arms and pouted in protest, but she obviously knew better than to argue with her father. She grudgingly said goodbye to both Chase and Desire before reluctantly following her brother to the door.

"She seems like a darling little girl, but boy, you have your hands full with her," Chase said with a smile.

"You have no idea. She's growing up too fast for my liking," Bryce said, before turning his attention to Desire, finally making her feel like she was a person, and a visible one at that. "Desire, you look absolutely stunning. Wow." His smile was genuine, admiring.

"I second that." Kaya touched her on the arm. "Such a beautiful dress. You look like a queen."

Desire felt warmth rising to her cheeks. "Thank you, both of you." She cleared the catch from her voice, marveling that members of the Summers and Fontaine families could stand next to each other, and compliment each other without an ounce of tension between them. They'd made remarkable progress.

"Is it a Joanne's exclusive?" Kaya asked, running a finger along the sleeve of the dress.

"Yes. It's a present from *Mr. B.* Along with the shoes, the purse, and the jewelry." Desire narrowed her eyes at Chase as she recalled his questions about her relationship with Bryce in the boarding house yesterday, when he was undoubtedly aware of the whole situation all along.

"He has exceptional taste," Kaya said, smiling up at Chase who seemed fascinated with Bryce's wife.

"Kaya, this is Mr. Bennett. Mr. Bennett, my wife, Kaya." Bryce made the introductions.

Bennett now? How thick could this plot get? Desired wondered.

"So you are the infamous and mysterious Mr. Bennett. It is an honor to finally meet you." She held her hand out to him.

"The honor is mine, Mrs. Fontaine." Chase kissed her hand. "You're even more gorgeous than your pictures."

She laughed. "Oh come on, no need for formalities, especially not after the last-minute stages and dance poles you added to our honeymoon cottages. They were perfect."

"So your husband tells me."

Desire watched Chase's face turn red. "You designed their honeymoon cottages," she asked, as the nature of his relationship with the Fontaines, and probably the other billionaires, dawned on her. So that's why he was able to land a table at Hotel Andreas tonight. "You've been working as an architect all these years?"

"You haven't told her yet," Bryce said.

"I'm telling her everything tonight."

"I didn't realize you two knew each other," Kaya said to Desire.

"We go way back." Chase said "We grew up next door to each other until she was fourteen, and then her family moved to Granite Falls."

"Really? Were you friends, or more?" she asked, tossing each of them a meaningful smile.

"More. Much more. Tonight is all about reconnecting, hopefully picking up where we left off years ago," he said in a deeply timbred voice as he smiled at Desire.

"We're trying to reconnect, too. At least I am."

"Reconnect with whom?" Desire asked.

"My mother. She's visiting. We had dinner upstairs in her room."

"Oh." Desire tossed Kaya a curious glance. Last year when Bryce and Kaya had visited Desire's parents to tear down the wall between them, Kaya had told them that her mother had abandoned her as a child and that she'd grown up in Florida's welfare system. As far as Desire knew, Kaya and her mother had never had a relationship since Kaya moved to Granite Falls to take care of her nephew and two nieces after their parents were killed in a car crash five years ago. This is where she'd met and married Bryce, who was the children's godfather at the time. Together, they were raising the orphan children, along with their own. "I didn't know you and your mother had reconciled."

Kaya uttered a soft chortle. "We're trying. I went to see her when I was pregnant with the twins, but she wasn't even ready to meet me halfway. We kept in touch, barely, but when I told her that I was pregnant again, she asked if she could meet her grandchildren."

"Why is she staying here, and not with you?" Chase asked.

"I don't want her in my home, not until she has proven that she can be trusted."

"And probably not even after that," Bryce stated, pulling his wife into his arms, and kissing the top of her head. "She will never have the opportunity to be alone with any of our children. Not as long as I live."

Kaya's eyes clouded with apparently sad memories. "She abused me physically and emotionally when I was a child, walked out on me when I was thirteen, then came back a year later, pretending she wanted me back in her life. But that didn't happen, thanks to my caseworker who found out that her then boyfriend was a registered sex offender. When the judge gave her a choice between him and me, she chose him. God only knows what kind of deal she'd made with that man, concerning me."

"I didn't realize how difficult a childhood you had, Kaya.

I'm sorry." Kaya's story made Desire appreciate her parents even more—despite the fact that her father had kept her and Chase apart for so many years.

"She's been going to counseling, and one of the steps is that she reconciles with me. She said she was sorry for what she did to me. I don't even know if I believe her. I'm not getting my hopes up. I don't need her to complete my life. When I needed her, she chose not to be there." She shrugged. "She can stay in Granite Falls as long as my children are interested in seeing her, but only in the presence of either Bryce and or me. I don't want them to grow up and resent me for keeping them away from their grandmother. I haven't told them anything negative about her. I'll let them draw their own conclusions when they're old enough. Hopefully, by then, she'll have really changed."

"Well, at least you'll be able to tell them that you tried," Chase said.

"Exactly." Kaya rubbed her hand over her stomach, a smile playing at the corners of her mouth as she caressed the child in her womb.

Desire felt a sharp contraction inside her own womb as Chase suddenly placed his hand on her shoulders and pulled her up against him. His hold was gentle, yet possessive. Very possessive.

"Pregnancy agrees with you, Kaya. You are glowing. When's the big day?" Desire asked.

"September eighth."

"Twins again?" Chase teased.

"Oh, God forbid. I don't think I would survive another set of twins. It's just one this time. A boy, which makes my husband very happy." She threw her head back and grinned at Bryce. "He says we need to even the playing field."

"It's only fair." Bryce bent way down to plant a lingering kiss on his wife's upturned lips at the same time that he placed his hand over hers, still resting on her baby bump. "Now, we have three sons and three daughters."

"Congratulations to both of you. I wish you a smooth

delivery and a very healthy baby boy," Desire said to the parents-to-be.

They smiled their thanks, then Bryce spoke. "I think we've taken up enough of your time. You have lots to talk about." He held a hand out to Chase. "We'll talk later." He brought Desire's hand to his lips. "Desire, it's always a pleasure to see you. Enjoy your evening. I don't have to tell you what a remarkable man you have here. Go gently with him."

Kaya held her hand out to Chase. "It's nice to have finally met you, Mr. Bennett."

"Actually, my name is Chase. Chase Hunter. 'Chase' will do just fine."

Kaya gaped at Chase like a college freshman girl meeting the senior hunk for the first time. "You're Azura's son? Oh my God! You are *the* Chase Hunter? I can't wait to tell Michelle, Shaina, and Tashi that I met you first. Oh, they're going to be so jealous."

From her reaction, Desire figured that Kaya and the rest of the billionaire wives knew all the little sordid details about Chase Hunter. His reputation would always precede him. Was this what she would be dealing with every time someone recognized him? She'd just drawn in a breath of relief and sent up a thankful silent prayer that they'd be dining in private tonight when the concierge appeared to tell them that their room was ready.

"Just in time," Bryce said, taking Kaya's hand. "My wife's becoming too excited. It was nice to see you, Desire. You should both stop by the estate sometime soon. It's only fair that you admire another of your creations up close, Chase."

"We will definitely pay you a visit soon, Bryce. Kaya, I look forward to chatting with you and Michelle, Shaina, and Tashi. Give them my best."

She grinned shamelessly. "I will."

Bryce guided his wife toward the playroom to collect their kids.

"You have a lot of explaining to do, Chase Hunter!" Desire slapped him in the gut.

"Yes, I do," he said in a winded voice. "But you heard Bryce. You're supposed to go easy on me."

"That depends on your explanation," Desire responded as Chase linked their arms. She felt a flush run through her as every head turned to gaze at them—both male and female—as they strolled through the lobby and in the direction of their private dining room.

They walked down a long ecru-colored hallway lined with a red carpet, a number of closed doors on the right, and round marble tables with tall crystal vases of red roses and white baby's breath on the left. Shimmering chandeliers lit their path. Desire was filled with awe at the elegance and beauty surrounding her. She'd visited this hotel several times to conduct business with wealthy clients, yet she hadn't even realized that this exclusive wing existed. This was definitely a different kind of world than the one she was used to. And now instead of serving in it, she was *being* served in it.

At the sound of a soft feminine laugh, Desire glanced behind her just in time to see a couple, dressed to the nines, enter one of the rooms they'd passed. She glanced up to find Chase smiling at her. He said nothing, but the tender look in his eyes told her that he found great joy in bringing *her*, of all women, into his new and sophisticated world. Despite the fact that she was peeved that he'd kept it from her, Desire's heart soared with love for him.

"Here you are," the concierge said, stopping at the very last door.

"Thank you, Austin." Chase placed his hand on the gold-plated lever. "I'll take it from here."

"Enjoy your evening, madam. Sir." Austin bowed and retraced his steps.

Chase opened the door, and stood back for her to enter.

"Chase! Oh my gosh!" Desire exclaimed, as she walked, not into what she'd expected would be a dining room, but into a little spherical garden with bed after bed of blooming flowers of every color and variety, hedged in by a green wall of Thuja Green Giants, one of the many evergreen trees that the town of Evergreen was named after. Hundreds of white votive candles separated the flowerbeds, and strings of white fairy lights strewn around the trees provided their only source of light.

The black outline of the Presidential Range loomed majestic in the background, and even though the privacy shrubs obstructed her view, Desire knew that the water trickling from the gold marble fountain fashioned into a representation of Gustav Klimt's "The Kiss" came from Crystal Lake, directly behind the shrubs.

As euphonious romantic tunes drifted from invisible speakers, Desire transferred her gaze to the middle of the garden where a romantically set glass-top table and two white, cushioned love seats sat under a white silk canopy that was decorated with red roses. Four large white pillar candles burning at each post crystallized the romantic setting. An amalgamation of savory aromas escaping from sterling silver serving pans warming on a buffet table a few feet behind the canopy reminded Desire that she hadn't eaten since breakfast.

Tears sprang to her eyes to think that this man loved her so much that he'd gone to all the trouble to make this night special for her. The fact that he'd hidden his rise to power and wealth these past two days didn't matter anymore. This dazzling slice of heaven that he'd given her exonerated every transgression he'd ever committed against her.

"Chase," she whispered in a broken voice, "I've never seen anything so romantic. It's almost surreal."

CHAPTER FIFTEEN

Chase grinned like a schoolboy who'd just asked the most beautiful, most popular girl to the senior prom, and she'd accepted. He stood next to her, his heart thumping at the awe and wonder on her face as she took in the romantic setting he'd planned. She shone with an ethereal beauty he'd never been able to find in any other woman. The fact that she loved him, that she was giving him a second chance to express his love for her rocked him to the core.

"Oh, it's real, baby. As real as you. Come." He felt her tremble when he took her hand and led her along the black marble floor toward the canopy. It gave him great joy to know that he'd never, ever done anything so splendid for any other woman. Hadn't even been tempted to.

"When did you plan all this?" she asked, as he helped her settle into one of the love seats.

"The planning began months ago when I knew for sure I was coming back home." He unfolded her napkin and spread it on her lap, being careful not to touch her thighs, and willing himself not to gaze too intently on the voluptuous swell of her breasts spilling from the top of her dress, or brush his lips against the softness of her neck and shoulders, or even inhale too much of her rousing perfume rising from her skin.

It wasn't easy being a gentleman around Desire Summers, but tonight, Chase needed to treat her like a sophisticated lady, beyond his reach, before he could strip her naked and treated her like the wanton seductress she was. He had to hold it together until after he'd told her everything.

He drew in a deep breath and limped around the table, wincing inwardly at the ache his growing erection was causing. He sat carefully down in the seat across from her. "I wanted to impress you," he said, picking up the bottle of Chateau d'Yquem chilling in the bucket at the side of the table.

"Consider me impressed." She laughed. "You were that sure that I would accept your invitation," she added, placing her clutch at the edge of the table.

He laughed, too, and proceeded to pour their wine. "I was, until I came home to find you engaged to my brother, which only made me more determined to win you back. And once I was sure of your feelings for me, I ordered the total execution of the plan after we left the boarding house last night. It was difficult, almost impossible at such short notice, but with a few extra hands, we were able to pull it off." He picked up his glass and beckoned to her to raise hers. "Cheers?"

"To what are we toasting?" she asked, placing an elbow on the table and toying provocatively with a strand of her hair falling across her cheek and down to her shoulder.

Chase fought the temptation to go and sit beside her, to caress her and kiss her and feel the warmth of her skin under his palm. "To new beginnings," he said hoarsely. "To love, marriage, babies—lots and lots of babies—and a lifetime of happiness together." He held her gaze, daring her to refute his request. He had to know if she was with him, willing to go with him all the way, even before he gave her the answers she was looking for. "I've always been in love with you, Desire. I've been with many women, but I've never loved any other woman but you. When I think of growing old, gray, and feeble, losing my teeth and my hair, you are the only woman I envision beside me. I want it all, and I want it with you, Desire Summers."

She stared at him for a few breathless seconds, and then she sat back, placed her hands on her lap, and stared at her glass of wine.

"Cheers?" he repeated, a tiny part of him wondering if all his effort was in vain. He realized that his concerns were premature when she smiled and picked up her glass with a trembling hand.

Her beautiful brown eyes were damp when she looked at him, and in their depths he saw a lifetime of love, love she had for only him. No other woman had ever possessed the power to move Chase with simply a glance like Desire Summers did. He couldn't wait to drown himself in her eyes while he was buried deep, deep inside her.

"Cheers." Her voice trembled as she continued. "I've never loved any other man but you, Chase Hunter. And I do want it all with you. Only you. I look forward to growing old and gray with you, lying beside you, toothless, hairless, and with my breasts sagging down to my waistline."

Chase laughed so hard, tears stung his eyes. "I promise you that my toothless mouth will still be suckling at your sagging breast and my feeble, crooked-from-arthritis fingers will still be trying to cop a feel."

She raised her glass and grinned. "To toothless mouths, feeble fingers, and sagging breasts, then. And penises," she added. "You won't be virile forever, love."

"Bite your tongue, woman. Haven't you heard of those magical little blue pills?"

Laughing, they clinked their glasses and drank their toast, gazing deeply into each other's eyes.

"Chase," she said, holding up her glass and staring at the dark gold liquid inside it. "This is by far the best wine I ever tasted. It's so smooth, like whipped cream and raspberry sliding over my tongue. It's almost exotic, if you can say that about a wine." She took another sip, her eyes widening and shimmering with appreciation. She glanced at the label. "I've never heard of this brand before. Where did you buy it? My mom loves white wine. I'm sure she'd enjoy this."

"Well, actually, it was a gift from Bryce and his friends. A 'thank-you' for the honeymoon cottages," he said on a smile. "And, you probably wouldn't find it in any stores around here, or anywhere else for that matter. This bottle of wine is over a hundred years old."

Her eyes grew wider as if that was even possible. "A hundred years old? And it still tastes so good?"

"It improves with time. This particular vintage was auctioned off some years ago. Adam was the lucky winner. He asked Bryce to mail it to me after they returned from their honeymoon." He took another sip, and relished the sweet, full-bodied taste of the wine as it glided down his throat. He'd done his homework, and he knew the bottle cost over a hundred thousand dollars. Ever since he'd received it, Chase had known exactly when he would pop the cork—on a night like tonight with Desire sitting across from him wearing a red elegant dress, and with diamonds sparkling around her neck and in her earlobes. He'd envisioned this intimate scene a million times over the past year. His fantasies paled in the light of the real thing.

"I personally have to thank Adam," Desire said. "I have to sip this slowly," she added, placing her glass down. "You are full of surprises tonight, Chase Hunter."

Chase set his glass down as he held her gaze. "I know you have a horde of questions about those surprises, so let's get dinner going. We'll talk while we eat. Is that fine with you?"

"It's perfect. I'm starving. What, no waiters tonight?" she asked when he got up and walked to the buffet table.

"Not tonight. I want no interruptions while we talk." He quickly filled two plates from the serving dishes. "Close your eyes," he ordered before turning around.

"More surprises?"

"Just one more."

"Okay, they're closed."

He smiled at the annoyance in her voice as he went back to the table and placed the plates down. "You may open them," he said, reclaiming his seat. "*Buon appetito, signorina!*"

Her face contorted into an incredulous expression as she stared at the plate he'd placed in front of her, then at him, and then at the plate again. "Really, Chase?" she said, slapping her hands on her hips. "You got me all dressed up in the most elegant dress I've ever worn, adorned me with diamonds, chauffeured me by limo to the most luxurious hotel in the northeast, organized the most spectacular dinner setting a girl could imagine, pour her wine from a hundred-year-old bottle, and then you serve her macaroni and cheese with grilled hot dogs. *Really?*"

"And a side of grilled vegetables," he said, chuckling. "Don't forget the veggies."

"This is a joke, right? That's why you're laughing. Ha ha." She wagged a finger at him, then glanced at the door as if she expected a waiter to enter, electronic pad in hand, ready to take their order.

Chase sobered up. "It's no joke, my dear." He unfolded his napkin and spread it across his lap.

"My mouth was watering for some lobster or steak or pheasant—at least one of the exclusive, delectable delights synonymous with the Andreas name—and you expect me to eat hot dogs instead." She sucked her teeth and glowered.

"I've heard they're the best hot dogs on the East Coast. I suggest you try them before you knock them." He picked up his utensils and prepared to dive into his dinner. "Go on, eat up. We have a lot to do tonight."

"Only because I'm hungry. I haven't eaten since breakfast. But I'm gonna get you for this, Chase Hunter."

"Some of your hard, lumpy, runny mac and cheese, and your uncooked hot dogs ought to do the trick. It put me out for a week the last time. But I'm hoping your culinary skills have improved over the years?" he said, amused.

She cut her eyes at him and picked up her fork and knife.

"Try this one first," he suggested, pointing to the one on the left side of her plate. "Add a little of this honey mustard sauce and a tiny bit of wasabi."

"Why?"

"Because I said so," he replied, filling their water glasses from the crystal pitcher on the table.

Her lips twisted skeptically as she cut a tiny piece off the end, added the condiments he'd suggested, and placed it into her mouth. A soft sigh escaped her, and then, "Oh my God," she crooned around the mouthful of food. "Chase, this is…oh, God…" Her lids fluttered shut.

As Chase watched her sexy mouth close around the delicious flavors, pleasure seared through him at the vision of her lips clasped around his shaft, working him into a quivering ball of passion. He shifted to ease the tension in his groin, anxious to take her upstairs to his penthouse and into his huge bed, naked and trembling under him, crying out, "Oh, God, Oh Chase."

The effect the erotic image was having on him was so potent, he almost choked on his own bite of hot dog. He swallowed convulsively and took a quick chug from his water glass. He cleared his throat. "How do you like it?"

She just moaned, as he imagined she would when he posed that same question later in bed. "Your mouth *is* watering, sweetie." He leaned across the table and licked at the trickle of honey mustard and juices running down one side of her mouth. His shaft pulsed impatiently.

She went rigid and her lids flew up at the touch of his tongue to her skin. She smiled wickedly, and pushed her tongue through her lips to curl around his. Guttural sounds escaped their throats as they sucked gently on each other, eating from each other, drawing out the last remaining flavors from their dogs until Chase reluctantly pulled back. If he didn't, he would have come right there in his tux. He had no intention of wasting any of his precious sperms tonight. Every last one of his little tadpoles was on assignment now—to beat all its little brothers and sisters to Desire's fertile eggs.

"That was delicious," she said, grinning at him, totally unaware of his lustful thoughts.

"Me, or the lobster dog?"

"Both," she said in a silken voice. "I didn't know that such a thing existed. It never crossed my mind that someone would come up with a lobster dog recipe."

"Anything is possible as long as your mind is open, love. All you have to do is let your imagination run wild. That one is made from Japanese Kobe steak, and this from duckling," he said, pointing to the other two dogs on her plate. "So you see my dear, you do have your lobster, your steak, and your duckling. Sorry about the pheasant."

"Nobody is perfect." Her voice dipped to a husky tone when she added, "Thank you, Chase. Thank you for making this night special for me."

"It's not over yet. There's still a lot to cover. Let's eat. I haven't eaten all day, either."

She giggled as she placed some macaroni and cheese into her mouth. "This is good, too. Way better than mine."

Chase watched her, debating how to begin, but knowing that the sooner he got through it, the sooner they could get on with the second act of the night. It was a relief to know that he didn't have to spend time trying to win her back, or make her fall in love with him again, although he would have enjoyed the journey, the *chase*.

His mother had said she'd named him 'Chase' hoping he would chase after his dreams and his purpose in life. Well, his dreams and his purpose in life were embodied in the woman sitting across from him.

And both he and Desire knew how precious and rare it was to find someone to love you, someone who would stick by you through thick and thin, someone you could never forget because that person had become part of you, and you part of them. They had a connection that no amount of time or space apart could sever. There was no need for them to pretend that they didn't love each other. For the first time in his life, Chase could say that his relationship with a woman was not a game. It was the real thing. Desire was his waking dream, loving her was his ultimate purpose in life.

"Why did you make me get all dressed up if we were dining in private?" she asked, lifting her head after they'd eaten in silence for a while.

Well, there, she'd started it for him. He cleared his throat. "You always talked about dressing up like a princess and going to the ball to meet Prince Charming when you were a little girl."

Her smile was tantalizing. "Yes. I remember. "But I'd already met my prince, my king."

Her words touched him deeply. "I'm glad to hear you say that, because I also wanted you to get a feel for what it will be like married to a billionaire king."

"Bill—did—did you say *billionaire*? With a B?" Her body went limp, and her fork slithered to the table. With trembling fingers, she picked up her glass and gulped down water as if her throat had gone suddenly dry.

"Yes, billionaire with a B," he said over the rim of his wine glass, delighted that she was more surprised at his financial status than the fact that he'd specifically mentioned that they would be married.

"Is that why you're using the alias 'Mr. B?'" she asked, when her composure was once again intact.

"Actually, I've been using 'Mr. Bennett.'" He chewed on some grilled vegetables.

"Azura's maiden name."

He nodded. "To the world, 'Mr. Bennett' is the CEO and owner of my company. Bryce suggested we used 'Mr. B' when I met Eli in his office yesterday. As you're aware, he talks a lot. Didn't want anyone putting B and Bennett together," he added for good humor.

She wiped her hands down her face and shook her head as if to clear it. "After the dress, the jewelry, the limo, and now this," she said, waving her hand around, "I figured you must have money. I thought you'd won the lottery or something. What I couldn't imagine was that you're as wealthy as Bryce."

"I've only made my first billion. I have a long way to go before I catch up with Bryce and his friends."

"So, I guess you also know Adam, Massimo, and Erik since you designed their honeymoon cottages?"

"I met them a few months ago on *Baia Degli Amanti*. They are building a family compound on the other side of the island away from the honeymoon cottages." He placed a slice of steak dog into his mouth.

"And here I was thinking you were a poor worker on an Iowa farm, who could hardly make ends meet, when you've been living the life of luxury all along."

He swallowed his mouthful then washed it down with some wine. "Not all along. I worked as a field hand on Carver Farm until I bought all six hundred acres. My employees run it. I just use it as my headquarters for DC Architectural Designs."

She tilted her head to one side. "DC?"

He held his humor as he recalled Lewis' *Dumb Chase* remark this morning. *Yeah, who was dumb, and who was laughing now?*

"I named my company Desire and Chase Architectural Designs, but I emitted the 'and' and just went for 'Desire's Chase' since that's who I really am."

Her hand went to her throat. "Chase, you named your company after us."

"Yes, Desire." He reached for her other hand lying on the table, and laced their fingers together. "It was the thought of coming back to you that gave me the drive I needed to be successful. I needed to be successful to take on and then take down the man who's responsible for tearing us apart. He's a devious little pig. I couldn't take the chance of him knowing I was coming for him. I had to sneak back into my own town. There was no other way to do it. I'm sorry I had to lie to you."

"You didn't lie."

"I did, by omission. Can you forgive me?"

She squeezed his fingers, sending joy spiraling through his veins. "I understand now. Since we're discussing him, and since you had no hesitation to tell Kaya who you really are, I guess you've dealt with him?"

He nodded. "I took care of him this morning. His company will be liquidated by the time the stock market closes on Tuesday."

"What did this man hope to gain from setting you up?"

"He wanted my designs."

"But you told me that I was the only person who knew about your dreams of being an architect back then."

"I'd told one other person before you, someone I thought was my friend. I was young and insecure about my ability, my purpose and direction in life. I wanted approval and feedback from him. I thought I could trust him, so I foolishly gave him my thumb drive. It was the only copy I had of my designs. He didn't give it back to me until the night of the show. I didn't have time to view it before I handed it to you."

"He switched out the drive for the one with you and…" Her voice faded and she dropped her gaze to her empty plate.

"Desire." Chase reached across the table and placed his hand under her chin, forcing her to meet his gaze. "He edited the timestamp on that video. It seemed he'd been after me for a long time. He used my weakness for sex against me. Yes, I was a hound. I did a lot of things that I wish I could take back. But I swear on my life that I never touched another woman after we declared our love for each other. I was celibate for a year after I left home. The thought of being with another woman made me sick to my stomach."

Her entire body shuddered as she drew harsh, deep breaths into her lungs. Finally she spoke. "I believe you, Chase. But I don't understand why you didn't stay and clear your name? You could have told everyone what he'd done."

Chase dropped his hand onto the table and sat back in his chair. "I couldn't, not without destroying my family—my mother's and my brother's worlds."

"What do you mean?"

Chase wished he could avoid dredging up his and Azura's past again, but a husband and wife should never have secrets between them. Since Desire would be his wife, it was only fair that she knew about his father. "He'd dug up some incriminating information about my mother's past," he said. "He threatened to make it public if I didn't leave town. He warned me that he would follow through with his threat if I came back. It killed me to leave you without an explanation. I wanted to stay to fight for us, but I couldn't let that man destroy my mother's world. What kind of son or big brother would I have been if I'd—"

"Oh, Chase," she cried, her lips trembling as if she were trying to combat her need to break down and weep. "I'm sorry that you were forced to choose between me and your family. You did the right thing, though. You had to protect your mother and your little brother, especially because I'd cut you out of my life. You didn't even know if we'd get back together if you'd stayed."

"I think we would have eventually, but I needed to go find out if what he'd dug up on my mother's past was true."

"You didn't know about it before? She never told you?"

"Nope." He dropped his gaze to the table.

"You don't have to tell me if you don't want to," she said after an awkward silence dragged out between them.

"I do have to tell you," he replied, raising his head to give her a smile he knew didn't reach his eyes. "It's only fair that you know everything about the man you love and the family you'll be marrying into."

He refilled his wine glass, and took a sip, wishing he had something stronger to ease the shame and pain he felt. "You sure you're ready for this?" he asked Desire. "It's heavy."

When she nodded, he began with the story Azura had told him last night. He left nothing out. Then he told her about his visit to the jail to face the man who'd sired him. When he was finished, tears were streaming down Desire's face, leaving two black streaks in their wake. "So, my dear, you are in love with the son of a rapist, a vile despicable murdering bastard, a jailbird. I'll understand if you don't want to be with me, if you don't—"

"Stop it. Stop demoting yourself." She was out of her seat and running around the table to sit beside him. She wrapped her arms around his neck and buried her face into his throat.

Chase closed his eyes tightly to stop the tears from falling, but they came anyway. He wished he didn't have to burden Desire with a tale so gruesome, but he knew she understood.

He held her close, breathed in her perfumed scent, and absorbed the warmth and comfort of her loving tender touch.

Way too soon, she raised her head, but kept her arms around him. Her damp eyes sparkled with a kind of fierce love and devotion Chase had never witnessed in another person's eyes before—at least not when they looked at him. She was kissing him, caressing him with her eyes.

"I will always carry that shame surrounding my conception. How do I live that down? How do I shake it off? Even though I never felt it, since I learned the truth, I often wondered if my mother resented me each time she looked at me. I'm the son of her rapist, and the murderer of the man she loved. She claims she's never once blamed or resented me, but I—"

"Of course she doesn't. Azura loves you. It's not your fault that your father is a rapist and a murderer, Chase. You're doing to yourself what the people in this town did to me after Victoria killed Pilar. You're no more responsible for your father's crimes than I am for hers. Our parents, our families, don't define us. I love you, Chase Hunter, and I don't care who your father is. It doesn't change the way I feel about you. I want to marry you and have your babies."

Chase was taken aback when she pulled his head down and pressed her lips against his. Her kiss was demanding, reassuring, and it sang through his veins—songs of dedication, loyalty, friendship, and eternity. Chase wrapped her in his arms and his mouth covered hers hungrily as he relinquished all the pain and heartache he'd been carrying for far too long. Desire loved him despite the fact that the blood of a rapist, murdering bastard ran through his veins.

He reluctantly broke their kiss, and said, "I told my mother about us, about that night in the garden, and about our reunion yesterday."

She eased out of his embrace and gazed at him warily. "She must think I'm an awful woman to be engaged to one of her sons and in love with the other."

He held her hands, stroking her wrist with his thumbs. "No, sweetheart. She understands. She knows true love conquers all. She's happy for us. She actually feels guilty that I had to sacrifice my happiness to protect her and Chad."

She quivered on a deep breath. "You never told me the name of the man who set you up. Who was it? I have a right to know."

Chase took a swallow of wine. "You remember I was working as a gardener for Carron Architecture."

Her fingers tightened around his. "It was Lewis Carron, wasn't it?" she said in a bitter tone. "It was him," she repeated, nodding in response to her own question.

Chase felt as if someone had dunked him into a tub of subtemperature water and was standing on his chest holding him under. "Yes. How did you know?"

She dropped her face into her hands and uttered a harsh groan. "That son of a bitch! I should have known. I'm so stupid!"

Chase could feel his breath solidifying in his throat. He pressed his hands to his chest to force himself to breath. If that bastard had touched her, he swore to God he would kill him. Now, he understood the rage that must have overtaken Troy when his sick brother, Roy, had raped the love of his life and then thrown it in his face. Chase's hands curled into fists. "Desire. What is it? What did he do to you? Did he touch you?"

She raised her head and gazed at him through eyes laced with torment and regret. "He found me crying in a room at the club that night. He told me how sorry he was that you'd embarrassed me, and that I didn't deserve it. He said he thought you were his friend, but that you must have been jealous of him and decided to hurt him by bringing disgrace on his father's company since your presentation represented them. He suggested we could help each other deal with the disillusion that you caused."

"How?" He ground the words out through his teeth.

She swallowed. "After you left town, he came to my house, to check up on me, he claimed. He asked me if I knew where you'd gone and if you were coming back. My father was all too happy that a nice young man was interested in me. He encouraged me to go out with him. After you told me about your letter, I know why he was so eager to pawn me off."

"Did you go out with him?"

She shook her head. "No. I was still in love with you. I wasn't interested in anyone. He was persistent though, calling me all the time. But then after Victoria killed Pilar, he lost interest, like a lot of the other men around here."

Chase let out his breath. "He was fishing for information about me through you. I didn't just abandon you, Desire. I left because I knew if he'd discovered I had feelings for you, he would have hurt you to hurt me, to threaten me into staying away. I'm so glad nobody knew about us. When I think of what he would have done to you…" He drew her to his side and placed her head on his shoulder. "He's no danger to you anymore. He's no danger to anyone," he said, stroking his hand up and down her arm.

"He works for Fontaine Enterprises. I've seen him around town with Bryce. They have lunch together often."

Chase laughed.

"What's so funny?"

He refilled her wine glass and handed it to her. "Here, you'll need this for a toast after I tell you how I met Bryce, and about the true nature of our relationship."

"I'm listening," she said, pulling out of his embrace and lying back against the cushions.

Chase ran his fingers through his hair, and tucked errant strands behind his ears. "I've known about Bryce since I was a teenager, but I'd never had the opportunity to meet him in person." He shrugged. "He was a few years older than me and we didn't run in the same circles."

"He was in the top circle in Granite Falls, and you were an underdog at the time, a busboy, a waiter, and then a lowly gardener," she said, tapping him playfully on the arm.

He appreciated that Desire could speak her mind freely to him without fear of upsetting him. She trusted in their love enough to know that he would get over it, and vice versa.

"Anyway, my first design, the one I gave to Lewis, was the blueprints for the building that now houses Fontaine Enterprises headquarters."

"Chase, you designed that?" she asked in awe. "That building has been voted the most beautiful in all of Granite Falls for the past ten years." She shook her head. "And Lewis has been getting credit all this time for your work. Unbelievable."

"I've had to sit back and watch him shine in my spotlight."

"How did Bryce learn the truth? Did you contact him?"

"No. It was sheer luck. About nine years ago, I was in Chicago with my girlfriend at the time. She was interviewing for a job there, so we'd decided to make it a little vacation away from the farm." He shrugged. "Anyway, Beth and I had an argument one night, so I went for a walk to cool down. I passed by this beautiful hotel, and was so awed by the structure that I wandered inside and went to the bar. I knew I could only afford one drink, so I nursed the hell out of it. And just when I was about to leave, guess who grabbed the stool next to me?"

"Bryce."

"I recognized him right away and we started talking about sports and women. I don't know what it was. Maybe it was the fact that we were from the same town, or because we'd both lost the loves of our lives—his by tragedy and mine by—well—I began unloading on him. I told him about Lewis, about that night and how he stole my designs."

"Did you tell him about me?"

"No, sweetheart. He wasn't ready to talk about any member of your family. He was still very angry, and still grieving for Pilar. I was sensitive enough to sense his pain." He took a sip of his wine. "He told me that he loved my work. I mean he chose my designs above everyone else's from the show. He just didn't know the true artist behind them, although he said he'd suspected that they weren't Lewis' since all his future drawings were—how did he put it? 'Crap.'"

They both laughed, and automatically clinked their glasses before taking sips.

"He told me success was the best revenge, but that I needed to be covert about it," Chase continued. "If my enemy doesn't know I'm coming, he can't counterattack. It was best Lewis didn't even know I was in the game. Bryce even put me in contact with a Hollywood makeup artist who created a face for Mr. C. Bennett."

"Like Ethan Hunt in *Mission Impossible*? Can I see it?" She grabbed his arm and stared at him like a kid begging for a dollar to buy cotton candy at the country fair.

He laughed and patted her hand. "Not that elaborate, my dear. She just made some minor alterations with makeup and props to make me look older when I played the role of CEO. I retired her when I left Iowa. It was time to leave that part of me behind. It had served its purpose."

"Oh well," she said with a deflated sigh. "Sounds like Bryce. He's smooth, yet shrewd when it comes to business."

"He's the kind of mentor every green entrepreneur needs in his corner. I was very lucky to have him in mine. To set me on my path of revenge, he encouraged me to return to college and offered me a full scholarship. So I stayed in Chicago, enrolled in Illinois Institute of Technology, and earned my master's and my doctorate degree in architectural engineering in five years."

"So you're a doctor? That's impressive, Chase."

"Thank you, baby. I worked my tail off. I didn't want to disappoint Bryce. I worked on the Fontaine Towers while I was in school, and once I graduated and moved back to Iowa, Bryce hired me to oversee the construction of his estate and the honeymoon cottages. It was kind of difficult not being on-site, but we kept in close communication and he would send a liaison to meet with me once in a while. He recommended me to many of his billionaire friends and acquaintances. Before long, I had more work than I could keep up with. Following Bryce's advice to stay off the radar, I founded DC Designs under the alias, Mr. C. Bennett, hired some of the best architects out there, along with a stellar staff to run my operation from Des Moines. I was Mr. C. Bennett in Des Moines, and plain old Chase Hunter on Carver Farm."

"That is quite a story, Chase," she said, in a voice bursting with admiration. "To Mr. Bennett and Carver Farm."

They toasted again then Desire placed her glass on the table. "When did you know it was time to come home? I mean what triggered the decision?"

He cleared his throat. There was no need to give her all the boring details about his and Bryce's Machiavellian machinations that finally caused the collapse and ultimate demise of Lewis Carron and his company. "As you know, Bryce started out in real estate. He owns half of Granite Falls and Evergreen. He's finally ready to develop some of the land around Cedar Lake and the Mannis River. He wants me to plan the communities. I'd been putting him off, but after I saw that picture of you in *Granite Falls People News*, I knew it was time to come home. Last year, I met him on *Baia Degli Amanti* to go over some last minute details."

"Their honeymoon island."

"Yes. When he told me that you would be planning the wedding, I thought it was only fair that he knew about our relationship, that I loved you, and have always loved you."

"Was he upset?"

"No. He seemed genuinely happy for me. He'd already spoken to your dad. He told me that he thought you were an intelligent, beautiful, and remarkable young woman, and that he could see us working out our differences and getting back together. He told me not to give up on you, on love."

She touched her fingers to her lips. "Bryce said those things about me?"

He nodded. "It was he who sent me the copy of the magazine with you in the garden, along with a note that it was time to strike down my enemy and come back to claim you before some other fool snatched you up now that you were famous."

She bit down on her lower lip, causing his heart to jump a mile high in his chest. "I didn't know he thought that much of me."

"He does. But I knew all those marvelous things about you

195

twenty-seven years ago when you crawled through the hedges from your yard to mine, wearing nothing but a pair of red cowboy boots, and branded me as your Chase. I've always been yours, Desire. I'd just been waiting for you to grow up, to understand the ways of love so I could teach you all the beautiful things, the lascivious acts that go on between a man and his woman."

She glanced around their little private outdoor cave, like a bird scouting a tree branch in which to build its nest. Her gaze came back to his. "Chase, do you have a room here in the hotel?"

He cocked his head to one side. "Why?" *Idiot, just say yes.* "Yes. I have a penthouse suite."

"A penthouse suite?" Her tongue rolled slowly and sensuously along her voluptuous lips. "I'm so turned on right now, baby. We should stop talking for the night, at least with our mouths. I just want…" She leaned in and whispered the most obscene requests Chase had ever heard fall from the lips of a woman, of anyone.

"Desire," he exclaimed as his cock swelled and throbbed. He had no idea she had those kinds of words in her vocabulary, those kinds of prurient thoughts in her pretty little head.

"What?" She fluttered her dark long lashes at him. "I'm done being a good girl. I want to be bad, and I want to be bad with you, Chase Hunter. Are you too good, too rich to be bad now?"

Only a wimp would run from a challenge like that. And Chase Hunter was no wimp. Without saying another word, he grabbed her purse off the table, took her hand, and practically dragged her toward the door they'd entered a few hours ago.

CHAPTER SIXTEEN

Chase hadn't said a word since they left their dinner table, but as he led her along the hallway with long purposeful strides, Desire could feel the sexual enticement in his tight grasp on her hand.

A secretive smile ruffled her lips at the curious stares they received as they whipped through the lobby and headed toward the elevators. She was certain everyone who saw them knew exactly what they were rushing upstairs to do. Desire bit down on her lower lip to keep from giggling. Maybe she'd had too much of that delicious hundred-year-old wine, or maybe she was just giddy from the thought of finally making love with the man she loved. She slurped in air as her body tightened in anticipation.

Chase pulled his key card from his pocket and veered her deftly through the throng of guests waiting for the attendant-operated elevators that stopped on selected floors, and marched them to the end of the corridor to an unattended set. The first one opened as they neared it.

As he stepped through the steel doors and dragged her in behind him, Desire heard someone shout, "Hold the elevator." She glanced back to see a middle-aged couple hurrying toward them.

Without a smidgen of hesitation, Chase shoved his key card into the slot, and then pushed the "close" button, causing the doors to shut on the stunned faces of the couple. He pushed the "stop" button, locking the elevator into place. They weren't going anywhere.

"Can you just stop the elevator like that?"

"It's mine. It goes directly to my suite. No one else is allowed to use it."

"Oh, I didn't know you had direct access. At least you could have—"

Before Desire could finish her sentence his hands encircled her waist, and he pushed her gently against the inside mirrored wall. "So you want to be bad?" he said, his eyes dark and wild with lust as his gaze slid slowly and seductively down her body, making her nipples harden and tingle against the soft material of her dress, and causing warm moisture to seep from inside her. He ripped off his jacket and his bow tie, tossed them on the floor, and then toed off his black Corthay Oxfords.

Desire's heart began beating out a vigorous rhythm in her chest. Dear God, he was going to take her in the elevator. Well, she'd whispered some pretty obscene things in his ear a few minutes ago. He was just giving her what she wanted, what she'd asked for. Yes, she wanted it, wanted him in all his rawness. They'd already talked about "protection," so there was nothing standing in their way.

When she'd said she wanted to be bad, she'd been thinking of the privacy of his bedroom, or hers, not here in a public place, where any random Joe or Jane Smith standing outside could hear them. What would people say? *The scandal.* "Chase," she whispered breathlessly, pulling on his arms. "They'll hear us. We should—"

"Shh. You said we should stop talking for the night, and that you wanted—" His lips spread into a dangerously sexy grin. "Well, you know what you said. Let's see how bad you *can* be, Desire Summers," he drawled.

A delightful shiver rushed through Desire as his hand snaked up her back. In one fluid motion, he pulled down the zipper of her dress, causing her breath to tighten at the mastery of his action. She quivered as his smooth warm palms skidded up her bare back to her shoulders to push the sleeves off and down her arms, slowly, ever so slowly. Her pulse quickened when the dress slithered noiseless down her body and ended in a soft pool at her feet, leaving her standing in nothing but a pair of red lace panties and her silver stilettos. As if on an afterthought, he undid her bun, causing her hair to fall like a black curtain around her shoulders, the ends brushing the hillocks of her naked breasts.

"Oh God, you are so beautiful. The most beautiful, desirable woman I've ever seen," he whispered as his gaze lazily slid down her near-naked body, and then up again, lingering on her nipples, hard and pebbled and tingling with desire.

She squeezed her thighs together as the walls of her sex tightened, then contracted sending warm sticky liquid into the crotch of her panties. She watched his nostrils flare as if he'd picked up the scent of the fluids gushing from inside her. His chest rose and fell as he seemed to struggle to breathe, and his Adam's apple moved frantically up and down as he tried to swallow. His hand clenched and unclenched at his sides as if he were fighting the urge to touch her. And the look in his eyes, well, it was hot, galvanizing.

So this was what it was like to watch a man in heat, she thought wildly.

Her heart pounded against her ribs, causing her achy breasts to bounce on her chest with the erratic rhythm of her shallow breaths. She wanted to tell him that she couldn't breathe, that her entire body was an aching, itching, tingling ball of flesh, that it was a feeling she'd never experienced before—a feeling that was driving her out of her mind.

Compelled involuntarily by her own driving passion, Desire reached her hand toward him. "Chase."

"Not yet," he said gruffly, taking hold of her hands. "Let me enjoy watching you a little while longer. You realize I've never seen you naked."

"According to you, you did when I was three."

He grinned. "Twenty-seven years is a long time to wait for you to grow up into such an exquisite, beguiling nymph." He raised her fingers to his lips, placed them one at a time into his mouth, sucking and releasing each while his eyes, smoldering with passionate and indecent promises, remained transfixed on her face. By the time he wrapped his hot lips around the last finger—the little one on her left hand—Desire's legs gave out from under her. She slumped forward.

He caught her and eased her back against the wall. And while she stood there weakly clinging to him, he raised her hands above her head and curled her fingers around a steel bar that ran the perimeter of the elevator—a bar she swore had been installed for this very purpose.

"Don't let go," he warned, taking a couple steps back from her. "Watch me prepare to be bad with you."

A hot ache grew in Desire's throat as Chase began to unbutton his shirt, starting at the top. She blacked out the thought of people listening outside, and, for the first time in years, she didn't care what anyone thought about her. Tonight, her only wish was to please her man. And if he wanted her in an elevator, he would have her in an elevator.

She stepped out of her dress and kicked it aside as Chase tugged his shirt from his trousers and pushed it off his body. She tightened her hold on the bar when he unfastened the clasp on his trousers, bent forward, and pushed them, along with his black silk boxers down to his ankles. He toed them off and kicked them behind him, his gaze never leaving her face. Before he straightened up to his full height again, she got a quick glance of the tight, dimpled cheeks of his buttocks in the opposite mirrored wall.

With her heart racing out of control, Desire's eyes feasted on the naked man standing in front of her—naked except for his silk black knee-high socks. Never had she seen anything so beautiful. They'd fooled around in the dark during that week of bliss, and wisely so. His chest, broad and muscular, and sporting two pink, pebbled nipples, was covered by a thin mat of curly dark hair. Her heart melted with love and affection at the sight of the pendant she'd given him so long ago. *He's really always been mine*, she thought, as her eyes traveled down to the ribbed contours of his eight-pack stomach, and his powerful hips—hips she knew would be swinging with earth-shattering force against her before the night was out.

But what set off a series of powerful contractions deep inside Desire's womb was the sight of his turgid shaft, long, thick, and crammed tight against his belly. A web of large veins, pulsing with blood, ran the entire length of him, starting at the hairy root of his groin to the broad red head, pointing toward the ceiling. "It's huge," she whispered, as her stomach tightened and seemed to catch on fire.

"Yes, it is," was all he said.

Her throat and mouth went dry when he stepped closer, bringing his raw heat and his natural man scent spiked with the intoxicating smell of musk, cedar, amber, and rum—the domineering fragrances of his *Straight to Heaven* cologne. From the enflamed look in his eyes, Desire had no doubt that his only mission tonight was to take her straight to heaven, right here on the elevator that was still locked into place on the first floor of Hotel Andreas while people walked back and forth outside.

"Now." He stepped closer still, so close that the heat from his body seemed to singe her skin. "Let's indulge in some of those dirty little acts you whispered in my ear." He dipped his head and began dropping feathery kisses on her cheeks, her eyes, and her forehead, while he slowly eased her panties down to her knees.

Shivers of delight followed his touch of exploration as he trailed his hands up the sides of her body, over her hips, and along her torso and arms until he came to her hands and curled his fingers over hers on the bar. Widening his stance, he crouched down, pressed his erection against her thighs and dragged it upward. He trapped her thighs between his knees, holding her immobile when he joined his shaft to her hot dripping sex. He pushed forward, pressing her derrière up against the cool glass and watched the play of emotions in her eyes as the fire blazed inside her. He held her there, panting, his breath hot and heavy on her face as they both savored the raunchy sensations of their sexes fusing.

"My Desire," he whispered as he rubbed against her, sending bolts of lightning catapulting through her entire body. The currents started at her toes and then swiftly spiraled up to her crown at the gentle circular massage he was giving her. As her passion grew, so did the pressure of his thrusts, making her acutely aware of the scope and strength of his flesh.

When she opened her mouth to scream from the force of the pleasure, his mouth closed over hers, devouring her hungry cry. He groaned deeply, and his heart drummed in her ears as he thrust his tongue in and out of her mouth, matching the rhythm of his hips grinding against her. Back and forth, side to side, he rocked her gently until her slick folds parted and the smooth hot ridge of his shaft glided along her sensitive little clit.

"Oh God, oh God, oh God." Desire moaned into his mouth as her body, trapped between Chase and the wall, began to writhe and frisson in unprecedented, unfamiliar, and unabashed rhapsody.

"Yes," he whispered against her mouth as if he was her god responding to her cries. "Yes."

Desire felt one powerful contraction after another building between her legs. Her toes curled inside her stilettos and her fingers tightened around the bar as she began to lose consciousness. "Chase!" she whispered in a breathless plea.

The throaty groan that escaped him went directly down Desire's throat and resonated deep inside her, sending her passion soaring so high, she exploded, screaming her ecstasy into his mouth as her body spasmed violently. She tightened her buttocks and pushed her groin into his as a fountain of hot juices gushed from inside her and ran down her inner thighs. She closed her eyes and held on to the bar as the turbulent waves of passion crashed upon her tender shores, time and time again until her mind went completely blank.

Desire had no idea how long it took for her to climb down from her euphoric ride, but when she opened her eyes, Chase's arms were about her, holding her up, and he was smiling at her, his eyes clouded with love and triumph.

"Did you like that?" he asked, returning her hands to the bar and curling her fingers around them again.

"Yes," she said on a nod. "I've never felt anything so hot and wild."

"That's because you've been playing with little boys who haven't been trained in the art of woman-pleasing."

"No, it's because—" She stopped when he bent down, picked up his shirt, and ripped it in half as if it were a sheet of paper. "Chase, what are you doing?"

"Do you trust me? You trust that I would never do anything to hurt you?"

"Of course, I trust you."

"I would like to bind your hands to the bar, render you completely helpless. May I?"

Desire licked her lips as her mind whirled with libidinous curiosity. "I don't know. It's kind of scary to lose control."

A dreamy intimacy appeared in his eyes. "You said you wanted to be bad," he reminded her. "This is what bad girls do. They relinquish control. They're uninhibited." He shook the two halves of the shirt, his eyes glowing with temptation and reckless audacity.

"There are people outside. I'm sure they heard us. They'll be talking about us." She could think a little more clearly now that some of the sexual tension inside her body had been released.

"What else is new, Desire? They've been talking about us for years. Want to give them something else to talk about? Something good and real."

At his challenge, Desire's sense of mischief suddenly returned. Her brain spun with thoughts of revenge, as Bonnie Raitt's "Something To Talk About" began playing in her head. It would be nice to get back at all those goody-two-shoes who'd ostracized her, condemned her for things she hadn't done, called her a pimp, among other debasing names.

Well, they could all go pimp this. "Oh what the heck. Tie me up, baby. Let's give them something to *really* talk about. Our love."

"Yes, ma'am." He took his time wrapping the two strips to her wrists and then binding them to the bar. "Is it too tight? Can you wiggle your hands?"

"It's fine. I can wiggle. Do I need a safe word?"

"No, darling. It's all pleasure and no pain. I promise. Don't fight it. Just relax and enjoy."

His hands were on her hips, drawing her into his body, his hot erection pressed into her belly this time. He showered kisses on her eyes, along her cheeks, and the corners of her mouth until finally his mouth closed over hers. Their sighs, their groans and moans of pleasure filled the small space around them. He kissed her deeply and thoroughly, his tongue exploring the recesses of her mouth, sending the pit of her stomach into a wild, fiery swirl.

Unabashed, Desire gave herself over to the ecstasy of Chase's tantalizing kisses and the feathery caresses of his hands on her back, her sides, her buttocks, and thighs.

She gasped when his hands crawled along her belly toward her breasts. Tingling frissons rushed up and down her spine when his palms continuously rubbed her hard sensitive nipples until she was panting and shaking from the titillating sensations.

The fire spread to her heart when he closed his hands around her breasts and began to mold, and knead, and stroke, and tweak, while his lips began a slow fiery trail from her mouth, down her chin, and along the sensitive skin of her neck, lower and lower…

Sliding his hands to the underside of her breasts, he cradled them, pushing them upward. He dipped his head, and began to lick and nibble each of her pebbled peaks in turn, rousing a melting sweetness within her, and sending a string of prickly sensations shooting from her nipples, down into her belly, and into her burning groin where his hard shaft was once again rubbing against her softness.

As she moaned and quivered from the onslaught of his lovemaking, he took one breast entirely into his mouth and sucked her ravenously, immediately turning the sweet tingles into powerful electrical shocks that zapped through her.

Desire had no idea that it was possible to derive different kinds of pleasure from different kinds of stimuli, but Chase obviously knew, and he was dishing it out with masterly fervor. She groaned aloud, her body arching, her legs slipping from beneath her as her passion consumed her, drawing her to a height of euphoria she never knew existed. The pressure of his thrusts against her increased as he dragged his lips to the other breast and idolized it as wholeheartedly as he'd done the first.

Her body vibrated with liquid fire, and waves of electrical pulses tunneled through her. Her mind went numb as the pleasure burst over her. She moaned and called out Chase's name, and as tears rolled down her face, and rivers of love juices ran down her legs, he eased away, dropped to his knees, and kissed his way down her heaving stomach. Lower and lower, his mouth feather-touched her with enticing appeal, until his hot lips brushed the dark thatch of neatly trimmed hair at her groin.

"Now. Let's see what you taste like." He spread her legs as far apart as her panties that had slithered down to her ankles would allow, then he parted her flesh with gentle fingers and touched the tip of his tongue to her wet, swollen clit.

"Chaaaaseeeee," she screamed as a flash of fire spread through her.

"Oh, God, you're so sweet." His groan vibrated deep inside her.

He spread her wider and pressed his nose against her. "You smell delightful. Delicious. Intoxicating." He clasped his hands on her buttocks, pulling her into his face as he began to lick her, flick her softly, teasing, from east to west and north to south. He kissed her like he'd kissed her mouth, his tongue going deep to stroke her until she began to come and come and come...

Hot tides of passion blazed through Desire's body when

Chase eased a finger partially inside her and began to move it back and forth as his tongue pirouetted upon her clitoris. She clutched the bar tighter. Her body undulated with each flick, with each stroke as she was heaved time and time again into one paroxysm of pleasure after another. The scorching sensations in her quaking sex mounted in volume and velocity, and moved higher and higher into her belly, across her constricted chest, and into her brain, infusing her mind. The small elevator spun and time and space dissolved as she was swallowed in a boisterous ocean of gratifying bliss. She was the epitome of fire, love, and *desire*.

Chase smiled at the guttural, rumbling sounds coming from Desire's throat. He glanced up to watch her body twisting and coiling, her stomach heaving, her head thrashing from side to side, her hair partially covering her face, which was contorted in rapture, her eyes closed, her mouth opening and closing in unintelligible blubbering as she was trapped in the heat, the vortex of one blistering orgasm after another.

Chase had never seen a woman climax so intensely, her body shake so violently, but then again, he'd never felt this basic, animalistic urge to be this bad with a woman before, and he'd never tied one to the stake, either.

The bad boy he'd put to sleep years ago had been awakened by a combination of facts. Most significant was Desire's eagerness to be restrained, and the fact that even though she was under the impression that they had a stunned audience listening outside, she'd abandoned all inhibitions and was brazenly shrieking out her pleasure, not caring what the world thought.

As another spurt of hot, tangy, musky juices filled his mouth and dribbled down his chin, Chase reluctantly pulled his lips away from Desire's pulsating heat. The harsh throbbing in his cock warned him that if he didn't get inside her soon, he would be coming on the floor of the elevator. He couldn't have that when they were on assignment to make a baby, a grandchild for her dying father.

He pulled her panties from around her ankles and pushed unsteadily to his feet. He lifted her limp, yet trembling legs off the floor, spread-eagled her, and wrapped them around his waist.

Her eyes flew open and grew wide with the knowledge that the time had come for their bodies to be carnally joined. Holding her gaze, he reached down between their bodies and placed the head of his shaft to the entrance of her wet heat.

They both gasped, their chests rising and falling against each other as they strove to breathe. He leaned in and kissed her mouth until the shock of that initial, raw, yet intimate contact wore off. Or had it?

Raising his head, he smiled at her as he pushed forward, in an attempt to get the head in. "Oh, God, you're tight," he hissed, as she stiffened, and her body seemed to push him out.

"Chase," she whispered. "I have— I need—"

"Shh. Don't worry, I'll be gentle," he said, hooking his arms under her thighs, and hoisting her upward until her legs were pressed against his chest, and her silver stiletto-clad feet were pointed straight up to the ceiling.

Satisfied that she was wedged securely between his body and the wall, he took hold of his cock again and glided it across her slick heat, moving it up and down from her opening to her clit and back again until she began to swallow convulsively and moans of ecstasy escaped from her throat. When her legs began to quiver and he felt a new dose of liquid coat his head, Chase pushed in.

She gasped as she arched, and her legs automatically tightened around his head as the succulent walls of her sex constricted around his cock. "Damn it, Desire," he drawled through clenched teeth as he felt the head of his shaft hit the thin resistance of her hymen. He tried to pull back.

"No!" she hissed, locking her ankles behind his head, and shoving her groin into him, the only way she had of keeping them connected.

His heart was full of joy that she'd waited for him, but he was irked that she hadn't told him. He could have hurt her, ripped her apart. "I should untie you," he rasped.

"No, just take me. I want you. This. Here. Now. I've been waiting for this, for you, all my life. I don't want to wait another minute."

He couldn't resist, not even if he wanted to. Placing his hand on her buttock, he gazed deeply into her eyes as he eased back and pushed solidly through the thin barrier. "We're one now," he whispered, and then closed his mouth over hers. He swallowed her scream of pain while his hands caressed her back, her thighs, and her legs in an attempt to ease the friction inside her.

God, it felt wonderful, and he moaned at the delight of her moist heat engulfing his engorged cock. Yet, he stood still, buried halfway inside her, waiting for her tremors to cease. He knew it was time when she began to move against him, gently and carefully.

She pulled her mouth from his and smiled erotically into his eyes. "The pain is gone. Now, make love to me, My Chase."

No other words were necessary.

Hot blood pumped through his veins as he pressed her soft damp body intimately into his, crushing her hard nipples into his chest. They were finally locked so closely together it was difficult to distinguish one heartbeat from the next.

Chase gazed silently into her beautiful misty brown eyes as he began moving back and forth with long, careful strokes, gaining deeper ground with each solid thrust and sheathing himself more possessively into her luscious body. Her stifled cries of pleasure bounced off the walls of the elevator as he pumped deeper and deeper into her.

Her flesh gripped him, squeezed him like a thirsty leech as they danced together to the music of love, burned together in the carnal flames of ecstasy. She was the Queen Bee in his honeycomb, his life's chocolate high, his sugar rush, his addiction, his backbone, the central element of his essence, his everything, his past, his future, *his Desire*.

"Desire," he called as he felt her tighten on the verge of another orgasm, seizing him in the turbulence of her own passion like a fish in a net. As she abandoned herself to the thrills of her own delight, he pumped into her, hard and fast and deep until he felt the familiar tingles begin way down in his groin, and the sharp electrical currents rush up and down his spine. His end had come.

He pulled back and slammed into her, shuddering for one exquisite moment before his hot seed rushed along the length of his shaft and shot with gusto into the welcoming recess of her womb. He pressed against her, giving himself freely over to the earthshattering climax as his body spasmed and his mind went black. He held her while their moans and sighs and labored breathing filled the air.

Once he slipped out of her, Chase untied Desire's wrists and slumped weakly on his back to the floor, pulling her down on top of him. He kissed her damp forehead and tucked her curves neatly into his own contours. As she sighed and burrowed into him, he closed his eyes and savored the lingering aftermath of their first love and baby-making session. It was long overdue.

After a while, Chase raised Desire's head from his neck. "Did I hurt you?" he asked, brushing her hair from her face and soothing her damp brows.

"Just for a tiny second," she said, her eyes drunk with passion.

"Why didn't you tell me you were still a virgin?"

"I wanted to surprise you."

"I'm surprised. And happy." He kissed her lips. "But," he added, slapping her playfully on her butt, "it was torture thinking of you with other men, especially my brother."

"Well, now you know how I've always felt at the thought of you with other women."

"I wish I'd waited for you, too."

A flash of humor crossed her face. "No, you don't."

Chase swallowed the lump in his throat as his heart began to hammer with love for her. "I mean it. You've always been My Desire. I was just waiting for you to grow up. You're all the woman I've ever wanted, needed. I love you, Desire

Summers."

Tears glistened in her eyes. "I love you, too, Chase Hunter." She bit down on her bottom lip as she traced a finger around the outline of the pendant lying on his chest, and then over the words, *Desire's Chase.* "I guess I should have had them engrave *Chase's Desire,* also."

"As a matter of fact, I had something made for you."

"What?" Her eyes sparkled with curiosity.

"I was going to give it to you after dinner and before we made love, but you hijacked my plans with your dirty little demands." He reached for his trousers and fumbled around in the pocket until he found what he was looking for. He pulled out a little black velvet box, and flipped it open.

"Oh my God!" She bolted up and sat on her knees staring at the twenty-four-carat diamond ring shooting sparks every which way. "Chase," she said, "it's huge."

He laughed as he pried the ring from its case. "I love the way you say that."

Her gentle laugh rippled through the air. "Yeah, you would."

Chuckling, he pushed to a sitting position. "See," he said, turning the ring so she could read the inscription on the inside of the white gold band.

She pressed her hands against her heart as tears misted her eyes. "It says *Chase's Desire, Forever and Ever.* Chase, the answer is, yes. I'll marry you."

He tilted his head and frowned. "I didn't ask you, yet."

"Actually, you did. Well, you implied. When you took my innocence, you whispered that we were one. Prove that you meant it." She held out her left hand, wiggling her fingers in his face. "Put your money where your…" She gave his semihard shaft a heated glance that made it throb with the anticipation of returning to her tight, sweet moistness, again and again. "Where your joystick had been," she finished, smiling provocatively into his face.

Chase threw back his head and let the laughter rip from his throat. "Such a demanding little hussy you are, and dirty minded, too."

"Don't start complaining now, mister. You got what you wanted. And if you know what's good—"

He leaned in and sucked on her lips, shutting her up. When he was certain she'd gotten the message, he pulled back and knelt in front of her. He took her hand, and gazed deeply into her eyes. "Desire Shelby Summers, will you take me, Chase William Hunter, to be your lawful wedded husband, to have and to keep, for better or worse, for richer or poorer, in sickness and in health, to whisper dirty little requests in my ears and commit lewd acts of debauchery in public places with me, to obey my every sexual command, as I have obeyed yours and promise to continue to obey for the rest of my life, to bear my children, to grow old with me, to love, cherish, and adore me forever, as I promise to love, cherish and adore you even beyond the shores of death?"

"Yes. Yes. I take you, and ditto."

Tears were streaming down her face, yet her body shook with laughter as he slipped the ring on her finger.

"I love you so much," she said, throwing her arms about him. "I promise to make you very happy, Chase."

"I already am, darling."

She pulled out of his arms and sat on the floor, staring at the ring. "It fits perfectly. How did you know my size? When did you buy it?"

He settled beside her and laced his arms around her. "I bought it with my first…" He paused. She didn't need to know that he'd spent his first quarter of a million dollars on her. "I bought it several years ago."

"You've had it that long? You knew we'd be together all that time?"

"I was hoping."

"I wish I'd known."

He placed a hand under her chin. "Don't. We are here now, right where we belong in each other's arms. We'll get married as soon as possible, and then spend the rest of our lives making up for lost time."

She kissed him. "I can't wait for the world to know that I belong to you."

"I think they already do, sweetheart."

"Oh my God, I can't believe what we just did. Suppose Adam throws you out of his hotel for indecent behavior?"

"Then he'll also have to kick out Bryce and Kaya, Massimo and Shaina, and himself and Tashi. They've all made love in one elevator or another in this hotel, among other semipublic places."

"How do you know all this?"

"I'm kind of one of the boys now. They inducted me into their circle when we met in *Baia Degli Amanti*."

She laughed. "I almost forgot you're a billionaire. I just made love with a billionaire."

"Want to do it again?"

"You bet. We have a lot of years to make up. We'll be doing it all night and all day tomorrow. I hope you took your vitamins this morning, Mr. Bennett, Mr. B, Mr. Hunter or whatever you call yourself tonight."

"I'm simply *Desire's Chase* tonight, love." He reached up and pushed the hold button, and as the elevator began to ascend, he pulled her in for a piping hot kiss that lasted all the way to the top floor. "By the way," he said as the doors opened, "I might as well tell you that the elevator is soundproof. Nobody heard us."

"Chase Hunter, you will pay dearly for that."

"I'm counting on it, baby. I'm counting on it." He pulled her to her feet, picked her up effortlessly into his arms, and walked out of the elevator, leaving their clothes behind.

When the automatic sliding doors of the penthouse opened, Chase carried his bride-to-be over the threshold and straight into the bathroom where he joined her in the Jacuzzi for some bubbly fun. Afterward, he carried her to his candlelit bedroom, laid her down on his enormous bed and took his time worshiping her sweet, brown body, pleasuring her over and over again throughout the night, and into the early morning.

CHAPTER SEVENTEEN

"Do you ladies need any help?" Chad asked as he stepped out of the bathroom next to the kitchen.

"No, we're good," Desire's mother said.

Desire gave him a nervous smile. "Why don't you join Daddy in the living room? We'll be right in."

"Yes, dear. Dinner was delish."

"Only because I didn't make it."

"I'm not marrying you for your cooking, darling." He blew her a conspiratorial kiss, and walked away.

"Poor man. He'll be eating out a lot," Desire's mother said in jest as she scooped blueberry-plum crisp into dessert bowls. "When you invited us over, I thought you'd be cooking, and frankly I was a little worried."

Desire smiled as she topped off the crisp with vanilla bean ice cream. "Like mother, like daughter, Mom."

"You got me there, baby." Her mother paused to look Desire up and down. "By the way, I've been meaning to tell you that I love your dress. It's gorgeous. Is it new?"

Desire blushed as she took a quick glance at her pink and black butterfly lace mini dress. Since she'd had no other clothes at the hotel but the gown she'd worn to dinner the previous night, Chase had gone down to the hotel's boutique to purchase this dress half an hour before she had to leave to meet her patents. "Yes, it's new." She licked a speck of ice cream from her finger.

"Is it a replica of one of our favorite designers?"

"It's an Alexander McQueen. And it's the real thing. Not a replica," she replied, deciding to be honest about at least one thing tonight.

Her mother dropped the serving spoon on the counter, her admiration turning to reproof. "Desire Summers, McQueen is one of the top designers in the country. It must have cost a small fortune. Remember what I told you about letting your overnight success go to your head, baby. You should be saving your money, especially now that you're getting married. What would your fiancé say if he knew you'd spent that kind of money on a dress?"

"He'd say that I look beautiful since he bought it for me."

"Chad bought you that? Wow, his practice must be doing a lot better than I thought if he can afford to throw that kind of money at a dress."

"Believe me, my fiancé can afford it. If he couldn't, I would have made him return it." Her heart skipped a beat as she glanced through the kitchen window to see Azura's car entering the Hunters' driveway. Soon, soon she'd be able to tell the whole truth. She picked up the tray with a stack of glasses and a pitcher of iced tea and headed out of the kitchen.

"Fancy takeout dinners and designer dresses. I still say you should be saving for your children's college," her mother said, following behind her with the tray laden with the bowls of dessert. "Kids are expensive."

Desire just smiled, happy she and Chase had thought to swap out the huge diamond for the simpler, more modest one Chad had bought her. It had been Chad's idea. The attorney in him had seen the potential problem and the barrage of questions that would have given them away. She wished she'd thought to change her dress before her family arrived.

The men stood up when they walked into the living room, but her mother shooed them back to their seats. "Sit, sit. You cleared the dinner table and put the leftovers away. This is ours." She placed the tray on the coffee table and began handing out the bowls, utensils, and napkins.

Desire poured the iced tea, grinning at her mother's take-charge attitude, a trait that had earned her Evergreen's Principal of the Year several years in a row. She was orderly, organized, and always did her fair share of the work, but her school had thrived because of her ability to match the right staff member with the right duty. She'd run her home the same way, and tonight, she'd taken charge of Desire's dinner party, doling out orders as if she still lived here.

"This brings back memories of when we used to entertain in our younger days, doesn't it, Ruth?" her father asked her mother.

"It sure does, honey. And just like Desire, we served takeout. Not as elaborate as this, but it was either takeout, or lose our friends."

Desire's heart warmed at her father's enthusiastic chuckle.

"Now, Chad and Desire are picking up the baton," he added. "Do you intend to live here, in this house, after you're married?"

Desire's hand shook as she set the pitcher down on the tray.

"We haven't planned that far yet," Chad answered, picking up on her hesitation to string another lie on to the chain they had already forged.

"Mmm. This is delicious," her mother stated around a mouthful of the crisp. "I'll have to walk an extra mile tomorrow, but that's okay. It's worth it." She rubbed her stomach. "I think I need to make a little room though. I gorged myself on dinner." She headed for the stairs.

"I should probably skip dessert," Desire said, as she sat down next to Chad on a mini sofa facing the porch. "I want to fit into my wedding gown."

"Since you brought it up, I'd love to hear about your wedding plans," her father said, as he took his first bite of the crisp.

She closed her eyes in exasperation when she realized she'd opened the door to the conversation she'd been trying to delay all evening. "Remember, Daddy, we have to wait until Chad's mom arrives before we start talking about the wedding."

"You could at least tell me where the ceremony will take place. Chad, you and your family are members of Evergreen Congregational, but I think you should get married at Granite Falls Community Church since that's where the bride's family worships. No offense."

"We're not getting married in a church," Desire said, in a low voice.

"Not in a church? You can't be serious."

"I'm—we're very serious, Daddy. We're exchanging our vows in Evergreen's Garden Maze."

He set his bowl down and sat forward, his hands on his knees. "The garden maze? Are you out of your mind? No daughter of mine is getting married in a garden maze. As long as I'm paying for this wedding, I have a say in where it takes place."

I'm not asking you to pay for it, and I know you won't when you hear whom I'm marrying. "No, you don't have any say, Daddy." Desire met her father's authoritative stare. A vision of him ripping up Chase's letter flashed across her mind. "It's what I want. What *we* want," she added, smiling at Chad.

Last night and earlier today, during their few breaks from lovemaking, Desire and Chase had discussed the details of their wedding ceremony, honeymoon, and her dinner party.

Chase had suggested that perhaps the Hunters should skip tonight's dinner. He wanted her to enjoy her meal with her family since it might be the last time the Summerses would dine together for a while—at least until her father's opinion of him changed. She couldn't argue with him, but she'd been concerned that her family would find it strange that Chad was absent during the discussion of his own wedding plans.

After a quick phone call, Chad had agreed to keep up the farce. Azura had deliberately taken a shift at the hospital so she wouldn't have to lie about declining the dinner invitation, and

Chase was keeping a low profile until Chad called to let him know that dinner was over.

Chase had also told her about his phone call with Lisa. He'd suggested that since Lisa was invited, Desire should talk with her before the party. Unfortunately, or perhaps fortunately for Desire, Lisa had left for Rhode Island early this morning to take care of a problem in one of her company's stores. She was not expected back until tomorrow. By then, Desire's family would have already been told, and she would break the news to Lisa herself.

With their conspiracy in motion, Desire and Chad had requested that they delay discussing the wedding plans until dessert when Azura would join them. Her parents still had no idea that Chase was in town. They'd talked about old times, about her and Chad growing up next to each other, work, careers, and a host of other pleasant topics while they feasted on a four-course meal that started with pomegranate spritzers, prosciutto cantaloupe bites, and a variety of seafood appetizers, followed by a tomato and watermelon salad. The main course, rosemary braised lamb, was complemented with roasted garlic mashed potatoes, and grilled vegetables.

Desire had ordered takeout from Ristorante Andreas on her way home. She'd chosen lamb because it was her father's favorite. From the way her family had devoured the dishes, she knew it wasn't just her mother who'd been happy she hadn't cooked. The meal wasn't cheap, but since she was about to marry a billionaire, money wasn't an issue.

Besides, if it weren't for that said billionaire holding her captive in his bachelor penthouse pad for almost twenty-four straight hours, she might have had time to throw some ingredients together. Butterflies fluttered around in Desire's stomach, but she quickly suppressed the visions of Chase and her tangled up in each other's arms in his penthouse. Neither of them had wanted to leave, but they knew that the sooner their families were aware of their intentions, the sooner they could get on with their lives.

"Are you challenging me, Desire?" her father asked,

breaking into her stroll down memory lane.

"Yes, Daddy," Desire said without a moment's hesitation. *I should have challenged you twelve years ago. If I had, the grandchildren you want so badly would be sitting at your feet right now.* "I love and respect you, Daddy," she added, meeting his belligerent stare, "but this is my wedding, and I make the decisions."

"We have a beautiful church. Even the billionaires realize the importance and sanctity of exchanging their vows in church. You planned that wedding, Desire. It's what made you famous."

"She just wants something different, Mr. Summers." Chad, who was aware of the significance of the garden, came to her defense.

"Enough with the 'Mr. Summers,' Chad. You're marrying my daughter. It's time you start calling me Dad."

Biting her lower lip, Desire looked away, out the window to the porch, praying silently for Chase and Azura to show up soon so she could stop lying to her family.

"What's wrong with our church that you don't want to get married in it, Desire?"

Turning her head, she recaptured her father's gaze. "Nothing's wrong with the church, Daddy. It's just that I want to exchange my vows in a place that means something to me."

"Are you saying the church means nothing to you?" He took a sip of iced tea.

"Of course not. The maze is where I first declared my love for Ch—for my fiancé. It's where I want to pledge my heart and my soul to him." *My body, too.* "Is that so bad, Daddy?"

"Is what so bad?" her mother asked, walking back into the room and taking a seat next to her father.

"Our daughter is planning to get married in the garden."

Her mother's eyebrows raised in question. "Evergreen Garden Maze?"

Desire nodded.

"I think that's very romantic, baby."

"Thanks, Mom."

"Why are we discussing your wedding?" she asked, picking

up her bowl of fruit crisp. "Weren't we supposed to wait for Azura?"

"The joining of two souls is sacred," her husband said, completely disregarding his wife's concern about waiting for Desire's neighbor. "A wedding ceremony should only take place in a church, by a minister, in the sight of God."

"Pastor Kelly will be performing the ceremony," Chad said. "I'm sure he'll bring God along, since they always travel together, sir."

"Good one, Chad," Desire's mom said on a snicker.

Desire giggled, warmly remembering Chad's uncanny ability to lighten any dark situation with his humor and wit. If she weren't in love with Chase, and if Chad weren't gay, she knew they would have found a way to make it work if she'd been pressured into marrying him.

Her father raised his hand, bringing her and her mother's humor to a halt. "When I said I want to walk you down the aisle, I meant it," he said. "The aisle is in the church where God is."

"Are you telling me that God can only be found in church? If that's the case, then I guess the millions of folks who can't go to church for one reason or the other are eternally doomed. Come on Gerry, even you know you sound ridiculous."

Defeated, her father grumbled something under his breath and cut his eyes at his wife, much in the same way Desire did when she was backed into a corner. Stubborn as he was, her heart warmed with affection for him, even as her anxiety grew about what his reaction would be when he came face-to-face with his future son-in-law.

Her mother took a sip of iced tea. "The garden maze is a very romantic place to have a wedding, and as the mother-of-the-bride, I give my approval and blessings. Since your father already opened up the discussion, have you begun working on a guest list yet? Who's coming to this wedding?"

"Well, we—" A mixture of feelings surged through her at the sound of footsteps on the porch steps. Finally, her reinforcements had arrived. She swallowed her panic when the door opened and Lisa walked in.

"Hey, everybody," she said in her cheerful Lisa voice. "Sorry I couldn't make dinner, but I'm here now."

"Lisa," Desire whispered. "What are you doing here? I mean, I thought you weren't coming back until around midnight."

"I thought so, too. But it turns out that I didn't even have to drive to Rhode Island, according to the boss of my boss." She stepped inside and closed the door behind her. "Seems I got back just in time for dessert." She eyed the bowls of crisp with a hungry glint in her eyes.

"You can have mine." Desire held out the bowl she hadn't touched. She hadn't eaten much at dinner either, but neither her parents nor Chad seemed to notice her lack of appetite.

Lisa snatched the bowl from Desire's hand. "You shouldn't be eating this anyway, not when you have to fit into that lovely wedding dress." She flopped down on the other end of the sectional, dropped her purse on the floor, and delved into the dessert.

"You found a dress already?" Desire's mother asked.

"Yes, Mom. I um—I placed one on hold at Princess Brides earlier today." The exclusive boutique was close to Hotel Andreas, so she'd stopped there on her way home and had fallen in love with the dress that had arrived yesterday.

Chase had told her that he wanted her to have everything and anything she wanted to make her wedding day perfect. He'd said that the sky was the limit and he'd handed her an American Express card with her name on it. Desire had wept when she realized that he'd been planning to include her in his life during the years they'd been separated. How could she ever doubt that he was devoted to her?

"Desire, that's the most sophisticated and expensive bridal boutique around. Their cheapest dress costs five times more than the most expensive one at Bride of the Day. How can you—"

"The groom is paying for it. He can well afford it, Mrs. Summers," Chad said with a smile.

"I hope so," Lisa said around a mouthful of dessert. "Because that dress is to-die-for."

"You already saw it?" Desire's mother asked with a trace of jealousy in her voice.

"Desire texted me a picture this afternoon. Wait until you see it, Aunt Ruth." Lisa reached for her handbag.

"Not yet, Lisa," Desire said hastily to stop her cousin from messing up her plan, even more than her unexpected appearance already had. She watched her mother's envious pout. "I sent it to Lisa when I thought she would miss dinner," she said. "I was planning to show it to everyone else at the same time once Mrs. Hunter gets here."

"Sorry, cuz. Me and my big mouth." Lisa gave her an apologetic smile. "But I still say 'Yes' to the dress." She grinned at Chad and gave him a thumbs-up. "You're the man."

"Thanks, Lisa. Desire's happiness equals my happiness. By the way, what was the problem with your company?" he asked, astutely and diplomatically taking the opportunity to change the subject, to Desire's delight.

"Several shipments we were expecting last night never arrived. The drivers of one of the shipping companies we use went on strike without notice. Inside sabotage of some kind. Anyway, I was told that all regional managers were expected at headquarters, but it turned out not to be true." She sighed and poured herself a glass of iced tea.

"So you drove down there for nothing," her aunt said.

"Yep, a huge waste of my day. Good thing they're paying for my gas. Headquarters is scrambling to find the truckloads of merchandise that were already en route, and trying to secure new drivers. But that's the big wigs' problem." She took a sip from her glass. "Let's not dwell on that. We have a wedding to plan," she said, grinning at Desire. "What did I miss?"

Desire's stomach tightened as her mind jumped ahead to the moment when Lisa would learn that she was in love with Chase and that they had slept together two days after he'd slept with Lisa. Lisa would have every right to feel used, but what was done was done. Desire couldn't let her cousin be humiliated in front of her family and the Hunters like this. Lisa didn't deserve it. Desire stood up. "Lisa, can we—"

"Your cousin is getting married in the garden maze." Her father waved his hand, motioning Desire to sit back down.

"What's wrong with that, Uncle Gerry?"

"Your uncle thinks it's unholy to get married anywhere but in a church, but I think it's romantic."

"I'm with you, Aunt Ruth. The important thing is that the bride and groom are happy. And they look pretty happy to me." She tossed a grin at Chad and Desire. "You all set a date yet? I need to start planning a bridal shower. I already have the perfect venue in mind. It's gonna be the bomb."

"That's right. You haven't given us a date." Her mother sat forward and placed her empty bowl on the coffee table. "Have you set one?"

Desire glanced at Chad who shrugged questioningly. Of course, he knew nothing about the details of the wedding she and Chase had planned. She dropped into her seat, her mind fluttering away in anxiety. "We're supposed to wait for Mrs. Hunter," she said, stalling. She'd hoped that Chase and Azura would be present by the time these questions were hurled at them. Chase had been alerted. Azura had been home for a while. So what on earth was keeping them?

"Oh come on, who knows when she'll get out of work? We're already talking about it," Lisa prompted.

Desire took a deep breath as all eyes trained on her, even Chad's. "It's on Tuesday, day after tomorrow."

"That soon? What's the rush? Are you pregnant, girl?"

The questions hit her simultaneously, but the one from Lisa packed a fierce punch.

Desire wrapped her arms around her stomach and stared cautiously at the stunned faces, including Chad's. She could have conceived last night, or this morning, or this afternoon.

"Oh my God, you are!" Lisa took her silence as confirmation. She waved her hands above her head and stamped her feet on the floor like a schoolgirl who'd just heard the boy she liked broke up with her biggest rival. "That's why you're in a hurry to get hitched. When did you lose it? Up until last month, you were a virgin. Well, at least that's what you told me. Tsk, tsk, tsk. Chad, you sneaky—"

"Lisa!" Desire's father stomped his foot, bringing silence raining down upon them.

While Lisa sat back and pursed her lips, Desire took in the look of astonishment on her mother's face. She had no idea if it was the fact that Desire had remained a virgin all these years, or the possibility that she was going to be a grandmother sooner than she thought that had rendered her mother speechless. Even though Ruth Summers had always been the one to remain calm when her family was in turmoil, it was hard to know how she was currently feeling. Her father's reaction was definitely a different matter, and true to his nature.

Desire held her breath as he placed his bowl down on the coffee table, took a sip of iced tea, and then pushed to his feet with a lot more vigor than she'd seen in him for a long time. In the next instant, he was towering over her and Chad. She held Chad's hand, ready to defend him if her father dared to attack.

"Chad," he began, "I always thought you were a respectable young man, so the other night when my daughter told me you'd proposed and that she'd accepted, I was filled with joy. But the thoughts of you making a baby—"

"Daddy!" Desire could not sit idly and let her father rip into Chad.

"I'm not done, Desire," he said, not taking his eyes from Chad.

"Yes, you are. I won't let you accuse Chad of something he—"

"Accuse him? I'm not accusing him of anything. I'm thanking him for making my last two wishes come true. Stand up, both of you." He stepped back and opened his arms.

Still reeling from the shock of her father's reaction, Desire looked at Chad, shaking her head, letting him know that he didn't have to pretend any longer, that it was over, but he pulled her to her feet and into her father's bear hug.

Her mother, with tears in her eyes, and Lisa grinning like an idiot, joined in the cheers, hugging and kissing and applauding them, patting her on the belly and Chad on the back until…

"I guess I missed whatever you're excited about," a voice said.

All eyes turned to the door. Desire's heart skipped at the sight of Azura standing just inside the screen door. She had changed from her scrubs into a striped blue and white summer dress. Chase was nowhere in sight.

"We're going to be grandparents, Azura." Desire's mother ran over to hug her.

"We are?" Azura's brows furrowed as she stared at her son, and then her future daughter-in-law. "Desire, are you expecting?" she asked, walking over to the group, still huddled together.

"I—um—I—" She dropped her gaze at the realization that Azura was the only person in the room who knew exactly where Desire had spent last night and most of today.

Chase had called to tell his mother where they were after she'd tried repeatedly and unsuccessfully to get in touch with him. Desire also knew that Chad hadn't yet told his mother that he was gay, and that she might be concerned that Desire didn't know the father of her hypothetical child, because at this point, that's all it was. *Hypothetical.* She could only imagine the thoughts running through the woman's head, especially since she herself had been caught in a vindictive, jealous war between two brothers.

Azura placed a hand on Chad's cheek. Her eyes were flat and burning with unspoken turmoil. "Are you claiming this, son?" she asked quietly.

Chad shook his head. "No, Mom. I'm not. I can't. It's not mine."

Azura dropped her hand and closed her eyes, her mouth moving in a silent prayer of thanks.

"Desire, what are you saying? What is he saying?" Her mother's voice was a dull cry.

"You've been sleeping with someone else other than Chad?" Lisa asked. "Dang, Desire. When you're out, you're out, huh?"

"How can you do this to us, Desire? How can you be engaged to one man and carrying another's child? I didn't raise you like this. Hasn't this family suffered enough already?" Her father's voice seemed to shake the very foundation of the house.

The disdain and accusations ripped through Desire, rendering her motionless. The fact that she'd been a thirty-year-old virgin didn't matter to her father. All he could see were the headlines with the Summers family name once again in the middle of a scandal.

She opened her mouth in an attempt to clarify the confusion, to tell them that if she were indeed pregnant she was in love with the father of her baby and that they were going to be married. There would be no scandal, but nothing came out.

"Who's the father of your child, Desire?" her father demanded.

"Okay, hold up!" Azura raised her hands in the air, demanding silence. "It's too soon for Desire to know if she's pregnant."

"Too soon?" her father shouted. "What do you mean by too soon?"

"You work in the maternity ward at the hospital, Azura," her mother stated. "Is Desire your patient?"

Azura smiled lovingly at Desire. "I had no idea you were a virgin all these years, that you'd kept yourself for him. I understand the bond. It's true love."

"What bond, and who are you talking about?" her mother asked.

Azura turned to Desire's parents. "Ruth, Gerry, I haven't consulted with your daughter as a patient. I haven't consulted with her at all. But I know this much, if your daughter is pregnant, the child belongs to—"

"Chase!" Lisa screamed.

CHAPTER EIGHTEEN

A chilling hush swept through the room, temporarily freezing everything and everyone.

Desire closed her eyes and fell back into her seat as she found herself swimming in a sea of nausea. This wasn't the way her parents were supposed to find out about her and Chase. This was...

"What are *you* doing here?"

At the sound of her father's incensed question breaking through the tension, she opened her eyes and turned her head in the direction of everyone's gaze. Hope soared inside her when she saw Chase's powerful figure standing at the door. He looked handsome, sexy in a pair of jeans and a white polo shirt. His dark hair brushing his wide shoulders added to his aura of strength and virility.

All her anxiety melted away at the vague sensual light that passed between them. Her nausea dissipated and happiness flooded her being. The walls of her sex contracted, and her nipples hardened and tightened as visions of the countless lewd acts they'd already committed together raced through her mind.

Her father dragged his gaze from Chase and stared judgmentally down at her. "Did you know he was back in town, Desire?"

Before Desire could respond, Chase strolled toward her father and extended a hand. "Hello, Mr. Summers. It's nice to see you again."

Ignoring his outstretched hand, her father turned to Azura, his eyes livid. "When did he return, Azura?" he demanded, as if Chase wasn't even present.

"Three days ago," Lisa interjected. "I picked him up at the airport. He didn't want anybody to know he was back. I guess the cat's out the bag, Mr. Bennett."

Desire wasn't surprised at the hostility in Lisa's voice or the rancid stare she gave Chase.

"Mr. Bennett?" her mother said. "Who's Mr. Bennett?"

"Oh hell!" Chad exclaimed, and then burst out laughing, causing everyone to stare at him as if he'd gone mad. He dropped down beside her and kissed her forehead. "I love you, you know that. I've always loved you, but it's time to end this madness."

Desire nodded. "I know, and I love you, too."

He stood and addressed her parents. "Mr. and Mrs. Summers, I should never have asked your daughter to marry me."

"But you just told her you love her," her father said in a voice that had lost its fury.

"I do, sir, but not in the way a man should love the person with whom he plans to spend the rest of his life."

"Chad," her mother whispered, "is it because of the baby not being yours? Did you think it was yours all this time?"

"No, Mrs. Summers. I thought nothing of the sort."

"I see what's happening here." Her father placed his hands on Chad's shoulders. "You're a good man, Chadwick. You're obviously marrying my daughter to keep her from falling into disgrace."

"I'm not a good man. I proposed to Desire for my own selfish reasons. She accepted because she loves you, Mr. Summers."

Her father shook his head. "I don't understand what you're

saying."

"You will, sir." Chad turned to his mother and took her hands. "Mom," he said, looking directly into her eyes, "there's something I should have told you a long time ago. The thing is—I'm gay."

There was a long brittle silence, and then Azura whispered, "Gay? You—you're gay?" She fell weakly on to the sectional, her hands pressed into her chest.

Poor woman, to learn about her son's sexual orientation in the middle of this chaos, Desire thought, as Chad dropped down next to his mother and began whispering to her, clearly in an attempt to calm her nerves.

Desire turned her attention to her family as each began shouting at will. "He's gay? Did he say gay? He can't be gay. He doesn't look gay. When did he start being gay? He's dated women. I don't believe this. He's been in the closet all this time? Oh my God…"

As the voices rose to a fever pitch, Desire shot to her feet and ran to Chase. He met her halfway. His arms folded around her and his sweet kiss immediately quieted her rattled nerves. She wrapped her arms around his waist and gave herself over to the heady sensation of his scent, his heat, the beating of his heart against hers, the calm that came from his comforting nearness.

Reluctantly, he raised his head and smiled into her eyes as if they were the only two people in the room. "I'm sorry. I should have been here sooner."

"You're here now. It'll all be over soon."

"Oh my God, you two are together?" Lisa's voice blasted through the din.

Desire turned, ice spreading in her stomach. When Lisa had shouted Chase's name a few minutes ago, Desire had thought Lisa knew that Desire and Chase had reconciled and had spent the night together. But her cousin's current question was a clear indication that Lisa's excited outburst had been a knee-jerk reaction to Chase's sudden appearance at the door.

Chase's comforting hands on her shoulders brought her

little relief. The very thing she feared most was about to happen. Lisa was going to spill the beans about her night with Chase in the trailer in Azura's backyard before Desire had a chance to explain her side of the story to her parents.

"Who's together?" Her father stared at her and Chase standing too close for his comfort, she imagined, but yet apparently still refusing to believe his eyes.

"Desire? You and Chase?" Her mother clamped her hand over her mouth.

"You told me you were over him," Lisa stated, walking up to them in a clearly belligerent manner.

"I thought I was. I'm sorry, Lisa. We're in love. We pledged our hearts to each other when I turned eighteen. We never stopped loving each other all these years."

Desire watched her father, standing next to her mother, his hands fisted, his nostrils flaring, and his face contorted as he tried to assess the barrage of information pouring into his brain. Desire held his stone-cold stare.

If the evening had gone as she'd planned, her father might have been inclined to give Chase the benefit of a doubt when he learned that Lewis Carron—the man he'd encouraged her to date—was the one who had caused her humiliation that night. He definitely would not forgive the fact that Chase had slept with his niece-in-law, and then his daughter in the space of two days. Well, as far as she was concerned, he had no one to blame but himself. If he hadn't destroyed Chase's letter, none of them would be in this mess.

"So he's the one you slept with," Lisa said. "And if you're pregnant, it's his."

"Lisa. I'm sorry." Desire took a step toward her. "I was going—"

Lisa shrank back. "Save it, cuz." She transferred her glare to Chase, who hadn't yet said a word during the entire ordeal. "You were in love with her, yet you had sex with me the other night? You used me. What kind of man does that?"

"A stupid one," Chase finally said. "It was a mistake. I'm sorry. I will regret it for the rest of my life."

"Oh, Desire. How could you?" Her mother collapsed next to Azura, who was now silently looking on, apparently dumbfounded.

"Take your hands off my daughter, you filthy bastard!" Her father charged toward them, his fists raised, ready to throw a punch.

"Daddy!" Desire placed herself between her father and Chase, but Chase pushed her behind him in one swift motion. From the corner of one eye, she saw Chad shoot to his feet and charge over to hold her father back.

"Mr. Summers, you should hear the whole story before you attack my brother. Things aren't always what they seem. It's not black and white here, no pun intended. There are layers and layers of gray in this conundrum," Chad stated, in a lawyerly manner.

Her father shook Chad's hands off his shoulder. "I don't give a damn about the gray layers. This son of a—"

"Hey!" both Chase and Chad shouted simultaneously.

Chase marched up to her father. "You can call me whatever ugly names you want, but don't you dare disrespect my mother, Mr. Summers. Or I will be forced to punch you, sir!"

"Stop it! All of you! Stop it right now!" Desire screamed at the top of her lungs.

The room went silent and everyone stared at her as if Medusa's head had suddenly grown out of her neck. This was the first time in her life that Desire had made a demand of anybody, and it felt damn good to be in charge, to be the center of attention, at her own command. She basked in the knowledge of her newly found power. "I am tired of all this bitterness, this contention among us. We're supposed to be friends, family—"

"But Desire—"

"Daddy!" She glared at him. Her patience with him had run its course. "I swear, if I hear another antagonistic word out of you, any of you, I will hop on a plane with Chase tonight and fly to the outermost corner of the world, and none of you will hear from us for a long time." She splayed her hand over her belly. "If I'm pregnant, you won't see your grandchild until he or she is walking, if ever. Is that what you want?" She spoke to all, but she held her father's infuriating gaze.

"Good," she said, when the silence continued. While they watched, she pulled Chad's ring from her finger and placed it in his palm. "Chad, thanks for what you did for me tonight, but in hindsight, I realize that we should have been truthful and not try to pull the wool over my parents' eyes. I was too afraid of how they would react, which is exactly how they did react. So it was all in vain. No situation founded on lies and deceit ever ends well. You just made a huge announcement about your life. Your mother didn't even get a chance to process the news before we were all caught in this hailstorm of hate."

"Oh, I processed it, Desire," Azura said, coming over to stand next to her youngest son. "It was shocking to hear, but he's my son, my baby boy. I love him, no matter what he is. What I'm upset about is that he thought he needed to hide it from me."

"I'm sorry about that, Mom." Chad kissed her on the forehead.

"I feel the same way," Desire's mom said, smiling at Chad. "You're still the same Chad, the little boy I watched grow up next door. The fact that you're gay doesn't change how I feel about you."

"Me, too," Lisa chimed in. "No wonder you always look so sharp. I'm gonna have to take you wardrobe shopping with me now."

"Anytime, Lisa," Chad said, grinning at her.

"How long have you known he was gay?" her father asked in a stiff voice.

"Since Friday." And that was all she was going to say. She turned to her parents. "Mom, Dad, I'm sorry for lying to you tonight. Forgive me."

Her father just stared at her.

"It's okay, baby," her mother said. "I understand why you thought you had to lie."

"Not really, Mom." She took Chase's hand and smiled up at him. "Can I have my ring?"

"With pleasure, darling." He fished it out of his pocket and placed it on her finger.

She held it up, sparks shooting across the room. "Chase and I got engaged last night. We're getting married on Tuesday."

"Do you see the size of that rock?" Lisa screamed.

The women flocked to her, ogling over the ring and congratulating her and Chase with hugs and kisses.

"Is it real? How can a farm worker afford a ring like this?" Lisa asked.

Desire swallowed and glanced from Chase, to Azura, to Chad, the only ones present who knew about Chase's success and the fact that he was a billionaire. "Um, I—"

"By eating lots of corn and saving his money." Chase winked at her. "But Desire is worth every penny."

"Gerry," her mother called to her father, who had begun marching toward the door. "Your daughter just announced that she's engaged, and getting married in a couple days. Can't you put aside your anger and congratulate her, show her you love her?"

"She knows I love her, but I will never consent to this—" He waved his hand in the air. "This, whatever you want to call it. Did you forget what he did to her, and then took off, leaving her here to be scorned and ridiculed? And the same day he returns, he sleeps with her cousin, and then violates Desire, too. What's there to congratulate? He was scum then, and he's still scum!"

"Chase had nothing to do with what happened at the country club, Daddy. He was framed, set up, and forced to leave town."

"By whom?" Her mother's voice was a choked whisper.

"By Lewis Carron, my former boss's son," Chase provided.

"The man you wanted me to date." Desire held her father's gaze. "He's the one who switched that thumb drive. He wanted Chase out of the way, and he had no qualms about hurting me to get what he wanted. Chase was just his first victim. He has committed a string of crimes since then. Embezzlement, money laundering, tax evasion, extortion, you name it; he's done it. He's the scumbag, Dad. Not Chase."

"Lies. Lies!" her father shouted, while the rest of her family just stared wordlessly at Chase. "Videos don't lie. You slept with those women a couple days before the talent show, after you supposedly told my daughter that you loved her."

"I confess to my participation in the video, Mr. Summers. The video was taken without my knowledge six months prior to the date on the time stamp. I was a stupid kid back then, but I did not publish it. What was I to gain from doing something that distasteful? Why would I want to hurt Desire and commit professional suicide when I was trying to make something of myself, prove to her that I'd changed, that I was the kind of man she could trust?"

"Then why did you leave? Why didn't you stay and fight for your reputation, for her?"

"I always wondered about that, too, Chase," her mother added. "Why would Lewis set you up, and why didn't you stay and clear your name instead of running off and hiding on a corn farm in Iowa? Desire had nowhere to run, nowhere to hide. It was very cowardly of you."

Desire took a quick glance at the members of the Hunter family. She read the tension on all their faces. "Mom, Dad, it's not—"

"He left because of me," Azura said.

"Mom, don't."

"Chase, I need to do this, son. You're marrying into a family whose scandal you already know. It's only fair that they know the secrets of the family their daughter is marrying into. We all have our skeletons in the closets."

"You can say that again, Mom," Chad stated.

A faint smile flashed across Azura's face. "Now it's my turn to step out of the closet." She sighed. "It's a long story, so I suggest we all sit down," she added, claiming the mini sofa that Chad and Desire had previously occupied.

Desire and Chase sat hand in hand on one side of the sectional, while her mother and Lisa sat on the other end, and Chad took a chair under a window. Her father folded his arms and kept his rigid position at the door.

Azura clasped her hands together on her lap. "I have one request before I begin," she said, gazing at her audience, who waited expectantly. "I need to get through this story without interruptions. Hold all questions until the end, or I won't be able to finish. I do need to finish. Understood?"

Everyone nodded in compliance.

She cleared her throat. "Chase was three years old when I first arrived in Granite Falls. I told everyone that I was from Iowa because that's where he was born. What I failed to reveal was that I'm originally from Arizona. The only person who was privy to that information was my late husband, Chadwick. I simply told him that I left Arizona when I was a teenager, but I didn't tell him why I left."

Desire felt tension ripple through Chase's body as his mother paused to glance at him. She wrapped her free hand around his waist and hugged him close to her side as Azura continued with her story that was punctuated every once in a while by sharp gasps and sighs from her audience. She left nothing out, and when she was done, there wasn't a dry eye in the room.

It was so quiet, Desire was certain she would have heard a pin drop on the carpet. Even her father, who was now sitting in a chair near the door, was affected. Sometime during Azura's story, his cold wall had cracked, zapping him of his strength to stand.

In fact, he was the first to break the silence. "Azura, I'm sorry you had to go through such a horrendous ordeal. I understand now why you were sympathetic to us during our family's painful period with Victoria. You were the only friend who stuck by us, and I can't thank you enough for that. But, he added, "I don't understand how your past relates to what your son did to my daughter that night."

Chase turned to face her father. "It does, Mr. Summers.

Somehow, Lewis Carron got wind of that story. He told me that my mother was a murderer on the lam. He threatened to go public with it if I didn't leave town. I had no choice. I had to protect my mother whom I thought at the time was a fugitive from justice. It was only years later, when I did my own investigation, that I realized she was a victim and not a criminal."

"Why didn't you come home after you found out that Carron was lying, instead of hiding out on the farm?"

"I wasn't ready, Mrs. Summers. I needed to put myself in a position to destroy Lewis Carron. He is—was a dangerous man. I had to take away his power, and the only way to accomplish that was to become more powerful than him."

Her father laughed sarcastically. "He's one of the most powerful men in the area. How can you, a simple farm worker, destroy him? What are you going to do, throw corn husks at him?"

"I don't merely work on Carver Farm, Mr. Summers. I own all six hundred acres of it. And not only that, but I built myself an empire. I also created and run DC Designs, one of the top architectural companies in the world. It's currently headquartered in Des Moines, but I plan to move it to Evergreen as soon as possible."

"He's a billionaire." Desire just had to say it.

Her mother and Lisa gasped in shock, then Lisa yelled, "He's a billionaire? I slept with a billionaire?" making Desire regret her rash declaration.

"I would prefer if we kept this information between us for now," Chase cautioned. "There are still some legal issues I have to figure out before I go public. Can I count on you?"

Lisa and her mom nodded, but her father remained unmoved.

"What does DC mean?"

"Desire's Chase," Desire responded to her mom's question, and then quickly related the story Chase had given her about their very first encounter, twenty-seven years ago. "That's when I apparently began calling him *My Chase*," she finished on a smile.

"I remember that day," her mother said, nodding with amusement in her eyes. "I'd left you at the kiddie pool and run back inside to get something, only to find you gone when I came back outside."

Desire grinned up at Chase. "So it was true."

"I've never lied to you, *Roni*." He gave her a quick peck on the lips that made her hungry for more.

"These two were truly meant to be together," Azura said in a voice laced with affection. "Don't you agree, Gerry?"

Her father flared his hand disputatiously. "It all boils down to the same fact. This man chose *you*, his mother, over my daughter."

"You forced Chase into that decision, Daddy. You kept us apart. You forbade me to see him, and you threatened to shoot him if he tried to contact me again."

"Gerry!" her mother cried. "Is this true? You threatened to shoot a kid?" She threw her hands up in defeat.

"You condemned Chase without hearing all the facts," Desire continued. "You turned me completely against him and then you destroyed the only evidence that would have helped me understand why he had to leave."

"Wait a minute, little girl. What evidence did I destroy?" His brows pulled into a frown.

Desire rose and walked over to stand in front of him. "The letter, Daddy," she said quietly. "Chase left me a letter the day he left. He explained everything about the setup. He wrote that he loved me and that he would always love me. He climbed through my bedroom window and left it on my bureau. But you found it, didn't you? You destroyed it. So here's another regret you'll carry to your grave. If you'd told me about the letter, if you'd given it to me, you would have had your grandchildren already. Chase and I were planning on getting married back then."

"Desire, darling." He held her trembling hands. "I have no idea what you're talking about. I never took any letter from your room." He shot Chase an enraged stare. "He obviously lied to you. And if I'd found him in my house…"

She pulled her hands from his. "No, Daddy. Chase has never lied to me. Ever. You're the one who's lying. You never liked him, not even when he was a kid. You did everything you could to keep us apart, including trying to destroy our love for each other, but it didn't work. Our love is stronger than ever. It's built to last."

Her father shot to his feet and glared down at her. "I refuse to sit here and have my own daughter call me a liar. As far as I—"

"Desire. Desire. Desire!"

At the third call of her name, Desire turned sideways and gave her cousin an irritated frown. "What, Lisa?"

"Uncle Gerry didn't take the letter. I did."

"Lisa?" everyone said in unison.

CHAPTER NINETEEN

Desire froze for a few seconds as the incredible information shot through her brain. "You? You took Chase's letter? Why, Lisa? Did you want him that badly back then that you were willing to stab me in the back? No wonder you slept with him a minute after he stepped off the plane. And no wonder you were quick to give me all the gory details the next morning. You *were* gloating. You are my best friend, my flesh and blood. You—"

Lisa jumped up and into her face. "I'm still your best friend, damn it, Desire. Yes, I wanted Chase back then. What girl with blood running through her veins didn't? But I knew you were crushing on him, so I kept my distance."

"Apparently not far enough. You got what you wanted. You slept with a billionaire."

Lisa grabbed her by the arm as she tried to move away. "You're going to hear me out," she demanded. "When I'm done, you can decide if you never want to see me again."

Desire glanced around to note that all eyes were now stationed on her and Lisa, standing in the middle of the living room. "Okay," she said grudgingly. "Let's hear it."

Lisa released her. "I'd come by the house looking for you. I just wanted to cheer you up a bit, you know. My mom had dropped me off at the curb and I was walking up the driveway when I saw Chase climbing out of your bedroom window, and heading to the back of the house. I thought you were in there with him, so I waited a little while before ringing the bell. When no one answered, I took the spare key from its hiding place and let myself in. When you didn't respond to my knock on your bedroom door, I went in, and that's when I saw the letter on your bureau."

She paused to take a breath. "Seconds later, I heard Uncle Gerry's car pulling into the garage. I didn't want him to know that Chase had broken into his house. It would have just added fuel to the flames that were already burning out of control. It was a split-second decision, Desire. I pushed the letter into my pocket, intending to give it to you when I saw you. But I forgot that it was in my jeans pocket. It got washed, and then I figured there was no reason to tell you about it. I just let it go."

"Did you read it?' Desire asked.

She shook her head. "I have no idea what Chase said in that letter. I didn't know you two were in love. I thought he was just trying to explain his side of the story since you wouldn't talk to him in person. I didn't know he was saying goodbye. I'm sorry. Can you forgive me?"

"Oh, Lisa." Desire pulled her cousin into her arms. "Of course, I forgive you. You were trying to help me." They clung to each other as the wall of tension that had been building between them for the past few days finally crumbled.

Lisa eventually broke free and turned to Chase. "I should apologize to you, too."

"No need," he said, pushing to his feet.

"Yes, there's need. The other night when you called to tell me that Desire and Chad were engaged, I didn't take the time to realize that you were in pain. I saw my opportunity to be with you, and I took it. I took advantage of your vulnerability."

"Are you kidding me?" Desire's father bellowed.

"Daddy," Desire held his hand, as tears rolled down her cheeks. "I'm truly sorry for accusing you of something you didn't do. When Chase told me about the letter a couple days ago, I thought it was you who'd found and destroyed it." She wound her hands around his waist and laid her head on his chest as she used to do when she was a little girl. "Can you forgive me?"

He hugged her close for a few breathless moments, before breaking away. "I forgive you, sweetheart. I love you."

"I love you too, Daddy."

Desire's mother was the first to remind them of the reason they'd all been invited to dinner. "Now that all this confusion is cleared up, and our differences settled, we have a wedding to plan."

"A billionaire one at that," Lisa said with a huge grin. "We're going all out."

"Amen to that," Azura said.

"Did you hear, that darling?" Chase grinned at Desire.

"Yeah, we're getting married with our families' approval. I've never been happier in my life." Her heart swelled with love and happiness as Chase's arms closed about her and his lips settled on hers.

"I haven't given my approval."

At the sound of her father's voice, Desire's heart raced with frightening intensity. She turned in Chase's arms to stare at the man whose dying wishes she wanted so much to grant. "Daddy—"

"I said I forgave you, my daughter, but I don't forgive him." His eyes were cold and hard as he stared at Chase. "I'm sure he was all too eager to incriminate me. I don't care that he was set up. I don't care that he felt like he had to leave town. I don't care if he's a billionaire. If he hadn't slept with that mother and her daughter, Lewis Carron would never have had the ammunition to use against him. Quite frankly, Desire, I question your principles, your intelligence. I thought you were smarter—"

"Mr. Summers, that's enough, sir!" Chase growled between clenched teeth, coming to her rescue as he'd done in the past.

"It's okay, baby." She braced her hand against his hard stomach, pushing him back. "I have this."

"Gerry, you can't mean that," her mother said. "Take it back!"

"I will not."

"How can you be so unforgiving, Daddy? Your daughter, my sister, shot and killed Pilar Fontaine." She quivered at the very thought of brining up that terrible period of their family's past. "Eleven years later, Bryce came to you. You didn't go to him. He came to you and told you that he forgave you for whatever part you played in his wife's death. And you're telling me that you cannot forgive Chase's youthful infractions?

"He was young and pumped full of raging hormones as all boys are. You were young once, and I know Mom isn't the only woman you've been with. You weren't married to Victoria's mother. I'm sure you have some stories you haven't shared with Mom or anyone else because you're ashamed of them. You weren't a saint in your youth, Daddy, and neither was Chase, but he has changed, just like you changed. I have forgiven him."

"He doesn't deserve your forgiveness."

"It doesn't matter whether he deserves it or not. You didn't deserve Bryce's either, but he gave it, anyway. You can't expect people to forgive you when you don't forgive others. That's not how it works."

"He slept with your cousin!" He pointed at Chase and then at Lisa. "I don't understand how you, any of you, don't see his depraved pattern. He obviously has a thing for sleeping with women who share the same DNA. How can you stand here and tell me he has changed? Money can't wash away his filth!"

"Mr. Summers, I—"

"Chase!" she cried, stopping him. This was between her and her father, and she didn't want anyone intervening on her behalf. "You're stubborn, difficult, and set in your ways, Daddy, but I can't help but love you. True love means loving someone in spite of his faults. Chase made a mistake, and he's owned up to it."

She paused to take a deep breath of composure. "You've always said that you want the best man for me, but it's not up to you to decide who that man is. I make that decision. I love Chase. I have loved him all my life. I've spent my entire adult life missing him, pining away for him because I allowed you to convince me that he was trash." She shook her head in regret and defiance. "I will not turn my back on him a second time because you think I should. If you make me choose between you and him, I will choose him, Daddy."

"So be it. You have made your decision, and I have made mine. I won't be at your wedding. I will never hand you over to the likes of him, and I will never accept any child you have with him. When you come to your senses and are ready to apologize, I'll be at home." He opened the door and marched out to the porch and down the steps.

"Daddy!" Desire called, running out behind him. "I'm sorry that you feel that way. I love you, but I won't be coming to you. I'm not apologizing for anything. It's your loss. All of it!"

When he opened his car, climbed in, and backed out of the driveway, Desire turned and walked back inside, straight into Chase's arms where she knew she would find comfort and joy and hope.

An amalgamation of emotions sped through Chase as he enveloped Desire into his arms. How could her father, the man she had looked up to her entire life, the man for whom she'd sacrificed her college dreams to stay at home, and nursed back to both physical and emotional health after his other daughter had destroyed it, be so heartless and cruel to her?

He was proud of her for standing up to him, for not running away, and for not collapsing into a helpless heap, which was probably what her father expected. Even though he'd always been ready to defend her, beat up anyone who threatened her peace of mind, Chase was happy to watch Desire stand on her own two feet. His heart had jumped with admiration when she'd pushed him back. The timid little girl he once knew had morphed into a fighter who'd taken on her chief adversary, and essentially turned him into a coward who ran.

"Desire, baby," her mother said, pulling her from Chase's arms. "I'm sorry for the way your father is behaving. Sometimes I don't even recognize the man I'm married to."

Chase swallowed a lump in his throat when she glanced up at her mother and asked, "Why do you love him, Mommy? What was it about him that attracted you to him? I need to know."

Ruth sighed, and held her daughter at arm's length. "When I met your father, he was sweet, and charming, and kind, and funny. He made me laugh. He had big dreams and plans that gave me hope. He worked to become the first black mayor in a town that was ninety-nine and a half percent white, and he was very good at his job. That's the man I fell in love with. But the scandals our family has suffered over the past years have broken him. Then his fight with cancer further weakened him. In the midst of all that, he's always wanted what's best for you."

"Then why can't he see that Chase is the best for me? He's who I want."

"Your father is a stubborn mule, Desire. But he always comes around after he cools down. You know that about him. And he'll come around again this time. I promise you."

"He'd better, and soon, because we don't have a lot of time. I do love him, Mommy." Her voice broke with apparent love and frustration. "I want him at my wedding. I want him to give me away, and I want him to hold at least one of my children in his arms before he dies."

"Then we all have to make sure he does," Azura said.

"We need an intervention," Chad suggested. "We only have one day to bring him around, and if he's as stubborn as you say, Mrs. Summers, we have to pressure him. I say give him the night to cool off and then pummel him all day tomorrow. We can do it one at a time or all together."

"Under the circumstances, I think it's best if I stay away from Uncle Gerry," Lisa said. "He needs to concentrate on why he *should* embrace Chase as a future son-in-law, not why he *shouldn't*."

"That's pretty wise thinking, Lisa."

"Thanks, Aunt Ruth. So while the rest of you gang up on him, the bride and I will start planning the wedding." She grinned at Desire. "How many guests are you planning on having?"

"You're looking at them, and hopefully Daddy too. And we do have to keep this under wraps until Tuesday night. Nobody can know Chase has returned or that we're getting married, or we'll be mobbed by the local press. We just want to enjoy a few hours of peace before the madness begins."

"I get that, but you're a wedding planner. Your wedding should trump all weddings. You're marrying a billionaire, for crying out loud."

"I don't want a big wedding. I just want the people who I love most in the world to witness me exchange my vows with the man with whom I've chosen to spend the rest of my life."

The smile she gave him rocked Chase to the core. How had he become so lucky?

"Seriously, Desire. You take all the joy out of being a maid of honor. I'm reduced to simply holding your bouquet and your train."

"Sorry, cuz."

"The garden maze is a public place," her mother said. "How are you going to keep it secret?"

"I've taken care of all that," Chase said. "I've booked the entire establishment. It's closed to the public on Monday and Tuesday. We'll set up tomorrow and marry on Tuesday."

"That's a sure case of money talking," Lisa said, shaking her head in disbelief. "I've got so much to learn. So let's get to planning."

Hope welled in Chase's heart as the women began to talk about weddings gowns, cake, food, themes, flowers, and more. He glanced out the window. The sun had set, and storm clouds were gradually spreading across the sky. It would be dark soon.

"You sure you're ready for this, big brother?" Chad asked, coming over to join him.

"I was ready years ago, little brother. You know you're my

best man, right?"

"Or I can give the bride away."

"I don't think that will be necessary. I know that man loves his daughter more than he hates me. Love trumps hate any day."

"He does love her, and he likes me, even when he thought I'd impregnated her out of wedlock."

"Really?"

Chad laughed. "Yup. He actually congratulated me for knocking up his daughter."

"Sick." Chase shook his head. "Desire has planned so many weddings. Hers should be perfect, but it won't be if her father doesn't show up."

Chad patted him on the shoulder. "You know I have the power of persuasion. I promise to do my best to make sure that Desire's father is present at your wedding to hand her over to you."

"Yeah, you owe me for Susie Connor."

They both laughed at the childhood shenanigans, then Chase tapped Chad on the shoulder. "Hey, what you did today—coming out like that—I'm proud of you."

"Brave me, huh?"

"What are you going to do now?"

He shrugged. "Maybe make a press release. Can I share your stage?"

"Any time, Chad, and thanks for helping out today. I guess I owe you now."

"I plan to cash in, especially since you're a billionaire. I have a long list."

"Bring it on. I already have mine of things to do for you and Mom. Plus, I will need a local attorney to look out for my interests. Know anyone?"

"I heard that guy Hunter is pretty good."

"Hunter, it is then."

Chad glanced at his watch. "Speaking of— I have to head to my office to work on a brief. I'll probably be there for the rest of the night. See you tomorrow?"

"Tomorrow." As Chad went through the kitchen and out the back door, Chase turned his attention to the women, still chattering away excitedly in their effort to make sure that Desire's wedding went off without a hitch. He loved them all, but he was ready for them to leave so he could be alone with his love. He crossed the room, crept up behind Desire, and wrapped his arms around her. She gazed up at him, and her tender smile, the faint tremor of her lips and the twinkle in her brown eyes sent pleasure radiating down his body.

His mother clapped her hands as if she'd read his mind. "Okay, folks. Let's take our wedding and intervention plotting next door. I think these young people want to be alone."

"Yeah, scram, you all," Desire echoed. "Chase and I have a lot to talk about." She wasted no time in escorting them to the door and practically pushing them out on to the porch. "Love you."

"Talk, huh?" Chase remarked, as he watched the women file across the lawn, his mother taking the lead.

"I had to tell them something," she said, with a sexy twist of her lips.

Chase closed the door, pushed her against it, and gazed into her eyes, already glazed with passion and hunger, the kind of hunger he'd recently learned to read, to feed, and to satisfy. Words were unnecessary between them. Actually, they had discovered yesterday that they enjoyed making love in total silence. Their sighs, their moans, and their eyes spoke for them. They knew what they wanted from each other, and neither of them was shy about taking it.

He cupped her face in his hands and his heart hammered foolishly as their mouths sealed in a kiss like the smoldering heat that joined metals. They tongued each other, while their hands caressed each other's bodies through their clothes in a frenzy. He smothered her lips with demanding mastery until their groans of ecstasy rang out around them, until it wasn't enough.

Raising his mouth from hers, Chase gazed into Desire's mesmerizing eyes as his hands reached for the hem of her dress and hers reached for the tail of his shirt. Somehow, they managed to undress each other in record time—shirt, dress, belt, jeans, bra, panties, briefs, and sandals flying across the room, some landing on lampshades, some on chairs, some in bowls half filled with dessert, and one over a glass of iced tea.

His gaze dipped to the heaving swell of her breasts and his mouth watered from the memory of their texture, their taste. His cock tightened and slapped against his stomach at the lovely sight of her dark nipples, hard and pebbled like raisins rising from the peaks of her swelling brown mounds. As if on cue, their mouths and hands went back to work on each other's upper body, molding, kneading, nipping, licking, sucking, caressing, while the rain began to beat steadily on the roof.

Their hands drifted south at the same time, trembling as eager fingers grazed the sensitive skin on their bellies. He cupped her hot soaking sex as her fingers closed around his turgid erection, not completely, but enough to make him moan and tremble from the pleasure of her grasp. He sucked in his breath and slid a finger inside her as she began to pump him up and down. He glanced down to the erotic vision of her slender hand moving along his hard pulsing cock, her palm gently rubbing his pre-cum over the head, and then back down to the root.

Their mouths collided on a long deep groan. Her hot wet kiss sang through his veins as their tongues danced to the tempo of their fingers working on each other's sex.

"Desire," he groaned as her soft wet walls clamped around his finger, contracting, releasing, over and over until his jealous cock pulsed with impatience to be inside her.

"Take me hard and fast. I want it rough," she whispered.

He picked her up and, stumbling toward the sectional, he placed her belly down on the back of it. He took a few breathless moments to admire and appraise her gorgeous body—brown, slender, and bootylicious—spread before him, with her long black tresses spread out above her head resting on the cushioned seat, her hands gripping the edge. *Gorgeous.*

Driven by a burning hunger to posses her, Chase nudged her thighs slightly apart with his knee. With one hand, he gripped his aching cock while he splayed the other over her firm derrière, and parted them. Stepping forward, he positioned the tip of his cock to her slick heat, and thrust, at the very moment a flash of lightning zapped across the sky.

She whimpered sexily, arched her back and flexed her buttocks as his cock drove deeper and deeper inside her until he felt the head lodged against her cervix. She quivered and locked her legs around his thighs securing him inside her feverish prison of soft quivering flesh. He emitted a guttural sound as chills zapped up and down his spine. Firmly lodged inside her velvety moistness, Chase leaned in, pressing his groin into her heaving buttocks, his belly into her back, and passing his hands beneath her to clasp her swollen breasts in his palms.

He squeezed her globes, rolled her hard nipples between his fingers, and feather-kissed her, teasingly, along her neck, across her back and shoulders as he began to pump in and out of her, swinging his hips gently at first, then with force and passion, matching the swiveling limited rhythm of her buttocks as she pushed back against his thrusts, meshing her butt into his groin, taking every hard inch of him. His shaft entered paradise again and again as he thrust as far as he could go, then pulled back just enough to feel the tight muscles of her entrance grip his head, before plunging in again.

Her body squirmed beneath him, testing, tempting, feeding his unmatched and unrelenting passion like no other woman had ever done before.

Sweat poured off his body, mingling with hers as their groans of pleasure were swallowed up in the claps of thunder that rolled across the sky, their passion ignited by the streaks of lightning that streamed through the window and danced across their damp heaving bodies, their thirst amplified by the deluge of rain beating against the roof.

She groaned at each deep satisfying thrust into her succulent body, the erratic and erotic sounds echoing deep inside her, traveling south into her pulsing sex, sending fiery and tingling vibrations into the tip of his shaft, up along its length into his groin, his belly, his heart.

The burning pressure in his cock was almost unbearable, but still he found the strength to ride her harder and faster until he felt her velvety walls constrict, felt her body tighten and arc beneath the powerful pressure of his, and felt her walls clamp down on him. The low guttural sounds he'd come to love signaled the onset of her orgasm.

His cock throbbed and jerked as she milked him. He trembled while wave after blistering wave of ecstasy crashed over him. He stiffened with maddening delight, then exploded on a clap of thunder, shooting his seed deep inside her welcoming womb before collapsing on her back. He moaned his pleasure into the soft hollow of her neck.

They clung to each other trembling fiercely in a sea of gratification as the storm raged on outside.

CHAPTER TWENTY

It was a perfect morning for a wedding. The sky was deep blue with hardly a cloud in sight. A pleasant breeze, perfumed with a fusion of floral scents, filtered through the white satin drapes of the bridal tent located at the end of the lane in Evergreen's Garden Maze, where Desire and Chase had shared their first kiss and pledged their love for each other.

It had taken them twelve long years of heartache and separation to get back to this place of love, but as the saying went: it was better late than never.

Desire stared at her reflection in the mirror, and tucked in a few strands of hair that had broken free of the tight bun Lisa had pinned it into, using Desire's own blue hairpin—her *something blue*. Her *something old* was a pearl bracelet her mother had given her on her sixteenth birthday, and her *something borrowed* was a silver butterfly broach Azura had pinned to her dress. Her *something new* was the pair of chandelier drop diamond earring dangling from her earlobes—a gift from her groom.

The women had all pitched in to help with her hair, makeup, and getting her into her dress without causing a disaster. They'd left her alone to take care of some last minute details in a nearby tent where the breakfast reception would take place. Ristorante Andreas had catered the food, and the smells drifting her way were already making Desire hungry. Too nervous to eat, she'd only had a cup of coffee earlier.

Desire felt blissfully happy, fully alive as she splayed her hands down her wedding dress—an Oscar de la Renta slim, strapless gown, fashioned from gorgeous Chantilly lace, and strewn with floral appliqués that clung to her curves all the way from the décolleté neckline to just below her knees, at which point it flared off into an enchanting, trailing trumpet skirt that brushed the ground as she walked. It was simple and elegant, and she felt like a modern-day princess.

Excitement filled Desire as she glanced around the elegantly furnished tent with a wall-to-wall gold and white Persian rug, a white vanity dresser and mirror, gold-plated nightstands, a divan, coffee table, a small dining table with two chairs, and a king-size bed covered with white silk sheets with red and white rose pedals scattered over it. A white liner, bordered by vases of roses and candles, extended from the door of the tent to the wedding trellis—located in the exactly spot where she and Chase had first kissed—and where they would officially exchange their vows.

A bathroom with a portable, flushable toilet, a sink, and a Jacuzzi were housed in the extension to the right of the main part of the tent. Chase had thought of everything when he'd built their honeymoon chamber.

Since her own employees weren't supposed to know about her marriage until it was over, Chase had gathered all the wedding ideas, and had anonymously hired her competition, Fae, to put them into place yesterday while Desire spent the day with the women from both families—a day he himself had arranged, because he didn't want her to worry about a thing, and he wanted her relaxed and rested for their wedding day and night, which they would spend in the tent. That addition to the plan had been a surprise to her. She was so happy she'd kept the wedding small and private. She'd heard many brides complain about being too tired to enjoy the first few days of their honeymoon. That would not happen to her.

After spending some time with her employees to make sure her business would run smoothly for the next couple days, Desire and her bachelorette party girls had started their day with an elaborate brunch at Ristorante Andreas, followed by shopping by private appointment for her honeymoon wardrobe, maid-of-honor, mother-of-the-bride, and mother-of-the-groom dresses at some of the most exclusive shops in Granite Falls. Afterward, they'd spent the afternoon in the spa at Hotel Andreas indulging in full body massages, manicures, pedicures, and facials. They'd ended the day in Chase's penthouse, dining on extravagant room service, while Chase had spent the night at his mother's house.

Even though Desire's joy had been clouded by the reality that her father might not be present at her wedding, she refused to let it destroy her. Her mother, Chad, and Azura had intervened on her behalf, but he was still being his stubborn self. She understood that he was scared of losing his little girl, that he wasn't the center of her world anymore, that she loved another man more than she loved him, and that he had no say in how she lived her life after she pledged her heart, her trust, her loyalty, and her love to Chase.

As a wedding planner, she'd encountered many fathers who'd expressed those fears, but some had eagerly and willing handed their daughters over to the grooms, while some had reluctantly done so. And then there were others, who for one reason or the other didn't show up at all. And like those latter brides, Desire was disappointed, but not enough to cause her to change her mind and go against her heart.

She was marrying Chase, with or without her father's blessings or his presence. But she held out hope in her heart that he would eventually come around when he found out he was going to be a grandfather. She hoped it wouldn't be too long.

Her mother was giving her away in her father's place. That was good enough for her.

Desire's heart fluttered as the melodious sounds of a harp signaled that the moment when she would make the most important declaration of her life was almost here. She and Chase had decided that a local harpist would commence with Don Henley's "Heart of the Matter" because it was apropos for the heartache and the separation they'd been through, and for the forgiveness and the healing that would follow them for the rest of their lives. Their playlist included "Conqueror" by Estelle and Jesse Smollet, "Written in the Stars" by Elton John, "My Love" by Patti LaBelle, Bobby Brown's "Good Enough," and of course "Roni," among other wedding-related love songs.

She hadn't seen Chase since yesterday morning when they'd enjoyed each other on both her kitchen floor and countertop. After making love all throughout Sunday night, they never thought they would have had the strength to come together again on Monday morning. But after a shower and a leisurely breakfast of western omelettes, fruit, coffee and toast—cooked by Chase—their strength and libidos had been revived. They probably would have headed back to bed if they didn't have to get their wedding plans underway.

At the sound of voices outside the tent, Desire picked up her veil, also strewn with floral appliqués, from a chair, and attempted to pin it on her head.

"Desire, let me help you with that."

She turned, smiling, as her mother walked into the tent looking beautiful in a Lunar three-quarter sleeve, sequined georgette gown with a V neckline that fitted snugly at the hips and tapered off into a bias-pleated bottom that swept the ground. It was a Jenny Packham.

"You look lovely, Mommy," she said, happy that her mother could finally wear an original from one of her favorite designers. She relinquished the veil to her mother and sat down on the stool in front of the vanity.

"Thanks, baby, but I still feel guilty for letting you talk me into buying it," her mom said, as she began pinning the veil into place.

"Get used to it. I plan to spoil you rotten. Uh-uh, don't argue with me," she added, when her mother opened her mouth to protest. She placed her hand over her mother's, which rested on her shoulders. "Thanks for giving me away. It means a lot to me."

Her mother kissed the top of her head. "I'm still hoping that your father will show up, baby. I just called him to let him know that he's missing out on the most important day of your life. I reminded him of how full of joy he was the first time he held you in his arms, thirty years ago. I reminded him that he'd promised to be there for you, to protect you and love you unconditionally. I reminded him of how proud he's been of you throughout the years. I told him it wasn't too late. Maybe you should give him a call, Desire. Give him a little more time to make up his mind."

"No, Mom. I'm not arguing with my father on my wedding day. I'm marrying Chase in half an hour. That's all the time he has to make up his mind."

Her mother lifted her veil away from her face and arranged it at the back of her head before taking a seat on the chair next to the vanity. "Well, the thing is, Desire, you do have to wait a little longer. Chase isn't here yet."

"He isn't? He was supposed to have arrived with Chad and Pastor Kelly ten minutes ago when the music started."

"Chad and Pastor Kelly are here. Chad said Chase had some last minute business emergency to take care of, but that he will be here in time. Don't worry, baby. You won't be one of those brides who are left at the altar. I'm sure of that."

"I'm not worried. Chase would never let me down. I'm sure whatever business he had to take care of couldn't wait." She glanced toward the door as Azura and Lisa came in.

Like her Aunt Ruth, Lisa had settled on an off-white Jenny Packham. Hers was a sequined georgette gown with a round neckline, capped sleeves and a scooped back. Azura had opted for a Pamella Roland gown, also off-white, with short sleeves, a jewel neckline and a straight hem. All of the women in Desire's wedding party looked exceptionally sophisticated, she thought with admiration.

"Did you hear that Chase isn't here, yet?" Lisa asked, as she came in and immediately began to fidget with Desire's bouquet that was lying on the coffee table.

"Yes, I heard, and—"

"Desire, may I come in?"

She stopped at Chad's request. "Sure, Chad."

A minute later he stepped inside looking handsome in a black and white tux.

"Wow," he said, his eyes bulging when he saw her. He walked over and gave her a hug and a kiss on the cheek. "I wish I wasn't gay," he drawled, making everyone laugh.

"No, you don't." She gave him a playful poke on the arm. "Where is your brother?"

"I left him at home. When the limo showed up to pick us up, he told me to go ahead, some emergency had come up."

"Is it serious?" she asked.

"Your guess is as good as mine, doll." He inclined his head. "I brought your butterflies and your doves, though. He had me stop to pick them up on the way here."

Desire pressed her hands to her chest as her heart began to flutter. "I told him he didn't have to fulfill that childish wish."

"My son loves you, Desire. He lives to make you happy. Just let him," Azura said lovingly.

Desire beckoned them close for a group hug. "Chase and I are so lucky to have all of you in our lives. I'm smart enough to know that it won't always be a bed of roses for us, but it warms my heart to know that we have your love, your encouragement, and your support in the good times and the bad."

"Always, sweetheart," her mother said, kissing her on the forehead.

Desire sighed deeply, feeling loved beyond imagination, but yet with a tinge of sadness that her father had chosen not to be a part of the most special day of her life.

***

Chase waited until the limousine carrying his brother and Pastor Kelly disappeared from view before he crossed the lawn to Desire's yard—garment bag in hand—and climbed into her car. Twenty minutes later, he parked the car in the driveway, grabbed the garment bag, strode up the steps, rang the doorbell, and stepped to the side away from the peephole.

Fifteen seconds later, he was face-to-face with his future father-in-law.

From the smile that quickly turned into a scowl, Chase could only surmise that when Mr. Summers had seen his daughter's car in the driveway, he'd thought—probably hoped—she'd 'come to her senses' and decided not to marry the man he loathed more than anyone on the planet.

Chase jammed his foot against the doorframe, preventing the older man from slamming it in his face. "I brought this for you, Mr. Summers. Your wife gave me your measurements," he said, holding up the garment bag. He pushed the door ajar, forcing Mr. Summers to retreat.

He stepped inside and glanced around the room. It hadn't changed much in the years Chase was away, and neither had the attitude of the man of the house. Chase had always felt unwelcome as a young boy when he'd visited both of the Summers residences with his mother and brother. He remembered squirming under the abhorrent stares from Mr. Summers when Azura wasn't watching. Mr. Summers wasn't the only father who'd shown contempt for Chase when he was a teenage, but strangely, he was the only one who'd made Chase uncomfortable.

Chase's eyes were drawn to an open book and a half-full glass on a table next to a La-Z-Boy chair. Chase wondered mildly what Gerald Summers had been reading, and whether or not they had anything in common. The answers to those questions would have to wait for another day. "Can we talk, man to man, sir?" he asked, hanging the garment bag on a coat rack near the door.

"Perhaps, if you were a man."

Chase bit back his retort. He hadn't come here to fight with his future wife's father. He'd come to ask for a chance to prove to him that he was good enough for his daughter, and that he would protect her, love her, and cherish her to the last day of his life. He hadn't had a chance to do that during the yelling, accusations, and threats that erupted on Sunday night. He needed to humbly plead his case. He owed it to Desire to try to make amends one last time.

"You are trespassing on my property. If you don't leave immediately, I will call the police and have you arrested. Perhaps they'll throw you in jail where you belong."

"If you think my being in jail would stop your daughter from marrying me, you don't know her very well, sir. I love Desire. She loves you. Today is one of the most important days of her life, and you are screwing it up for her."

"How dare you talk to me like that?" Gerald's hands balled into fists.

Chase held his scathing gaze. "Go ahead, hit me. Take out your anger on me, Mr. Summers. I would gladly take a beating from you if that's what it takes for you to make your daughter happy."

He released his fists. "You're not worth the trouble."

"Dead right. I'm not, but Desire is. She has spent her entire life trying to make up for the aftermath of Lewis Carron's vendetta against me, and for all the hardship your family has gone through. She gave up her college and stayed at home to help nurse you back to health. She restored your family's name. She loves you, unconditionally. And the one day she needs you to be there for her, you have abandoned her."

"I'm not abandoning her. I'm rejecting you."

"Believe me, I do understand. If I were in your position, I might feel the same way about the man my daughter was about to marry. But the truth is that we both want the same thing for Desire. Her happiness is paradoxically tied to both of ours. She was willing to marry a man she didn't love just to give you the grandchildren you want so much. I'm not asking you to trust me. I'm asking you to trust your daughter. Trust what you know about her. Be the father she knows and loves."

"She's selling herself short."

"That's just your opinion, Mr. Summers. Desire thinks

differently, and only what she thinks, what she wants, matters to me. She thinks I'm worthy of love, and of being the father of her children. We will have many children. Your grandchildren."

Chase paused as he recalled Kaya's words about not speaking negatively about her own mother to her children, and of her determination not to keep them away from their grandmother for fear that they might grow up to resent Kaya. "Desire and I will teach our children to love you, Mr. Summers, even if you choose not to be in their lives. I pray that you beat this cancer, and that you're around when they do come into this world. But let me ask you, what will you tell them years from now when they're looking at our wedding photos and you're not in any of them? Will you tell them that you didn't walk their mother down the aisle because you didn't think their father was good enough for her?"

"It would be the truth."

"They would be living the truth. They will respect me and honor me because I will be the best and most loving father to them, and the kindest, most devoted husband to their mother. That is the truth, sir. I will never hurt Desire again. I would die for her and kill for her, simply because I love her. What are you willing to do for her after all she has done for you?"

Gerald's eyes narrowed as he stared into Chase's, and for the first time in his life, Chase realized that Desire had her father's eyes, and that some of his children would also be staring back at him with those same eyes. He swallowed, and before he knew what he was doing, he was on his knees in front of Gerald, his hands crossed over his heart.

"Mr. Summers, I'm asking your permission and your blessings to marry your daughter. Give me the chance to make her happy, and the honor to take care of her for the rest of her life, long after you and your wife are gone."

He paused waiting for a response, when none came, he gave it his last shot. "Desire told me that 'Adrian' is your first name, but that you've always preferred to be called 'Gerald.' Well, we have decided to name your first grandson 'Chase

Adrian Hunter' in your honor. Our decision is not conditional. Desire loves you. She will honor you whether you accept me or not."

When the older man just continued to stare him down, Chase took a deep breath and got to his feet. He turned, opened the door, stopped and then turned around again. "One more thing before I go. It is said that the mind has the power to heal the body. You beat cancer once because you felt you had something to live for—your daughter. You can beat it again, but only if you give yourself a reason to fight. Grab on to hope and live. Get out of the way of your own happiness, Mr. Summers."

He stepped outside and closed the door behind him. He was halfway to the car when a voice behind him yelled, "Chase, my name is 'Dad' to you."

Chase broke out into a wide grin.

***

"He's here." Desire shot up from the divan and raced toward the door of the tent when the harpist began playing El Debarge's "Second Chance," the song she and Chase had chosen for their wedding march.

Her mother grabbed her hand and pulled her back. "You can't let him see you. It's bad luck."

"You don't really believe that, do you, Mom? I've witnessed countless grooms talk to their brides in their wedding dresses, and most of them are still married. That's a myth." Her lips trembled with the need to smile.

"Myth or not, you're staying put." Lisa picked up the bridal bouquet of sunflowers and daffodils and thrust them into her hands. "You bilked me out of a lot of duties as your maid of honor. You're not bilking me out of my honorary march. I'm not taking any chances. Somebody's gotta see me in this dress."

Desire grinned and stood motionless as Lisa arranged her veil over her face, and then, with the help of her mother, attached her six-foot wedding train to the shoulders of her dress and spread it out behind her.

"You are absolutely lovely." Lisa said, placing a kiss on her cheek. "See you outside." She grabbed her own bouquet and sashayed toward the tent door.

"This is a great honor, Desire," her mother said, hooking her arm into Desire's as they prepared to follow Lisa.

"I think that honor belongs to me."

Desire froze, her hand going to her mouth to stop her squeal as the dark figure of her father, dressed in a black and white tuxedo, appeared in front of her.

"Gerry," her mother whispered. "Thank God."

"Daddy!" Desire dropped her head onto his chest, not caring that she might be ruining her makeup or leaving mascara smudges on her veil or his crisp white shirt. He didn't seem to mind either as he pressed her closely to his heart. "What changed your mind?" she asked, lifting her head to gaze at him.

"Chase. The thanks belongs to him this time," her father said to her mother before returning his attention to Desire. "Chase did the one thing I didn't expect."

"What did he do, punch some sense into you?"

"He got down on his knees in front of me and asked for your hand. He promised me that he would take care of you long after I'm gone. He also promised to name your first son after me."

Desire bit down on her bottom lip. "He's a good man, Daddy. I'm so glad you two are making an effort to get along. It means a lot to me."

"I'm proud of you, Gerry." Her mother kissed him on the cheek.

"You look beautiful, Ruth. I hope you saved a dance for me." His eyes shone with appreciation and devotion as he gazed at his wife.

"All my dances have belonged to you since the first moment I met you, Gerry. You know that."

Desire hugged both her parents. "I hope that Chase and I are half as in love as you are with each other when we're your age."

"I have no doubt, Desire," her father said.

Her mother sniffled. "Then we'd better get her hitched to that wonderful, handsome, smart, intelligent, wealthy man."

"I wholeheartedly second that," her father said, with a grin as he watched his wife leave.

It was the kind of grin Desire hadn't seen on his face for a very long time. "Daddy, I'm so proud of you for taking the high road."

"And I'm proud of you for waiting for the one man you truly love. I guess I did something right, after all."

"You did a lot of things right, Daddy." She cleared the croak from her throat and forbade her eyes to shed another tear.

"Oh, by the way, I've decided to fight this cancer, to kick its butt so I can hold my grandchildren in my arms."

"We'll kick its butt together, Daddy." Warmth spread throughout Desire's entire body as she hooked her arm in her father's and stepped out of the tent.

Her heart rocked as she looked straight ahead and into the gray eyes of the man of her dreams, who was dressed in a white tux and looking sexier, yet more sophisticated and handsome than any other man she'd ever known.

She was so lucky that he'd allowed her to love him. If she had to go through the same pain, the same humiliation, the same separation to get to this moment again, she would do it in a heartbeat.

She was *His Desire*.

He was *Her Chase*.

EPILOGUE

"Grandpa. Look, Mommy, it's Grandpa."

"Yes, Hope, that's Grandpa." Desire glanced at her two-year old daughter, sitting at her feet on the floor in the nursery, flipping through the family album Desire had recently put together.

"Why did Grandpa go away, Mommy? Doesn't he love me no more?" she asked, shaking her head of black curls, her little mouth pouting, and her gray eyes sad, as she looked up at her mother.

"Your grandpa still loves you, darling." *Even beyond death.* "He loves you and Adrian very much." She kissed the brow of her seven-month old baby boy, who was staring at her through big brown eyes, her eyes, her father's eyes.

She shivered on an intake of air. Her father had kicked cancer's butt long enough to hold his granddaughter, Hope Shelby. She and Chase had named their daughter Hope to give her father hope. He'd lived to see her, to hold her in his arms, to rock her to sleep, bounce her on his knee, watch her crawl across the floor, take her first step, walk, and then run into his open arms in this very room after he and her mother had moved in with her and Chase.

It had been a hard and rough fight, and many times Desire

had wanted him to give up, just so he could be at peace and not suffer anymore, but when he'd learned that she was pregnant again, somehow, he'd dug deep and found the strength to hang on for another year for the chance to meet his grandson, Chase Adrian Hunter, before he succumbed to cancer, two months ago.

Desire squeezed her eyes, but the tears slid down anyway. She stifled her sob in a desperate effort not to upset her daughter.

"Why are you crying, Mommy?"

Her heart rocked as she felt Hope's small hand cupping her chin, and her warm body press against her thigh. "You miss Grandpa?"

She opened her eyes and smiled through her tears. "Yes, Hope. I miss my daddy."

"I miss my daddy, Mommy. Where's my daddy?"

"He'll be here soon, baby."

"I'm not a baby, Adrian is a baby."

Desire chuckled as she hugged her with her free hand. "You'll always be my baby, Hope, no matter how old or big you get." She bent down and kissed her smack on the lips.

Her gaze followed Hope as she skipped over to the window that overlooked the playground of their sprawling Mount Reservoir estate. Chase had bought the Forsythes' property, leveled the main mansion, and built their dream home. And after living in his penthouse suite since their wedding day, they were finally able to move into the estate earlier this year. They had servants and maids and gardeners and a butler, but no nannies. Desire wanted to raise her children herself. When she needed a break or intimate alone time with her husband, their grandmothers, their Uncle Chad, and cousin Lisa were all too happy to step in.

Desire was still trying to get used to the idea that she was now neighbors with the LaCrosses, the Fontaines, the Andrettis, and the Andreases, and that their children played together, visiting each other's homes. But most amazingly was the fact that Bryce and Kaya's children called her Aunt Desire.

Never in a million years would she have thought that possible. In fact, they had become so close that Bryce had given the eulogy at her father's funeral, and he and Kaya were the godparents of her son. It was all still so surreal to her, but that was the power of forgiveness and healing.

She glanced down at her son to find that he'd surrendered to sleep after nursing at her breasts for far too long in her estimation. He was just like his father, she thought, cradling him close as she rose to place him into his crib.

She stood gazing lovingly down at him, her heart throbbing at the little face that already looked so much like his father's. It was still hard for her to believe that it was three years since she and Chase had exchanged their vows and begun their life together, and that even after all this time, her body tingled every time she saw him, thought of him, or was near him.

She loved the life they had built together. No matter how crazy things got, Chase had always put his family first. He had been her Superman, her superhero, her rock of Gibraltar during her father's illness. He'd skillfully juggled running back and forth to Des Moines to take care of his company while overseeing both the construction of their new home and the new building for DC Architectural Designs where Carron used to be. Then, a year and a half ago, he'd finally and officially moved his headquarters to Granite Falls with a satellite office in Evergreen.

One of Chase's first local projects was to restore Wheaton Boarding House and transform it into Wheaton Estates, an exclusive assisted-living home. Their special room that had a spectacular view of the Mannis River was opened up, enlarged, and turned into a maze conservatory that housed an array of plants, fruit trees, vegetables, and of course flowers and a butterfly garden. The Gerald Summers Conservatory was now the most popular place for children to spend time with their aging grandparents, and great-grandparents, for some.

As for Lewis Carron, instead of taking Chase's advice to leave town and never come back, he'd tried to take Chase down. Consequently, many of his victims started coming forward one after the other to accuse him of fraud, extortion, theft, and many other serious crimes. But the most damaging was his involvement with some local politicians and government employees whom he'd bribed in order to receive special favors involving several real estate deals.

The news of Carron's arrest, and Chase's new identity broke just days after they were married. It had been crazy, and with the local media hounding them, they'd wanted so much to just fly away and leave it all behind, but they couldn't. Her father had started his chemotherapy the day after he gave her away, and Desire didn't want to miss one single day with him. But now that he'd been laid to rest, she was looking forward to spending some time alone with her husband. They were planning their long-awaited honeymoon trip, traveling across Europe in one of his private jets.

She sighed in anticipation and pride. Chase's business had quadrupled overnight when he was finally given credit for all the Fontaine buildings in Granite Falls, including Fontaine Enterprises Headquarters. He was now a multibillionaire, who was contributing tremendously to their community, training and hiring young architects, some of whom had gone out and started businesses of their own, both locally and nationally.

Contrarily, she'd had to turn most of the responsibilities of her business over to her capable employees during her father's illness. With two pregnancies and everything else that was going on with her life, Weddings by Desire had had to take a backseat. It was still thriving, still very competitive, and she was certain that once she got past the grief of losing her father, she would return to it. Only time would tell.

Life was also going well for the other members of their families. Chad and John had both come out publicly after John confessed his infidelity and sexual orientation to his wife, Teresa. She'd been devastated, ridden with shame, guilt, and low self-esteem at his disloyalty and treachery. She'd immediately divorced him and had forbidden him to see their son. After being shunned, John had resigned from his position at the parochial school, and had begun studying law so he could advocate for victims who were forced out of their jobs for one reason or the other. John moved into Azura's house with Chad after Azura moved in with Chase and Desire. And just a few months ago, John's ex-wife had found it in her heart to forgive him, for her son's sake, she'd told Desire.

Desire smiled as she thought about her cousin, and still her best friend, Lisa. Lisa was now married to Beau Cadwell, one of Chase's executives who'd move to Evergreen from Des Moines. Their first child, a little girl, was due to arrive in five months. Before her father died, he'd given the Evergreen house to Lisa, so she could begin her new life without a mortgage hanging over her.

A heavy ache settled in Desire's chest as visions of her father sitting in the chair she'd just vacated, rocking his grandchildren to sleep overwhelmed her. God, she missed him so much. She hurt so much. She bit down on her lip and gripped the edge of the crib as grief threatened to cripple her.

"Daddy!"

Desire turned as Hope flew across the nursery floor and into the arms of her father, who scooped her up, hugging and kissing her unabashedly, tossing her into the air, catching her, and blowing bubbles on her tummy.

The tears of deep sorrow that had started to pool in Desire's eyes were instantly washed away by tears of joy at the sight of her handsome husband, dressed in a suit and tie, striding into the nursery.

Needing to feel his arms around her, she hurried across the floor, and when she found herself wrapped in his warm strong arms, she turned her face upward to receive his passionate kiss.

"Chase," she whispered. "I'm so glad you're home. I missed you so much."

He chuckled and gazed down into her eyes with so much love, so much devotion, her heart literally stopped for a second.

"You're acting as if I've been gone for weeks. It's only been eight hours, *Roni*."

"I'm greedy. I want you all to myself all day, all night, all the time."

"Now that's the kind of greeting a man appreciates from his wife when he comes home from a hard day at work." He dipped his head to kiss her leisurely on her mouth, their tongues dancing around each other in light play, promises of the heat and passion that were to come later.

"Give me kisses, Daddy." Hope's little hands clasped their faces, pushing them apart.

"You're as insatiable as your Mommy, aren't you?" he said, releasing Desire's mouth to plant a series of kisses on his daughter's face, which made her squeal with delight.

Desire groaned as Adrian began to whine. "I'd just put him down."

"He wants to see his daddy," Chase said, passing Hope into her arms as he walked over to the crib and picked up his son, who immediately stopped whining when Chase kissed his chubby cheeks and then pressed him to his chest. "Daddy's home, my little boy. Daddy will always come home to you, your sister, and your mommy. Always."

With her daughter clinging to her, Desire looped an arm around her husband as he cradled their son to his chest. She glanced to the floor to see her father smiling back at her from the album Hope had left there.

Desire's heart beat with a bottomless peace and satisfaction as she, her husband, and her children huddled together, wrapped in a cocoon of love and hope.

THE END

FROM THE DESK OF ANA E ROSS

Dear Reader,

I hope you enjoyed following **Chase and Desire** on their journey to love and *Happily Ever After*. I wish you all the best in your search to find a love that stands the test of time and separation. If you've already found that kind of love, then Kudos to you! Love him/her with all your heart.

Also, if you enjoyed **Desire's Chase**, you will also enjoy **The Mogul's Reluctant Bride**, Bryce and Kaya Fontaine's love story, and also **With These Four Rings** where Desire was introduced as the wedding planner for the billionaire brides' wedding of the decade.

Blessings,
Ana

Connect with me: www.AnaERoss.com
www.facebook.com/Ana-E-Ross
Twitter@anaeross

OTHER WORKS BY ANA E ROSS

Billionaire Brides of Granite Falls Series:

The Doctor's Secret Bride – Book One
The Mogul's Reluctant Bride – Book Two
The Playboy's Fugitive Bride – Book Three
The Tycoon's Temporary Bride – Book Four
With These Four Rings – Book Five: Wedding Bonus

Beyond Granite Falls Series:
Loving Yasmine (Robert & Yasmine)
Desire's Chase (Chase & Desire)
Pleasing Mindy (Galen & Mindy) 2016/2017

Short Stories:
Her Perfect Valentine Birthday Surprise
The Brit Who Loved Her
His Amber Sunset

ABOUT THE AUTHOR

New York Times and USA Today Bestselling Author, Ana E Ross, was born and raised in the Caribbean where she began indulging in romance novels at a very early age.

A former Writing and English Literature teacher, Ana writes steamy contemporary romances featuring sexy, alpha heroes and strong, feisty heroines who fight and love with equal passion.

Her published works include three short stories, five books in her *Billionaire Brides of Granite Falls,* and two of three books in the spinoff series, *Beyond Granite Falls.*

Once her *Beyond Granite Falls* series is completed, Ana will begin work on her *Billionaire Island Brides* series. The sky's the limit when it comes to her writing career.

Ana lives in the northeast, and loves traveling, tennis, yoga, meditation, everything Italian, and spending valuable time with her daughter.

Connect with me: www.AnaERoss.com
www.facebook.com/Ana-E-Ross
Twitter@anaeross

Made in the USA
Lexington, KY
11 September 2016